FLASHPOINT

*When his client becomes the prime suspect
in a murder case, political consultant Dev
Conrad's campaign is thrown into chaos*

When Tracy Cabot's body is found in Senator
Robert Logan's fishing cabin, the police are
certain that he killed her. But Conrad finds
numerous suspects in the Senator's mansion
and in the somewhat comic but dangerous
figure of political saboteur Howie Ruskin.
With the campaign hotting up and the battle
for votes becoming increasingly brutal, can
Dev find the real killer and win the election
for his client?

A Selection of Titles by Ed Gorman

The Dev Conrad Series

SLEEPING DOGS
STRANGLEHOLD
BLINDSIDE *
FLASHPOINT *

The Sam McCain Series

THE DAY THE MUSIC DIED
WAKE UP LITTLE SUSIE
WILL YOU STILL LOVE ME TOMORROW?
SAVE THE LAST DANCE FOR ME
EVERYBODY'S SOMEBODY'S FOOL
BREAKING UP IS HARD TO DO
FOOLS RUSH IN
TICKET TO RIDE
BAD MOON RISING

* available from Severn House

FLASHPOINT

Ed Gorman

Severn House Large Print
London & New York

This first large print edition published 2014
in Great Britain and the USA by
SEVERN HOUSE PUBLISHERS LTD of
19 Cedar Road, Sutton, Surrey, England, SM2 5DA.
First world regular print edition published 2013 by
Severn House Publishers Ltd., London and New York.

British Library Cataloguing in Publication Data

Gorman, Edward author.
    Flashpoint. -- Large print edition.~ -- (A Dev Conrad
    political thriller ; 4)
    1. Conrad, Dev (Fictitious character)--Fiction.
    2. Political consultants--United States--Fiction.
    3. Murder--Investigation--Fiction. 4. Suspense fiction.
    5. Large type books.
    I. Title II. Series
    813.5'4-dc23

    ISBN-13: 9780727896711

Severn House Publishers support the Forest Stewardship Council™
[FSC™], the leading international forest certification organisation. All
our titles that are printed on FSC certified paper carry the FSC logo.

Printed and bound in Great Britain by
TJ International, Padstow, Cornwall.

*To the Charter Members of the Lunchtime Hall
of Fame Deb and Dale Jones Melissa
Sodeman and Ricky Sprague*

Acknowledgements

I would like to thank the Multiple Myeloma Foundation whose support keeps all of us with this incurable cancer alive as long as possible. I would also like to thank my longtime partner in crime (and first editor) Linda Siebels for her contributions and friendship.

PART ONE

At any other time this trip to Northern Illinois would be a pleasant break from the chaos of my office in Chicago. Dev Conrad and Associates is involved with five different candidates in this election cycle and now, in mid-October, each campaign is only three weeks from the finish. And in this election cycle nothing can be taken for granted.

So leaving my office for the day, jumping into my Jeep for a fast drive upstate, for an even faster drive through heavily forested land that showed the gleaming golds and burnished browns and elegant reds of autumn, should be an enviable twenty-four-hour vacation.

But I am still hearing Senator Robert Logan say: 'We both know this phone may be bugged, Dev. You know where my cabin is. I need you up here now.' And after that he hangs up.

Neither the sweet, piney breeze nor the sight of a mother deer helping her awkward fawn across the asphalt road can quell my sense of dread. Logan spent two terms in the House and is now running for his second term as a senator. He is a professional politician. He is one of those inherited-wealth men who votes generally to help those less fortunate.

He has the rangy looks of a small-town

Midwesterner; the way he talks and walks and handles himself suggests a quiet self-confidence that is offset by his easy self-deprecating humor. He can afford this humility because he's both handsome and bright. Third in his law school class at Princeton. He worked for eleven years in Chicago as a defense attorney, a soldier for the machine we have. He enjoys the brawl and the bravado of big-time elected office. Face it. There are few clubs more privileged than the United States Senate. People of every race, color and creed stand in line to kiss your star-spangled ass.

So what the hell is going on? He's at his cabin and he's obviously in some kind of desperate trouble. I start to think of all the possibilities, then I force myself to stop. Borrowing trouble, as my father said – he was a political consultant too, a very successful one – is a waste of time because your clients will just bring it to you free of charge.

Suddenly, through a sparse line of jack pines, I see the sparkling lake. I've spent a few weekends up here with the senator and his staffers. We fished and hiked the hills then settled in for a night of eating and drinking and working on the campaign. The lake lent everything we did a rich blue backdrop. And it was just as beautiful at night; I'd sit on the dock with a couple cans of beer and watch the stars as their lights were vaguely detailed in the water. My ex-wife still says that my years as an investigator for army *intelligence made it impossible for me to relax, that as soon as we finished making love my mind went back to churning through the case I was working on. I always wished that she could have been with me on this big-ass dock at midnight.*

I needed GPS because I hadn't been here in some time and I had to reach my destination as quickly as I could. To the east was a deep forest. I recognized an ancient rusted CAMEL CIGAR-ETTES *sign on a field gate from my trips here. Turning right would take me down a twisting road that would switch back on itself and end a few hundred yards from the cabin.*

I speed up now.

When the road ends you turn and drive on sandy soil to reach the back of a large A-frame house that by agreement everybody calls a cabin. It was big enough for a family of five and stocked with all the furnishings appropriate for life in the suburbs. 'I'll leave the roughing-it to Teddy Roosevelt,' the senator once joked to a reporter.

I pull the Jeep up next to the cabin. As I get out I can smell the lake; fresh and chill. No sound from inside, no TV or music. Robert is a big fan of eighties music. I think he still wants to be Simon Le Bon when he grows up.

Then I hear the front door of the place open-ing, followed by footsteps on the roofed porch that spans the width of the house. 'Dev?'

Even before I get around the corner and see

him I can tell from the timbre of his usually deep voice that he is even more tense than he was on the phone. He speaks now a full octave higher.

Blue chambray work shirt, Levi's, dark hair mussed and brown eyes those of a man barely in control of himself.

'What the hell took you so long?' he snapped.

'I couldn't get my jet pack to work so I had to take a regular plane.'

I think his smile surprised him as much as it did me. He shook his head then ran big, wide hands through his mess of hair. A splash of dark red caught my eye on the left sleeve of his shirt. 'I don't sound too crazy, do I?' Then, 'Thanks for coming, Dev. This...' He waved his hand. And stopped talking.

I walk up on the porch as he just stands there staring out at the lake. A red speedboat is bouncing roaring sounds off the high cliffs on the far side of the water. Since he isn't paying any attention to me I pause at the framed window next to the door and look in. Hardwood floors, an enormous fireplace, leather couches and chairs, a plasma TV screen that even an upscale sports bar would envy and a kitchen a Gold Coast chef gave him tips about building and stocking.

Out of sight are the two Murphy-like beds that can be pulled down near the back of the place. This is not to mention the shower downstairs and the two bedrooms upstairs. Oh, and the *additional shower as well.*

Something like a sob catches in his throat. His back is to me and now I see how stooped his shoulders are. I see again the inch-long trail of red darkness on his sleeve. My stomach clenches automatically. A few of my cases as an army intelligence investigator involved violence. What the hell is going on here?

'Robert.' Still not turning around.

'What?'

'You need to talk to me.'

'Somebody set me up, Dev.'

His remark is close to the one uttered by the infamous Washington, DC, politician Marion Barry when one of his many mistresses cooperated with the feds in busting him for drugs.

But I know that Robert isn't thinking about any such ironies now. He is lost in panic and helplessness. In some respects he has ceased to function.

'I can't help you unless you tell me what happened.'

His head hangs even lower. He won't be looking out at the lake now. If his eyes are open he'll be staring at the ground. 'The back porch.' Even speaking these three words seems to exhaust him. The head drops lower.

There is nothing to say. I can't clap him manfully on the shoulder and say, 'It'll be all right, Senator, just let me handle it.' That's what they all want to hear, that's what they all think they're paying you for. Sometimes you can help them. The help may not be quite legal or even honorable, but as any operative will tell you that is the game and if you are unwilling to play the game then you're quickly dealt out. In our silence birds cry out and somewhere in the forest I can hear a dog bark.

He turns and looks at me as I put my hand on the doorknob and push the door inward. Our eyes study each other. I can't tell what he's thinking. In his gaze there's just frenzy.

My first impression is of some kind of overly sweet odor. Some kind of air freshener spritzed to a toxic level. All the windows are open, too. It's actually cold in here. Autumn cold; even a hint of winter. The odor and the open windows means he's trying to cover a smell. Given his crazed alarm, given the streak of blood on his shirt I saw, given his remark that somebody set him up, I know now what I'll find on the back porch.

My stomach clenches again and despite the cold I know there's light sweat on my face.

Oh, yes, sometimes you can walk on the dark side and keep your candidate from self-destructing. That is, if what you're covering up falls within certain parameters.

I have the feeling that I'm about to see a dead woman. I also have the feeling – knowing now that he has probably been lying to me all along – that I know who she is.

Or was.

ONE

Fifteen days earlier I'd sat on a folding chair in a high school gymnasium watching Senator Logan conduct a town hall meeting. Given the state of the economy, mixed-to-racist feelings about the president of the United States and the leader of Logan's party and the prospect of unions being busted, not to mention gay marriage, there was plenty to discuss.

The gym was decorated with yellow and black crepe paper and large papier-mâché images of a lion's head. Apparently there had been a pep rally here earlier today. Hard not to think of your own pep rallies, the slap of basketballs on the shining floor, the feel in your arms of your first love knowing that all too soon she'd break your heart; and how small it would all seem when you visited it a few years later.

Logan was in his usual casual attire, the chambray shirt and jeans plus a gray tweed jacket. He addressed the crowd of perhaps a hundred through a stand-up microphone. The meeting had started promptly at seven and now, at eight, showed no signs of calming down.

Even though some of the questions were pointed, none had been personal or demeaning. The entire country was pissed off and generally with good reason. The citizens of Linton, Illinois, population 31,600, had every right to be just as pissed, especially given the fact that within the past two years three of its manufacturing plants had been relocated in the South.

But then came the inevitable.

If this was a movie role you'd cast somebody burly and menacing. He'd have wiry black hair and need a shave and maybe his teeth would be bad. His eyes and his voice would belong on the violent wing of the nearest psych ward.

You would not cast a maybe one-hundred-and-thirty-pound, fortyish man with thick glasses and a faint lisp as your choice to drop the birther bomb. He wore a short-sleeved shirt buttoned to the neck and tan pants that reached to his ribcage. He was a parody of a type and when he stood up my first response was to feel sorry for him. You could imagine the bullying he'd had to endure in school and the invisible sort of life he'd had as an adult.

But then he started waving a bunch of papers and that was never a good sign. People who wave papers announce upfront that they are going to say something crazy. George Bush was behind 9/11 had become a popular myth once again. A lot of papers had been waved at Robert about that.

'Senator Logan, my name is Stan Candiss and

I have proof here that your president is a Communist spy.'

Before Mr Candiss had grabbed my attention the gymnasium had been inspiring some high school memories of my own. I'd been thinking about the girls I'd taken to my junior and senior proms respectively, wondering what they were doing now, wondering if they ever wondered about me. But when Mr Candiss had stood up I'd sensed – despite my feeling a little sorry for him – that we were about to witness the inevitable moment in all town hall meetings: the conspiracy accusation.

Mr Candiss was apparently a known commodity locally.

'God damn it, Stan; sit down and shut up.'

'We're trying to have a serious discussion here, Stan.'

'Somebody should throw him out.'

Mr Candiss, it would seem, was not a beloved figure. Which did not stop him from continuing to wave his papers from his position in the last row of folding chairs – or from saying, 'Whether or not the senator wants to hear about it, there is a website that proves that after the president was born in Kenya he lived for eight years in Moscow. If any of you have ever seen *The Manchurian Candidate*, you know how communists can turn human beings into assassins. This website documents how the president – *our* president – is going to turn our entire arsenal of nuclear bombs on our own country.'

Though there were a few giggles, the general response was cursing, grumbling and even threatening.

Logan handled it calmly. 'I've actually seen that website. I believe you called my office in Washington a while back, Mr Candiss. You actually made our receptionist so curious that after she hung up she went right to the site and then started showing it to the staff. We were very intrigued.'

This time there was laughter. It wasn't hard to imagine congressional staffers chortling over some whacked-out crap about the president nuking America.

'These people laugh because they're ignorant. Are you ignorant, too, Senator Logan?'

Candiss went back to waving his papers but was forced to stop when a huge man in a Packers sweatshirt and jeans reared up from his seat and stalked to the last row of folding chairs. Most of the people had swiveled around to watch the action.

You can never tell how something like this will play out. Harsh words can lead to violence. There is always the chance, given the fact that the NRA wants to arm everybody over the age of three, that a gun might appear.

'We need to stay calm,' Logan said. 'Sir, if you'll take your seat again—'

Logan's local people had hired two off-duty police officers to handle security. They now appeared from their posts at the respective doors of the gym. They moved quickly toward Mr Candiss. They would stand next to him in case the big man tried to charge him. Then came the surprise.

'Stan, I stick up for you all the time at the lumberyard,' the man said, and there was real sympathy in his tone, 'and I even listen to all your stupid stories at lunchtime. But we're trying to have a serious talk here so please just sit the hell down and shut the hell up.'

Just about everybody in the gym applauded. Mr Candiss knew enough to look embarrassed and sit down. As the Packers man made his way back to his seat other men stuck their hands out to shake his. I admired the way he'd handled the situation. I'd have shaken his hand, too.

Logan had a few awkward moments but finally assured everybody that he was still interested in taking questions. His enthusiasm for the task only reminded me and his staffers of how our fortunes had changed in the last twenty-three days. The other side had dumped more than eleven million dollars in negative TV advertising into the state and we had started to feel its effects. For the previous two months we had managed to stay two-to-three points ahead, but now our internal polling showed that we were in a tie. Our opponent was a man named Charlie Shay, a folksy multimillionaire insurance executive who had once been considered too conservative for even this election cycle. Insurance people were not beloved in this country. But his bullshit Huckleberry Finn persona, created by a public relations team in Washington, was starting to take hold. There was one especially unctuous commercial where he was sitting with his grandson at sunset along a stream where he pretends to be fishing while handing out numerous lies about Logan. The closest Shay had ever gotten to fishing was opening a can of tuna.

'Who's she?'

Not only the question but the tartness of the voice brought me out of my thoughts about the election.

I was sitting between two women on the ass-numbing folding chairs. On my left was Caitlin Conners, who ran the day-to-day operations of the campaign for my firm. Caitlin was long, lean and red-haired, a college star in track with a pretty prairie-girl face and a sly smile. On my right was Elise Logan, Robert's wife, a striking if somewhat ethereal woman you had to be careful with. She had suffered a terrible childhood trauma, so terrible that she had been sent to psychiatric hospitals throughout her life, most recently three years ago. Shay's people couldn't talk about this on paid media but their printed material coyly referred to it many times. I liked Elise more than I did Robert, actually. She was one of those wan beauties you always read about in Agatha Christie; I wanted to protect her.

I had to scan the crowd to see whom she'd referred to. I didn't see the woman until my eyes reached the back of the gym.

From this distance she looked wrong not only for a town hall meeting, but also for a small burg like Linton. Just the way her hip was cocked, the way she smiled so obviously at Logan and the way her white silk blouse and tight dark skirt clung to her suggested that she likely had a big-city life somewhere. Not that she seemed obvious in any way; on the contrary, she was the kind of young woman – from here I guessed her age at around thirty – you saw in expensive clubs in Chicago and Washington, DC. I would have bet that the hairstyle had cost her three or four hundred and the duds an easy fifteen hundred. And if her facial features up close were as elegant as they appeared to be from here, I would probably be in danger of falling in love for an hour or two tonight.

The concern in Caitlin's response surprised me. 'She's nobody, Elise. She's probably press or something.'

The conversation ended when a cranky older woman in the crowd stood up and barked, 'What are you going to do about high school girls sending pictures of their boobies to their boyfriends?'

Hilarity, as they say, ensued.

The next morning I flew back to Chicago, and in the battles that awaited me forgot all about the woman at the back of the gym and Elise Logan's angry response to her. In fact, if I remembered anything it was the way the senator had responded to the booby question. He'd laughed and said, 'My only solution is to bow our heads and pray.' He'd gotten a big ovation. Then he'd gone on to make the correct pious noises.

Eleven days later I was with Caitlin and the senator again. I had talked to him every day, Skyped with him every other day or so and poured over the daily internal polls. We were up with women and African-Americans, but getting a miserable twenty-two percent of white working-class males, which was terrible for us, and trailing substantially behind with college-educated males, a group that tended to vote. Our opponent was a believer in taxing the grubbing poor and helping the much misunderstood but deserving rich. I suppose that explained it.

And now we were back in Chicago at a major fundraiser. My one and only dinner jacket was fraying on the left cuff but I assumed I could get through the evening without causing a social catastrophe. As I had been without woman since my friend of several months had decided to go back to her faithless husband after all – this time he'd be different, she'd said, and I cared enough about her to let the lie go un-challenged – I had vague hopes of meeting somebody tonight.

Combing my hair in my room before the festivities I puckered my lips then smiled at myself in the mirror. I almost always did this before a fundraiser where wealthy people were the targets. Some of them expected Olympian-level ass-kissing and always got it. They wanted you to know how important they were to the campaign and what they expected the senator would do for them when and if he returned to Washington for an additional six years. The Pope doesn't get the kind of servility they expect. Fortunately that's a small number of them.

This being Chicago, a small troop of security men with guns had been hired to make sure that nobody was packing and that everybody who walked through the front door was on the approved list. Assassination was not exactly unknown in America.

I arrived early and was met by James-never-Jim Logan, the younger and less successful brother of the senator. They were near twins physically. Tall, lean, lanky and both graying some – nice-looking if not quite handsome in traditional manly ways. Mid-forties, my own age.

But there the similarities ended. Their father had spent his life in communications – radio, mostly – and at the time of his death owned a large number of small and mid-size radio stations across the country. That was the basis of his sprawling fortune, a fortune Robert had overseen quite well before entering politics, where he was equally successful.

James was the swashbuckler. Fast cars, faster women and three failed start-ups in a three-year period. At that point, his own inheritance depleted, he patched up a quarrelsome relationship with Robert and began to live off his older brother's charity. First he worked as a staffer for the then Representative Logan. But Robert made him do the kind of scut work most staffers have to do. So James did what every right-thinking American lad does who loves to sit and drink and toss the ol' shit back and forth. He became a lobbyist, spending most of his time working for firms that were interested in snagging his brother's vote. But it turned out that Robert's charity didn't extend to selling his vote to James' firms so they fired him. Unhappily he went back to work on Robert's staff.

'I saw the internals, Dev. Not looking so good.' James was friends with another group of consultants. He had tried to convince Robert to dump me and go with them. All this took place two years ago. He still took every opportunity to challenge me. Everybody knows somebody who's better at a particular job than you are; consultants are used to that. But James makes it personal. Had I been less of the considerate gent I am, I would have brought up the subject of the loan he'd been begging his brother to make him. I'd caught them wrangling about it several times. James had another dumb idea for a dumb business – a public-relations agency for raccoons or something – and Robert was understandably sick of hearing about it.

'I don't like the internals either but we're

holding our own. And we have three weeks to go.'

'What's that expression? Whistling past the graveyard?' Then he turned his attention to the doors and the sudden influx of sparkling high-end donors.

More than a dozen women in evening dresses were filing in on the arms of their husbands. James had two reputations – one as a heavy-drinking hothead and the other as a chaser. He was one of those mysterious males you run into occasionally. He didn't have the looks or the charm to be successful with women but some-how he was. It could have been his brother's money or his brother's status as a senator, but somehow I didn't think so because there was also the matter of the mysterious *female*. Wo-men you credit with intelligence and judgment become slaves of a kind to men who treat them terribly. So maybe it was the bad-boy syndrome that kept James in contention. But fortunately I don't know that many women so inclined, so most kept their distance from him. He special-ized in treating women horribly; there had been a few lawsuits, in fact, and one abuse incident in which police had been called but the woman refused to press charges. This was after, I was told, Robert offered her a good chunk of change.

'I'm a lot more comfortable in a union hall than I am in a place like this.'

I wanted to laugh but I couldn't, of course. It

was alleged by James he had the 'touch' (his word) with the working class, so he actually went to some meetings in union halls in Robert's district. A union guy I knew who'd worked with James said, 'He came to a meeting and left after twenty minutes. He claimed he had another appointment. But you could see that we kind of freaked him out. Like we'd give him an infection if he stayed long enough.'

An angel of mercy in the comely form of Caitlin Conners appeared in a strapless silver gown. Very fetching. She slid her arm through mine and said, 'I hope you're planning to dance with me tonight.'

'If you'd ever seen me try to dance you wouldn't be asking me that.'

She stuck her tongue out at me. I'd always loved her occasional immaturity.

'I'll dance with you,' James said. 'In fact, I already have.'

'Yes, I remember. And by the time we were finished I'd wished I'd had my rape whistle.' She obviously wasn't joking.

Most men would have been embarrassed to hear a woman say that about them. Not James. He just grinned. 'Oh, I forgot you're a virgin.'

Caitlin's laugh was piercing. 'You're such a clown, James, and you don't even know it.'

Then she was brushing her lips against my cheek – all perfume and warm woman flesh – and hurrying away.

'Bitch.'

'She's a friend of mine. And she's not a bitch.'

'They're all bitches, Conrad. And when you grow up someday, you'll realize that.'

He smirked and walked away.

A few dozen men and women in white coats were finishing their work with the tables that filled three-quarters of the small ballroom. The walls were hung with large color photographs of our senator doing various things including being sworn in, waving to people at a Cubs game, whitewater rafting in Colorado, looking somber as he delivered a speech to his colleagues, standing between a rabbi and a priest, shooting baskets with inner-city kids and hugging Elise and his teenage daughter Maddy to him. If we could have gotten a photo of him ascending into heaven we'd have had our victory in our pocket.

There was a stage with a six-piece band of mostly bald men in shiny red dinner jackets and blood-red cummerbunds. They called themselves the Cavaliers; four of them were lawyers and two worked at the same brokerage firm. Not rock-and-roll rebels but I'd heard them play several times before and they were just right for gigs like this.

There were enough small chandeliers to blind you and enough flowers to give you a sinus infection. The peach and red décor was smart and the red chairs comfortable. I'd tried one. I'd also scanned a menu. I was up for the Grilled Marinated Salmon with Roasted Red Pepper

Sauce and Saffron Rice. For fifteen thousand dollars a couple – half that for singles – would you expect any less?

Within half an hour the place was filled with people of various ages and various colors all shiny and fine in their evening attire and almost immediately klatching up in groups of friends. Young men and women in red jackets – replacing the first battalion of white jackets – flitted about the room like worker ants offering cocktails while the Cavaliers tuned up.

When Elise and Robert appeared fifteen minutes later, everybody turned to the doors. They made their way toward the front of the room, throwing out smiles and nods the way royalty had once thrown out roses. A standing ovation was inevitable since everybody was standing anyway and little effort was required.

At an appropriate distance behind them, like a courtesan, came Caitlin. The problem was her smile. She'd obviously had to wrench it out of herself and I wondered why.

I'd hoped to talk to her before we both took our seats at the small table nearest the dance floor – just the five of us, Elise and Robert, Caitlin and I, and of course my good friend James – but there wasn't an opportunity because exactly on time a burly guy from the Chicago machine grabbed the microphone that Robert would be using for his speech and proceeded to inform us of what a buncha great people we were and how we were gonna break the legs – so to speak – of our opponent. I exaggerate, of course, but not by much.

Dinner, it seemed, was served.

By the time both Robert and Elise had finished their first cocktail it was clear that they, too, were wrenching paparazzi smiles out of themselves. Robert kept glancing at her nervously and she kept glaring at him in return. Then they'd become aware of me observing them and up would come these rickety bullshit smiles like fading footlights.

James had excused himself after gulping down a drink. He was making the rounds of the tables, no doubt searching for tonight's lucky woman, married or not. That he'd be interrupting people's dinners wouldn't bother him – not James. Or maybe he was smart. Maybe he just wanted to get away from the tension at the table. But whatever, he'd be hitting on women all through the night, taking what he considered the trophy back to his Michigan Avenue condo. The gossip columnists in Washington loved him. He was always good for a couple of sleazy lines. I'd finally convinced Robert to rein him in by threatening to fire him. James had gotten all in my face about it; like I gave a shit.

Caitlin kept telling Elise how pretty she looked and she did, her pale elegance in her mauve gown all the more endearing because of her palpable sadness.

What the hell was going on?

'Excuse me,' Elise said. I tried to pretend that

I didn't notice the tears in her pale gray eyes. 'I need to visit the ladies' room.'

As soon as she was gone Robert said, 'Well, this is some goddamned night, isn't it? I could've just stayed home if I wanted to hear her tear into me.' Then, quickly: 'I shouldn't have said that. I love her. She's the love of my life, in fact, and I was the one who screwed it up.' Then he was on his feet and tossing his heavy white cloth napkin on the table. 'I'm going to the john myself.'

'All right,' I said to Caitlin once he'd disappeared. 'What the hell is going on here?'

'He's right. He screwed it up and he's paying for it.'

'Screwed what up?'

'His marriage. He had a little affair three years ago and she's never been able to trust him since. They've tried to keep it quiet but one night when we were in a private plane they woke me up with their arguing. I was able to figure it out in pieces. Some waitress in a Washington pub. Georgetown, I guess. The woman was crazy enough to call him – drunk, of course – late at night. Elise was able to find the number on the phone in the morning and called it. The woman answered. It took her a week to work on him – Elise, I mean – but he finally admitted that he'd slept with the woman three times. Which meant it was probably ten times or more. It really destroyed Elise. You know how fragile she's always been anyway. It runs in her family.

A lot of mental issues.'

'Robert told me about that. What's she so upset about tonight?'

'Just seeing all these beautiful women, I guess. She starts thinking about him sneaking around again and kind of loses it. She feels threatened all the time. She's seeing a therapist and taking anti-anxiety meds because it's getting worse, but they don't seem to be helping much.'

The first time you meet a potential client you expect to hear nothing but what a wonderful swell man or woman he or she is. You expect that. The problems come out in the following meetings when you've begun to work together. *Oh, didn't I mention...? Oh, I didn't think that would be a problem! That was just a misunderstanding with the IRS.* Eventually you get most of it but not all of it. When George McGovern ran for president in 1972 his vice-presidential choice, a man named Thomas Eagleton, forgot to mention the teeny tiny fact that he had spent time in a mental hospital for depression. McGovern probably hadn't had much of a chance of winning anyway but getting stalled like that right at the start of his campaign sure didn't help him.

Some of my clients don't like the fact that when I hire opposition researchers to comb the past of our opponent I also pay them to comb the past of my candidate. I also tell them if I ever learn that they were involved in a felony that has come to light I will in turn inform the police of it. So if they ever have anything to hide tell me upfront so we can deal with it. I have been fortunate thus far; most of the things they haven't wanted to tell me about dealt with infidelity.

Robert was back. He started to talk but by the time he was seated a small group of well-wishers had gathered around our table and were telling him how much they were enjoying themselves tonight. He was good at the blarney. Not a hint of anger. The men shook his hand and the women kissed his left cheek. He smiled as if he'd gone to acting school to learn how.

All this time the machine man had been introducing other machine politicians. The applause had diminished considerably after the fourth or fifth one. People got tired of seeing the farm team. They wanted to see the star of the World Series and tonight that was Senator Robert Logan.

When his name was announced everybody stood. The applause was fulsome and lengthy. The senator took the stage. And just as he did so Elise came back. She sat down without a word and turned her attention to the stage where the senator was just beginning his speech. The gray eyes were dry now, though the rims looked wounded.

Having had a hand in writing the speech there were no surprises for me. I wished I was sitting at the back. Watching people was a lot more interesting than watching the stage. Elise was one chair away from me. When I saw her start to lean forward I wondered what she was going to do. Then I realized she was putting her hand out for me to take. I was glad to hold it for her. I'd known a few people, including men, who'd been thoroughly devastated by love affairs gone bad. One of the guys had tried to cut his wrists. I'd visited him twice a week on a psych ward for two months. Elise and I smiled at each other.

Robert got another standing O when he finished his speech. The band waited for everybody who wanted to rush to the stage to congratulate him on solving all our national problems in just under seventeen minutes. Then the lights went low over both the dance area and the bandstand and they broke into the ballad 'Laura', which they hyped up just a bit.

I watched Elise stare in the direction of Robert. Though he'd moved off the area where couples were already dancing he was still surrounded by well-wishers.

Elise said, 'Would you dance with me, Dev?'

Caitlin said, 'Every woman in the office has tried to get him to dance for years.'

I said, 'Is your insurance paid up, Elise?'

She had a sad, shy smile. 'Robert stands on my feet. You couldn't be any worse than he is.'

I must have done all right because she didn't scream and there was no sign of bleeding. I did the old box step I'd learned in Catholic school. A rather buxom nun had taught the boys before letting us loose on the girls.

I was several inches taller than she was so she had no trouble placing her head against my chest. She was so slight and fine-boned I had to be careful of hurting her in some way. She was the flower-like princess out of a boy's tale of noble knights. And soon enough she did what I'd known she wanted to do. Talk.

'I'm such a child sometimes.'

'We all are, Elise.'

'I can't imagine you being childish.'

'You can ask my ex-wife.'

'How's she doing, by the way?'

'Just about two years out now and she's doing fine. Knock wood.' Just before my ex-wife's breast cancer operation she'd asked me to fly to Boston to be at her bedside along with her new husband and my daughter. I was kind of wary of him at first, but he turned out to be a hell of a nice guy and we got along fine.

I gave Elise an update.

'It's so nice you can still be friends. I'm sorry you had to split up.'

'I wasn't a very good husband.'

'You put yourself down a lot, have you ever noticed that?'

'I'm just stating a fact, Elise. I was on the road so much it was inevitable.'

She put her head against me again and we danced for a while without talking. I was back in high school or college with a pretty girl in my arms. I liked the feeling. Then she leaned back and said, 'I know he loves me.'

'I know that, too.'

'It's just that I'm so damned suspicious. My therapist said that this may become a self-fulfilling prophecy. I'm afraid I'll lose him but my behavior is pushing him into leaving me.'

'Talk to him.'

'That's all I do. Talk to him. Or talk past him, really. He's heard it so often he doesn't even listen anymore and I don't really blame him.'

As the song came to its end we started walking back to our table. She had some of the same problems her husband did in navigating the ballroom. People kept rushing up to her and squeezing her hand and kissing her cheek and throwing bouquets of flattery at her. She didn't handle it as well as Robert did but she tried; the smile never left her lips and the voice gushed appropriately in gratitude. Only the anxiety in the eyes revealed her discomfort.

'That's one of the things I've never liked,' she said when we were alone again. 'Being on public display.' But as soon as she said, 'Maddy's here!' she hurried on ahead of me to the table where her nineteen-year-old daughter sat talking to Caitlin.

Maddy Logan was the same fragile size as her mother and every bit as beautiful, but there was a robust quality to her movements that lent her a vitality her mother lacked. Her mother was the immortal image in the portrait; Maddy was the living version. In her wine-red dress with the red flower in her fine pale hair, she was all demure sexuality and amused dark eyes. She rushed up to embrace her mother and they stood hand-in-hand talking to Caitlin and me as I sat down next to her.

'Maddy's in a play at Northwestern,' Elise said. 'She wasn't sure she could get away to be here.'

'I have a very tiny part. Two lines. They didn't miss me at all.'

Elise was downright bubbly. 'No wonder you and Dev get along. Trying to give either of you a compliment is impossible.'

Maddy laughed. 'I'll take any compliment you want to give me.'

There are many worse fates than sitting at a table with three attractive women. The waiter came by, we all ordered drinks and Caitlin, Maddy and I talked about how well the night was going while Elise, of course, scouted the territory for sight of her husband. The brief joy she'd shown with Maddy was long gone; I could see the tension in her shoulders and jaw line. Terrible suspicions would be crackling through her mind like summer lightning illuminating her worst fears.

And you had to give the dark gods their sense of humor, because as a group of people retreated from the dance floor after another song ended, there stood the senator and a woman who looked oddly familiar to me. Then I recognized her. The mystery woman who'd stood at

38

the back of the gym during the town hall meeting eleven days ago.

'It's her again, Caitlin.' The desperation was back in Elise's voice.

Maddy clutched her arm. 'It's all right, Mom. He's just talking to her – whoever she is. That's all.'

Caitlin shrugged pretty shoulders. 'This is the fifth time she's shown up at our recent events. The last two times she's managed to talk to the senator. He says he doesn't even know her name.'

I didn't like any of this. An elected official, from small town council member to president of the United States, is a target for so many people with bad intent. There's always the possibility that the other side is setting a trap for you or that the very ordinary-looking person wishing you well is actually an assassin who managed to slip a weapon past security.

'I'll be right back,' I said, already on my feet.

The two of them stood just outside the shadows of the dance floor. In the lighted area, which was at least three-fourths of the ballroom, people were sedately partying. You did not see a lot of ladies ripping off their clothes and dancing on tables at fundraisers, though something like that would be more than welcome on nights when the speeches were interminable.

The closer I got the more I realized that she was not quite human. She was a fashion magazine icon pretending to be flesh and blood. She had been cleaned, painted and dressed to please one of those photographers who are more famous than the women they shoot. In her shiny black dress her perfect body was almost a match for her perfect face. But nothing could quite match it. God had been in a very good mood the day He'd created her.

She sensed me before Robert did and was already luring me to her before he turned to watch me close in on them.

Five times at the senator's recent events. She was wrong in every way. Before Robert could say anything I reached out, took her hand and said, 'The senator needs to go back to his table, so how about having this dance with me?'

For just a moment consternation shone in those blue eyes; she knew she was in some kind of trouble but it had come on so quickly she hadn't been able to prepare for combat. Then, 'Why, of course. I'd never turn down a handsome man.' To Robert, 'It was so nice seeing you again, Senator. My group really appreciates everything you've done for women's rights.'

'Senator, your wife and daughter asked me to ask you if you'd come back to your table. Your daughter wants to tell you about the play she's in.'

Robert, confused, embarrassed and angry, said, 'It was very nice seeing you again.' Then to me, restraining himself with great effort: 'I'll talk to you later, my friend. Be prepared.'

Then he stalked off.

She was a pro for sure. She was already sliding her arm around my waist as she said, 'He's bigger than you are. Think you could beat him up?'

'I have an agreement with my clients. I don't beat them up unless they don't pay their bills.'

'You're a practical man. Good common sense.'

'So just who the hell are you?'

A faux Southern accent. 'I do declare, Mr Conrad, that you just might give me the vapors. I like strong, tough men.'

She knew my name, meaning that she would also know everything else about me.

'Your name.'

'Tracy Cabot. See, I'm easy.'

'And you do what?'

'Are you going to beat me up if I don't tell you?' At least she'd dropped the accent.

'And you do what, Tracy?'

'Oh, you're no fun.' And then she brought us together in a most pleasing way and as we held each other, the feel and shape of her body forced me to close my eyes for a time and just enjoy the touch and smell and urgency of her. She led me onto the dance floor and we danced.

'Now, see, isn't that better?' She was having fun with the dumb guy. Give him an erection and he was your slave.

'Who do you work for?'

'Would you really expect me to tell you?'

41

'No. But at least we're cutting through the bullshit. I don't want you around the senator anymore.'

'Jealous? Want him for yourself?'

'I want him to win. That means avoiding any setups.'

'Maybe you haven't heard. Women can vote now. They also have the right to go to political events and support their candidates.'

'You must have quite the job. You have free time to track the senator all over the state. He was upstate the night before last and way downstate last night. And here you are now in Chicago.'

'That's another thing you mustn't have heard about yet. They're called airplanes. And sometimes women who have the right to vote ride those airplanes when they want to go somewhere.'

'All I care about is that we understand each other. I don't want you around the senator anymore. Period.'

She started to say something but I eased myself out of her clutches and started walking briskly back toward our table. I didn't look to see how she was handling the unthinkable situation of somebody dumping her on a dance floor. Her irritating Southern accent came back to me; if being dumped on a dance floor didn't give her the vapors nothing would.

The table was as cold and silent as a mausoleum. Caitlin was the only one who looked at me. She was tense and unhappy. Maddy held her mother's hand and Robert scowled off into the distance. As subtly as I could I signaled Caitlin with a head nod.

'Would anybody like to go to the ladies' room with me?' she said.

'That sounds like a good idea,' Maddy said with a fraudulent smile. 'C'mon, Mom.'

The way she helped Elise up reminded me of the time I'd spent with my father in his last days. I'd held on to him even when he just wanted to cross the room. But Elise was only forty-two and as far as I knew in good health.

After they left, Robert said, 'I should fire your ass.'

'Go ahead and fire me. I don't like working for morons, anyway.'

'What the hell's that supposed to mean?'

We both knew we had to keep our voices low and our body language friendly.

'This Tracy Cabot is following you all over the state. You've no doubt been photographed together at least three or four times when she comes up to talk to you. Right there's a story.'

'What story?'

'A beautiful, mysterious woman in three or four different outfits photographed next to the sitting senator seeking re-election. I'm surprised nobody's picked it up yet.'

'Nobody cares.'

'Elise cares.'

His cheeks became a deep red. 'My wife is

none of your goddamned business.'

'And I care even if you don't. The woman is a plant. How can you not see that?'

'The woman is an admirer and nothing else.'

'Robert, you've been in politics quite a while now. You know how this works. The other side sets out all kinds of traps. And you're walking right into one.'

'Bullshit. She's just a woman with some money who appreciates how I vote on women's issues.'

'Have you ever been alone with her?'

He had to take the bullet between the eyes before he could speak. 'What the hell? What kind of question is that?'

'A simple one. Have you ever been alone with her?'

'Of course not. I don't play around. You know that.'

For now I had to let the lie go, ludicrous as it was. The list was long of elected officials who toted their mistresses and girlfriends along on the campaign trail. The ladies usually had protective meaningless titles to explain their presence. But I didn't expect Her Highness Tracy Cabot to have a cover story that mundane.

The waiter took our order for a couple more drinks and we sat there not talking while we waited for them. Not talking to each other, I should have said. The senator had to play senator for his admirers, some of whom were starting the procession home. I wondered if he was as tired as I was. The situation with the Cabot woman and the confrontation with Robert had ground me down. I was still worried about Tracy Cabot. One thing I'd learned as an investigator was that a good share of the time your instinctive response to a situation was correct. And this whole thing just felt bad. Maybe very bad.

When the women came back, Maddy said, 'Mom wants to go home, Dad.'

'Of course, honey. Let's go.' He started toward Elise but her look stopped him. 'We'll see you later, Caitlin.'

Their departure happened quickly, so quickly that he only had time to snap at me, 'My brother knows a consultant who could start work tomorrow morning. You'd better keep that in mind.'

As we watched them make their slow way through admirers, Caitlin said, 'You must have really pissed him off.'

'I did.'

'That woman?'

'Uh-huh.'

'I warned him about her. He told me it wasn't any of my business.'

'He told me that he's never been alone with her.'

'Wow. You asked him that?'

'Yeah.'

'You believe him?'

'I want to,' I said. 'I really do.'

TWO

I admit to being single-minded; selfish if you insist. My first thought seeing Tracy Cabot lying twisted on the floor four days after my run in with her was nothing as noble as a human life had been wasted. No, my first thought was *There goes the election.* I could justify this by saying that the party and thus the country needed this seat. That if one more representative of the Tea Party gets into the Senate the average American will grow ever closer to living in poverty. We will be on our way to oligarchy. So you could – could if you were being kind – see my first response as somewhat noble. But who would be that foolish?

She was dressed in a red silk blouse, stylish jeans and three-inch black heels. She hadn't come out here to go hiking.

The wound hadn't bled that much; somebody had hit her with something heavy on the right side of the head. Those dazzling eyes were dulled now and the mouth shaped in the form of an objection. Or curse. The most certain proof of death was the stench. It often is. From the looks of things, she'd been dead since last night.

Very soon the room would be full of police personnel performing forensic investigations of various kinds. There would be a traffic jam of reporters' cars and vans. For now these would all be local. But Chicago wasn't far away and the networks would have people up here within two hours. The circus would be in town and within six hours press from foreign countries already posted here would be striding the midway.

Sex. A senator. A murder. An international orgasm.

I was careful not to touch anything, including her.

The back porch was not only screened in but stuffed with plump comfortable furnishings, a dry bar and a corner packed with fishing gear. You could sit here and watch the sunset with all the melancholy sights and sounds of the dying day and share it like a prayer with your wife or lover. The best days of my marriage had been like that, that kind of shared peace and unspoken love.

But as I stared at it now I remembered for the first time that on the other side of the hill, maybe six or seven miles away, was the Logan family mansion. Civilization was only ten minutes away.

I looked for signs of a struggle and found one easily – a small bronze statue of Jack Kennedy. The upper portion was lurid with blood and hair.

My eyes found her again.

In most cases I would have wondered about her. Not as a character assassin paid by somebody to take down a damned dumb senator, but as a person, because behind the beauty and the expensive work – in natural light, without the heavy make-up, I could see that she'd had some done on her nose and cheeks – there had been a person of some kind. Somebody's daughter – maybe even somebody's mother, though that seemed unlikely. I'd wanted to bust her ass and then shove her in the face of her masters but I hadn't wanted – nor certainly expected – this. Not this at all.

There was nothing else for me there so I went back to where Robert sat in a leather chair before the great dead fireplace. His right hand held a tall, clear glass that appeared to be filled with bourbon.

'Go easy on that. We need to call the police.'

'Oh, this'll be great, won't it?'

'Robert, you lied to me. You were involved with her.'

'No, damn it, not the way you say. We never had real sex.'

Just what I needed. I was in the company of Bill Clinton, Jr. We were going to parse words.

'Hand job? Blow job? What the hell are we talking about here, Robert?'

He stupidly gunned his drink then shook his head miserably. 'We, uh, laid naked together one night but nothing happened.'

'You both had a religious conversion at the same moment?'

'Fuck yourself, Dev.'

'I need answers, Robert. We need to call the police and we need to get Zuckerman up here.' Ben Zuckerman was the go-to criminal lawyer for our side in Chicago. He was a master.

'I didn't kill her.'

'All right. That's a start.'

'You believe me?'

'Yes.'

'Oh, God, Dev, thanks for believing me.' I thought he was being sarcastic until I saw the tears in his eyes. He was coming undone.

'You need to pull yourself together, Robert. We need to get your story straight so it's coherent.'

'I know, it's just—'

'How many times did you see her alone?'

'Twice. The first time was in her hotel room. We had room service and made out a little. That was all.'

Microphones, video cameras...

'How about the second time?'

'A different hotel room. That was when we— When I couldn't do anything.'

Microphones, video cameras...

'Why couldn't you do anything?'

'I don't know. Why can't you get it up sometimes? Maybe it was guilt. About Elise, I mean. But that's why I got so hot and bothered in the first place. Our sex life hasn't exactly been

49

great. Since I had that little fling, I mean.'

Your sex life isn't very good since you stepped out on your wife so you step out on her again.

'Now I want you to tell me everything you did so far today.'

His expression said that I was tormenting him and he resented it. But he spoke with forced patience. This was the man of privilege talking to a hired hand.

'She was supposed to be here waiting for me. I'd made the mistake of telling her how great our cabin is, so she asked if she could spend a night here. She said she liked waking up in the country. She even managed to con me into giving her a key to the place. I didn't want to but I was in no position to say no.'

'God, Robert, she was probably planting cameras.'

'I'm not *completely* stupid, Dev. I finally realized you were right about her. I was going to surprise her. She thought we were meeting to have sex. But I was going to tell her that she could go to hell and that I wouldn't stand still for blackmail. I was going to dare her to go to the media. I was ashamed as hell and thought I'd finally gotten my brains and my balls back.'

He formed a fist to shake at the dark gods. 'I was so stupid, Dev. I can't believe how stupid I was.' A sob; then the tears. Not for the dead woman. 'All I can think of is what this'll do to Elise. I never told you but she was in a kind of rest home last year after she had a hard time dealing with things.'

'"Things" being your affair?'

'I'd give anything to take that back. Elise is ... She had psychological problems as a child. She saw a shrink for most of high school and half of college. It runs in the family. Her mother committed suicide and she always blamed her father.' He made a face. 'The old man was in love with somebody else and about a week after he told her, Elise's mother killed herself. With a gun. Elise got all her anxiety attacks and depression from her mother.' Then, 'And she'll leave me now, for sure. She deserves to leave me.'

More tears.

I went out on to the porch. I had Ben Zuckerman's number on my speed dial. His personal assistant answered.

'Hi, Stephanie. It's Dev Conrad.'

'Hi, Dev. I hope you're in the city. It's such a beautiful day.'

'Actually I'm upstate for the day. But it's nice up here, too.'

'I love fall so much. My favorite time.'

'Mine, too. Say, Stephanie, is Ben there?'

'Yes he is. He's got one of our temps in with him. I can buzz him if you'd like.'

'I'd appreciate that very much. Thank you.'

The wait took about a minute and a half.

'Hi, Dev.'

'Hi, Ben. Listen, you've been to Robert's cabin.'

He laughed. 'I got the worst hangover of my life the weekend I went up there, supposedly to fish.'

'I can't say any more than this: we need you to fly up here now. Take a private plane if you need to and charge it to us. There's an airport nearby. Call me back when you have the arrangements made.'

'Hey, Dev. You're scaring me, and I mean it.'

'Nobody's more scared than Robert is.'

'I'll have to blow off a couple of very important clients.'

'You know how badly we need this seat.'

'Damn it!' he said and took a deep breath. 'I really am dreading this. I'll be on a plane as soon as I can. Give me your cell number again, huh?'

THREE

Detective Frank Hammell stood with me on the porch as we watched a green Chevrolet two-door sedan come around the corner of the A-frame and stop. He and two of his uniformed men had been here for just over half an hour now. Bright yellow crime scene tape clashed with the more autumnal colors of the trees and grass.

He had made it clear from the start that he considered me at best a nuisance. I'd warned Robert three different times that after his brief explanation of how he'd come to find the body he didn't have to say anything else until his lawyer showed up. He'd given me the name of a local attorney who was also a strong political supporter of his. He felt she could handle things until Ben got here.

'There she is,' Hammell said, watching a woman get out of the Chevy. 'She's a pretty one. And if you don't think so, just ask her.' His spiteful tone suggested a lot but since it was in code I didn't know what he was talking about.

Her name was Jane Tyler. Everything about her, from the cut of her blue suit and starched white blouse – and certainly including her pretty, freckled face – suggested that she was a smart, confident woman who'd be good in a courtroom. This impression faltered for just a moment when her blue eyes met Hammell's.

She came up onto the porch toting a slender briefcase. She nodded to each of us and then said, 'Hi, Frank.'

'It's Detective Hammell these days, Jane. You should've figured that out for yourself.' He was a tall man who might have played basketball in his high school days. At least, the graying crew cut suggested something like that. He wore a gray suit and black tie and blue shirt. He kept squeezing one of those little rubber balls that help your grip get more deadly.

'All right, Detective Hammell. I'd like to talk to the senator if I may.'

'Then this is the man you want to talk to. He seems to be giving the orders.'

I put out my hand and we shook. 'I'm Dev Conrad. I work with the senator on his campaign.'

A good, open Midwestern smile. 'Oh, yes. He talks about you all the time.' Then to Hammell: 'Detective Hammell, I'd like ten minutes alone with Senator Logan. And since I imagine you've got a couple of men inside I'd like to request that they wait outside while I talk to him.'

'Why, hell yes, Jane. You and this Conrad are making my work easy for me. All I got to do is

54

take orders and not worry my pretty little head at all.'

For the first time her blue eyes showed concern. 'Detective Hammell, I'm not asking for anything irregular and we both know you don't have to go along with it. If you're against it just say so.'

'Now how could I say no to a former family member?'

This time her look was one of exasperation. A soap opera was playing out but I still didn't know the plot.

He moved from us to the door and said, 'Carter and Banes, get out of there right now.'

As he spoke another car came around the side of the house. This one was a new silver Buick and had a doctor's tag on the license plate. Probably the medical examiner.

The two uniformed men came out of the house. Both of them carried small evidence bags. All the bags were filled. 'Our good friend the lawyer needs to talk to the senator.'

Neither of them showed any particular emotion. They were likely competent officers doing their job. They didn't seem to share their boss's enmity toward Jane. In fact, one of them was bold enough to nod to her and offer a whisper of a smile.

I heard one or maybe two vehicles making their way down the slope leading to the house. The place was getting busy.

'You better get in there right now,' Hammell

said to Jane. 'You know how Doctor Wilhelm hates to be kept waiting.' His moderately civil tone surprised me.

Jane hurried inside.

The man who came up on the porch appeared to be in his fifties with graying hair that had once been red. He wore a V-neck blue sweater with a button-down white shirt underneath. Jeans and tan cowboy boots. Somewhere he'd bought himself a pair of mean green eyes, maybe at a gun shop. It was hard to imagine him comforting a patient.

Even before Hammell had had time to introduce him, Wilhelm leaned into the detective and grinned. 'Looks like I'm gonna get the senator I want after all. Sorry about that, Detective Hammell.' Hammell grunted but said nothing. Then Wilhelm glared in my direction. 'Who's this?'

'Logan's consultant.'

His hand went out. I took it automatically. Shockingly weak for such a medical cowpoke. I wanted to punch him in the mouth.

'A little joke there, Conrad. My name's Tag, by the way.'

'Uh-huh.'

'I'd never let my politics interfere with my job.' He was covering his ass in case I wanted to give the press his name and repeat what he'd said. 'Well, I'd better get in there.'

There were numerous cases around the country where medical examiners had been bought off. Most notorious was the case of the Chicago-area detective who'd allegedly murdered three of his four wives.

'You'll need to hold off ten minutes, Tag. Jane Tyler's in there.'

'Tyler? What the hell's she doing here?'

'The senator asked Mr Conrad here to get her. They've got some hotshot lawyer flying in from Chicago and she's holding down the fort until he gets here.'

'She's about as cold a little bitch as they come.' The word cold was, I suspected, attributable to the possibility that he'd hit on her and she'd spurned him. Why, here was a stud popular enough to be both a husband and a player – how could she turn down a prize like him?

An ambulance pulled into view, followed by another squad car. And right behind them, still coming down the slope, was another vehicle that was soon enough revealed to be a Channel 8 van. Like Jane and Wilhelm, they'd all have to park outside the yellow tape.

'You have any ideas yet, Frank?' Wilhelm asked.

'Not yet. Way too soon. I'd like to talk to the senator but our friend here doesn't think that's a good idea.'

A man and woman in white came up from the ambulance. Hammell checked his watch and said, 'Jane Tyler's got four more minutes in there. We'll just wait.'

'This is really bullshit, Frank. I've got a lot

to do.'

The ambulance woman rolled her eyes when Wilhelm said this. He was clearly a beloved figure in medical circles.

Jane beat her deadline by a couple minutes. She walked out with her briefcase and glanced around at the new arrivals. When her eyes stopped on Wilhelm her face tightened perceptibly. Then, 'Detective Hammell, the senator would like to talk to you but I'd like to be with him when you do.'

She was being polite. She had the legal right to be with her client.

But a cop is a cop. 'That's fine. But I want to do it at the station.'

'Are you serious?'

'Yes, I am. For one thing, Tag has to get in there, and for another the ambulance folks have to do their job after he finishes.'

A hefty man in a Bears jersey with a camera on his shoulder was shooting an attractive blonde woman in a tan Burberry who was talking into a hand-held microphone. The reporters who'll go on to better gigs are the ones who know stories like these are the ones that will get them there. So they play it big.

'I'd like to speak to Mr Conrad for a second,' Jane said.

'Then you can do it around the corner of the house, lady, because I'm going inside right now. Some of us have more important jobs than covering up for a lying politician.' Wilhelm didn't wear righteous indignation well at all.

Hammell nodded and Jane led me down the steps of the porch and a few feet around the house.

'The senator would like you to drive over to his house and explain to his family what's going on.' She was good at reading faces. 'It's a terrible job and I told him that. But what he's afraid of is that Doctor Wilhelm will call the senator's brother, James, and all the information will come from those two. They're big friends.'

I couldn't help myself. 'Wilhelm and James? Man, that James sure is a loyal guy.'

I was graced by the warmth of her smile. 'I shouldn't comment.'

'You just did.'

'Anyway, they really need to hear everything from somebody they trust and like. Elise and Maddy despise James. And Doctor Wilhelm started hitting on Maddy as soon as she turned eighteen. They all go to the same country club. The board there warned him he'd be kicked out if he kept it up.'

I thought of Elise's angry and anguished face when she'd spotted Tracy Cabot at the fundraiser. I was afraid to think about how she would react to this. All I could hope for was that she was stronger mentally than she appeared.

'To be fair, I have to tell you something about Wilhelm. He's a wonderful doctor. My brother was in a car crash and we thought he wouldn't live through the night. Wilhelm saved him through surgery. His problem is with younger women, and one of these days it'll catch up to him.'

'I still don't like him. But I'm glad you told me he's competent.'

'More than competent. He's very good. Now, I need to tell the senator that we have to go to the station. He's not going to like it.'

'I can come along if you want.'

She humored me. 'Anything to get out of going to tell Elise and Maddy, huh? I don't blame you for that. They're very sweet people and they deserve a lot better than this.'

I went to my car wondering about her relationship with Detective Hammell. Speculation on the soap opera kept my mind off Elise.

FOUR

The mansion was a Shingle-style home with a gambrel roof that lent it a Victorian look. It had always been referred to locally as 'the mansion,' even though it really didn't qualify as one. The Logans had liked the fact that it was more than a century old, despite all the renovations it had required before they moved in. The lovingly-tended lawn stretched from the top of the hill on which the house sat all the way down to the rural gravel road below. The driveway was paved and widened in front of the house.

Mrs Weiderman answered the door. She was a tall, somewhat overweight woman with pure white hair worn short and one of those sweet faces that grandmothers order online right after they get the news about the forthcoming child. I had seen her raise hell with reporters, nasty drunks at parties and anyone who spoke ill of any of the Logans, James, unfortunately, included. After she opened the door she stood smiling at me. 'One of my favorite people.'

'Let me say the same. How are you, Mrs Weiderman?'

'Well, I suppose I'd be even happier if I was

thirty years younger, forty pounds lighter and fifty times smarter, but I guess I'm doing all right. Now get in here and let me get you some coffee. Are you hungry?'

The house was quiet, though somewhere I could hear a muffled TV. Once she'd brought me into the living room she sat me down and said, 'I believe you take it black.'

'Thank you. I could use some coffee.' I heard the anxiety in my voice and caught myself. 'When it's as good as yours it doesn't matter what time it is, Mrs Weiderman.'

It was a large room of framed Monet prints, comfortable deep- red matching couches and chairs, a stone fireplace large enough to roast a buffalo in and a grand piano in front of the floor-to-ceiling windows that looked out onto the forest. There was a dry bar tucked away; I had taken advantage of it quite a few times.

I got up from my chair, sat down again and once more got up. I was just sitting down again when Mrs Weiderman brought me my coffee and said, 'Maddy wants to see you, too. I told you last time I think she has a little crush on you. They'll be down in a few minutes.'

I thanked her then stood up again. This time I went all the way over to the grand piano and stared out at the woods. Whenever I got into trouble with my folks as a boy I imagined that I could run away and live in the forest. I never had a clear sense of what I'd do there, especially after nightfall, but eating leaves and tree bark sounded better than facing my parents' disappointment.

When I heard them I turned around and saw that they knew. They didn't know what, but they knew it would be bad. Maddy wore a tan crew-neck sweater, jeans and merrily striped socks; Elise was in a white blouse, black cardigan and jeans. Her feet were in black slippers.

'I'm almost afraid to hear, Dev. I have to tell you that. You could have phoned – Maddy and I both know that this is going to be terrible.'

Maddy and Elise sat on a couch in front of the fireplace. I sat in the chair opposite them.

'I called Dad's cell,' Maddy said. 'A strange man answered and then let Dad talk. Dad said he was being taken to the police station and that he loved Mom and I very much. And that you were coming over to explain everything.'

So they did know some of the details in broad stroke. A police officer answering and a father telling a daughter that he was being taken to the police station was ominous.

The more difficult part for me would be telling Elise about Tracy Cabot.

'I want to say right upfront that I believe he was set up by somebody to make it look as if he murdered someone. We all know Robert and we know that he would never kill anybody.' I tried to establish my professional and moral authority but I doubted they even heard me. They wanted the facts.

Elise was ahead of me. 'Someone was

actually murdered?'

'Yes.'

'My God, Dev. A murder. I can't believe it. Who was it?'

'A woman.'

'A woman?' A subtle shift in her expression and tone of voice. She was figuring out the elements of the equation here. A woman, the police and Robert.

'Was this a woman Robert knew?'

'Only slightly.'

'I see.' And she did see. All too clearly. 'Where did this happen?'

'At the cabin.'

'Our family's cabin?' She emphasized the word 'family.' 'Where Maddy and I always ride our bikes? Where Maddy had her birthday parties when she was a little girl?'

I nodded.

'I have the feeling, Dev, that you're not telling me everything.'

'I've told you everything I know, Elise.' I spoke softly because I could sense the agitation growing within her.

'If I didn't know better, I'd think you were protecting Robert.'

'I'm not, Elise. I don't believe he had anything to do with the murder, if that's what you mean.'

'You know damned well what I mean.'

'Mom, please—'

'Be quiet, Maddy.' Elise did not take her eyes

from mine. 'Was my husband having an affair with this woman?'

'No.' I wasn't about to go into the finer details.

'Did you ask him that?'

'Yes. That was the first thing I asked him.'

'And he said he wasn't having an affair with her?'

'Yes. And I believe him the same as I believe he didn't have anything to do with her death. I don't blame you for being angry and hurt, Elise, but our main concern is keeping him from being charged with murder.'

'In other words, you're worried about the election.'

'Yes. No point in lying, I'm worried about the election. That's my job in this. But we're friends, Elise. You and I and Maddy. I hope you understand how much I care about you.'

'And we care about you, Dev, you know that,' Maddy said.

But Elise was having none of our Oprah hug. 'Who was the woman?'

'Her name was Tracy Cabot. Somebody hit her on the head with something heavy and killed her.'

'She probably deserved it.'

'Mother!'

Elise brought her slight hand to her face and touched fingers to her forehead. 'Oh, God, forgive me for ever saying such a thing. I apologize to both of you.' Then, as if she'd already forgotten the tone of her apology, the anger was back in her voice. 'Dev, I don't believe what Robert told you and this time everybody will know he cheated on me. It will be all over the news.'

Maddy angled herself so that she could see her mother straight on. 'Mom, there's no point in going through all this. There was a woman involved and she's dead and the police think Dad did it.'

'He was the one who found the body. Before the police got there I called Ben Zuckerman. He's probably on a plane coming up here right now.'

'I have a right to know if my husband was sleeping with another woman.'

'He wasn't.'

I was back to Bill Clinton word parsing. He would have if he'd been able to get it up but since he couldn't he didn't.

'He told you that?' It didn't matter that we'd gone through this a minute or two before. She wanted to convince herself that he hadn't so she could find some relief from the turbulent emotions that were suffocating her; but her history with men in general and her father and husband suggested otherwise.

Maddy flung herself back against the couch and folded her arms across her chest. Her mother's persistence was obviously starting to grate on her.

'Elise, listen to me. That's exactly what he

told me.'

'He said to you, "I didn't sleep with her."'

'Yes, he did. They weren't, of course. But things were bad enough already.'

'But he was going to meet her at the cabin.'

'He was going to set her straight. That's why they were meeting there.'

'And now the police think he murdered her.' Was there the faintest note of satisfaction in her voice?

This time when she leaned forward she put her elbows on her knees and buried her face in her hands. Maddy took her in her arms but Elise stayed hidden. She probably wanted to crunch herself into the smallest configuration possible. And maybe just disappear.

I remembered the dry bar in the far corner straight behind the grand piano. I walked over there and filled a small glass with bourbon and water. When I got back Elise was sitting up again, but from the gaze I wondered if she was in shock. The dullness of her eyes suggested it.

She took the glass with both hands. Like a child. She began drinking right away.

Maddy thanked me *sotto voce*.

'That's all I need. To become an alcoholic.'

'Oh, yes, Mom. You drink so much. What're you up to now – two drinks a month or something like that?'

'Honey, you know how many alcoholics are in my family.'

'Yes, but you're not one of them.'

Elise had drunk most of the small glass. She set it carefully on the coffee table and then sat back and closed her eyes.

'Are you tired, Mom?'

'Uh-huh. Very.' Eyes still closed. Willing the world away and I didn't blame her.

'How about if I take you upstairs and tuck you in for a while?'

'It's funny, Dev.' Her eyes suddenly opened and she was staring at me. 'I knew there'd be a woman. My father was like that. He'd make promises to my poor mother but he'd always go back to whoring around. And then one day he announced he'd fallen in love with some girl at his office. I'd actually met her several times before that and liked her. Very pretty and smart. I felt so guilty that I'd had those thoughts when my father told my mother about her. As if I'd betrayed my mother somehow.'

'I'm sorry, Elise.'

She stood up abruptly. But she was uncertain, almost falling over, which she would have done if Maddy hadn't bolted up and grabbed her around the waist.

'Just lean on me, Mom. We'll take it easy and get you tucked in.'

Mother and child, roles reversed.

As if I'd already gone, and as Maddy began slowly walking her out of the room, Elise said, 'Tell Dev I'm sorry if I was a bitch.'

'You weren't a bitch, Mom. And Dev is our friend. He wouldn't think anything like that.'

She accompanied this with a glance over her shoulder. Another *sotto voce* thank you.

Suddenly Mrs Weiderman came into the room and Elise broke from Maddy and rushed to the much larger woman, embracing her and putting her head to Mrs Weiderman's chest. Elise began sobbing and the woman started stroking her small, fine head the way she would a child's. Maddy stood in place watching them, a fond smile in her eyes and on her mouth. After two or three minutes Mrs Weiderman gently eased herself back from Elise and nodded to Maddy. Then Maddy took charge of her mother again.

I watched them leave. I felt bolted to my chair. I was getting like Elise. I didn't want to stand up and meet the world again. The world I knew was always a harsh and deceitful one, but this new situation was a treachery I'd never faced before. My footing was anything but sure.

Mrs Weiderman came into the room and said, 'I heard some of it, Dev, but I didn't hear all of it. The police think that the senator killed a woman?'

'Well, since she was found in his so-called cabin, they're certainly interested in talking to him.'

She sat down with prim dignity on the edge of the couch, facing me. She lowered her voice respectfully. 'Was he seeing her, Dev?'

'I'm afraid so. But he told me that they had never slept together.'

'Oh, Lord. Poor Elise. Her father and then her

husband – and now her husband again. I feel so sorry for her.'

'I don't think he had anything to do with her death – that's what I have to focus on now. I like Elise very much but I can't worry about his marriage. Within a few hours the press will be out here en masse and the way they'll cover it will help to hand the other side the election.'

'Lord, I hadn't even thought about the election.'

'Let me ask you something, Mrs Weiderman: how many people had keys to the cabin?'

'Everybody. The whole family. I have one. And old Mr Stokes, the handyman we use for lighter work.'

'Does James have one?'

'James...' Then, 'My Lord, you're not thinking—?'

'No, I just want to be sure I know of everyone who has a key.'

'Oh.' But I could see she still didn't believe me. 'Yes, James has one, too. He takes some of his women there. As Elise says, "That's all right with us because it means he isn't here bothering us." I probably shouldn't say this but right now I'm more worried about Elise than I am about the senator. Thank God Maddy's strong. I think they would have divorced if it hadn't been for her. She would sit with her mother for hours and listen to the same thing over and over and never complain. And she would question her father from time to time to make sure he wasn't seeing that woman anymore. He resented it but he understood so he never got angry with her. And now—'

I suppose I heard the gunshot first but in my memory it and the scream are simultaneous. There was that second or two delay – it was the same with Mrs Weiderman – when we sat letting our ears inform our brains of the real meaning of the sounds ... and then we were lurching from our sitting positions and racing to the sound of more screams from upstairs.

I recall staring up the flight of stairs in front of me; it might have been a mountain. I went up them two at a time with Mrs Weiderman, gasping, close behind me.

PART TWO

FIVE

Because I'd slept in the guest room a number of times, I knew where I was going. I took the steps of the winding staircase two at a time and when I reached the landing on the second floor I saw Maddy already pounding on the door of the master bedroom. She'd just started shouting to be let in. 'Mom! Please let me in!'

As I ran toward her, her voice got even more urgent and her fist against the door louder. When I finally got a glimpse of her face, the shock and dismay she'd kept hidden downstairs – I'd admired how coolly she'd handled the news about her father; perhaps because she understood she'd needed to hold it together so she could help her mother – were clear on her pretty features now. She was frantic, fearing that her mother might be dead.

When I reached her she said, 'It's locked, Dev! It's *locked*!' She stepped aside. She wanted me to be the magic man, to fix this. I wished I could.

I tried the fancy filigreed doorknob knowing it would be no use. Then my voice joined Maddy's in calling out for Elise to let us in.

'Kick the door in! Kick the door in! Hurry, Dev!'

Thanks to the movies and television – not to mention at least a century of fiction – people have the impression that a kick or two will pop a door open in under a minute. And true, there are some old doors that probably wouldn't put up much resistance. But any reasonably well-made door in any reasonably well-made frame requires energy and a little time. Especially if the door resides inside a home as expensive as this one.

So while Maddy continued to scream I set about throwing myself against the door a few times, then slamming my foot into a space just under the doorknob.

Then a funny thing happened. It shouldn't have been funny – after all, we might find a dead woman in the room, and maybe it was only funny to me anyway – but just as I raised my leg and leaned forward to assault said door again it was opened from inside and I went stumbling head-first across the threshold, then slammed drunken-moose style into Elise and ended up sprawled across the floor.

'Oh, God, Dev, I'm so sorry.'

So she wasn't dead. Or wounded.

'I'm fine,' I said. 'What the hell happened?'

Maddy was already holding her mother, which was fine with me. That way they were too busy to watch me scramble to my feet. I do, after all, have my dignity. I'll always be the seventh-grader who lives in fear of being humiliated in front of girls. Who gives a shit what boys think of you.

Elise had started to cry again. 'I tried to kill myself, Maddy. Or that's what I thought I was doing. I put the gun to my temple but at the last minute I jerked it away and the bullet just went into the wall. I'm so sorry. Then I was too ashamed to come to the door!'

Her arms dangled over Maddy's shoulders. Neither of them appeared to realize that Elise still held a Smith & Wesson .45 in her right hand. She didn't even seem to realize when I slipped it from her fingers.

By now Mrs Weiderman had reached us. 'Are you all right, Mrs Logan!'

'Oh, Mrs Weiderman, I did such a stupid thing!'

'You did no such thing, Mrs Logan. Now I'm going to take you into the guest room and turn the covers back for you and you're going to lie down and relax while I bring you some hot cocoa with those little marshmallows you like so much. Isn't that right, Maddy?'

But Maddy was too distracted to respond. Her mother had fainted dead in her arms.

SIX

When I reached the desk at Linton's only decent hotel – and the only likely place where Tracy Cabot would stay – I joined a group of four men and one woman who were doing everything except climbing over the registration desk and throttling the nervous-looking young man who was spit-and-polish enough to pass the meanest corporate test.

The reporters were local. They had no idea who I was, which was to my advantage. A Chicago man or woman might recognize me because I'd been around so long.

The clerk said, 'This gentleman would like to get through. I'd appreciate it if you'd stand down the counter, please.'

They were not happy, the dears. I was interrupting the fun they were having tormenting the kid.

'Welcome to the Regency. May I help you, sir?'

'Thanks. I'll need a single for a few days.' By tomorrow morning there would be no rooms to let.

I'd brought a suitcase with two changes of

78

clothes and balled-up underwear and socks. After signing my credit card slip, I carried the suitcase over by the elevators where a bellman who appeared to be in his sixties watched me suspiciously. He was a sharp and cynical sixty and he probably watched everybody suspiciously. He'd seen it all and maybe done it all and he knew that we've all got it in us.

'You want some help, sir?'

His jacket was ruby red with gold-sprayed buttons and epaulets that looked in danger of slipping off. His tan trousers were as faded as his blue eyes.

'Not with my bag.' I set the suitcase down and said, 'But I do need to ask you about a woman.'

'You mean to hook up with?'

Nice to know I looked like the kind of guy desperate enough to have to pay for sex. 'No. Somebody who might be staying here.'

'Oh. Good. Because I could lose my job otherwise. So who's the lady?'

I described her.

'Sounds like the Cabot woman. That's why all those reporters are over there. A cop said somebody killed her out at the senator's cabin.'

Amazing how quickly and how much the press had already picked up on. Amazing and terrifying for us.

'So she's been staying here?'

'Oh, yeah. I'd have to check to be sure but I'd say four, five nights offhand.'

The Regency would probably get a B rating in

one of those travel guides. It had a kind of worn opulence like a grand dame on her uppers. The other bellmen I'd seen were much younger than this guy and much more clean-cut. I suppose every hotel needs a crafty old bastard. He would know where all the bodies were buried, sometimes literally.

'She get many visitors?'

'Lots of guys around the restaurant and bar who wanted to be visitors, if you know what I mean.'

'How about anybody who actually got into her room?'

'One. This little bastard. Thought he was pretty important. Like they say, you can tell a lot about a guy by the way he treats the help.'

'He have a name?'

'She called him Howie.'

'Howie? Howie *Ruskin*?'

'Oh, yeah. Come to think of it, that's what that candy-ass desk clerk called him. Mr Ruskin. He some kind of big deal?'

He obviously didn't understand the implication of what he'd just told me.

Ruskin. Howie Ruskin. I'd never met him, but I'd heard way too much about him. In college he'd been a supporter of our party. Then, or so the story goes, he switched parties because a girl he loved dumped him. She'd been on our side. In revenge he spent his years as a political saboteur doing everything he could to demolish us. He was especially good at opposition research and at using the press to spread rumors. He was equally good at setting up traps for unwary politicians. His specialty was using women (or men on a few occasions) to seduce said politician and then outing the relationship. This had worked at least nine times in critical elections. It had brought down six of the nine, which was a damned good record. Throughout this time he'd paid a ghostwriter to concoct three bestsellers for him.

Then there was Howie himself. Good Catholic boy/man in his late-thirties now. He was five-four and weighed around two hundred pounds. He was losing his hair and insisted on fitting his ball-like body with the latest fashions, said fashions being designed for teen-gaunt bodies. Once or twice a year you could see him on TMZ or in one of the supermarket rags on the arm of a model or a starlet. A publicist had always set it up for him. I was told that, pathetically, Ruskin had convinced himself these women actually wanted to go out with him.

My favorite Ruskin story involved Mensa, the organization for people whose IQ registers in the top two percent of all humanity. He qualified as brilliant; the problem was he also qualified as one of the most obnoxious self-promoters the group had ever had to deal with. There were so many stories about his jerk-off behavior at various functions that his publicist had pulled him out of the organization.

Among his other problems was his gambling addiction. By all accounts he was a terrible poker player but insisted on spending hours with some of the pros. He'd lost a lot of money – he'd also tried to welsh by claiming he'd been cheated. One of the pros, obviously a man of little sensitivity, sent a goon after Howie baby and gave him a black eye. Another apparently suggested he might meet with a fatal accident if he didn't pay up within twenty-four hours. It was whispered that at any given time somebody in Vegas had it in for him.

The one thing his publicist hadn't been able to do was disarm him. Because of his connection to the other side and its connection with judges all over the country, Ruskin was always armed with a Glock, insisting that 'they' (meaning us) were out to get him. Any time he got hassled by law enforcement he just made a call, and whoever he talked to made a call and Ruskin went back to spending his time wooing fabulous babes – another one of his problems.

'Is he staying in the hotel?'

'Four thirty-eight.'

'How many times did you see them together?'

'I work four to midnight. The last week I'd say I saw them together every night around dinner time. And a couple of times in the bar.'

Howie Ruskin. I was going to meet the bastard.

'You see her with anybody else?'

'Hey, seems you're getting a lot of talk for

nothing. I'm a working man.'

I eased my wallet out of my back pocket and laid a fifty across his open palm.

'I've seen her with about a couple dozen guys since she was here who tried to pick her up.' The grin gave him a satanic look. 'She's probably the most beautiful woman who's ever been in this town, if you want to put it that way.'

'Any of them succeed?'

'I don't think so. She got rid of them pretty fast. She wasn't much of a flirt. She'd shut them down fast. She wasn't mean or anything; she just wasn't interested.'

This was the woman who'd come on to Robert so openly and seductively. But that had been her job. Robert's mind had gotten caught in his zipper and he hadn't figured it out until it was too late, despite my warning.

'Did you ever see the senator in the hotel?'

The grin again. 'Talk about somebody whose ass is in a sling, huh?'

'So did you ever see him here?'

'No.'

'Was she ever involved in any kind of incident?'

'What does that mean?'

'Any kind of trouble or anything. Did she just have a nice, quiet stay?'

'Quiet except for everybody who wanted to sniff her panties.'

'How about her room? Have the police been up there yet?'

'I don't know.'

'Could you get me in if they haven't?'

He took a deep breath. 'That'd get me fired for sure.' He was working both sides of the street. He was genuinely worried about losing his job while setting me up for a big raise in pay. 'You'd really have to pay me.'

'How much?'

'Three hundred.'

'Two.'

'Two seventy-five.'

'Two-fifty.'

'Hell, I guess I might as well take it.'

After I paid him all I had was a five and two ones in my wallet.

'How about putting my suitcase in my room after?' I was still lugging it along.

'Oh. Yeah. Right.'

He took it and surprised me by not asking for more money.

Except for a maid in a light-blue uniform pushing her cart down the hall, this end of the fourth floor was quiet. I could see from here that the room had not been sealed, though likely it would be very soon. In the elevator Earl Leonard – he'd finally told me his name and it hadn't cost me a cent – had begun breathing in tight little spurts. There was the gleam of sweat on his wolf face. He really was worried.

'I'm going to make this easy for you, Earl,' I said now. 'You let me in and then you take off. If I get nailed I'll say that I was able to open the lock.'

'You know how?'

'Maybe.' I was good but not great.

'I'd appreciate it. And you won't mention me?'

'Not to anybody.'

So now we stood at the door. He looked both ways, advertising that we shouldn't be doing what we were doing. When he got it open he pushed it in and said, 'It's all yours, man.'

Then he was double-timing it to the elevator. What he hadn't remembered and what I hadn't wanted to bring up was that the hall was undoubtedly on security cameras. But I was hoping it wouldn't come to that. There'd be no reason for anybody to check the tape. I expected to stay no longer than a few minutes in her room.

The room was done in contrasting blues. Twin beds, an open closet area packed solid with clothes and at least a dozen pairs of shoes below. Cosmetics and perfumes clouded the air with intoxicating aromas and dresses and blouses were strewn across one of the beds.

The phone rang once and scared the hell out of me. It was as loud as a shriek in the hotel room.

I needed thirty seconds to relax and then I went back to work, conscious of needing to get the hell out of there.

I quickly went through both the desk drawers and the closet and didn't find anything useful.

The small blue carry-on piece of luggage shoved under the same bed as the clothes was another matter.

I counted fourteen articles from various Internet sources about Senator Robert Logan. Long articles that went into his entire life; one article was an interview with some friends of his from high school. Then there were overviews of his time as a wealthy businessman and finally his decision to enter politics and how this led all the way to the United States Senate. She had taken her masters in the subject of Senator Logan.

In the manila envelope I found a dozen photos of her and the senator. All but one of them was staged at his rallies. Each of them gave the unmistakable impression that she and the senator were more than what you might call mere acquaintances. She made sure of that by looking as though she was about to go down on him. She knew what she was doing. And he stood there looking smitten like a horny tenth-grader.

In another drawer I found a white number-ten envelope with photographs of Tracy Cabot at various ages. The photos spanned maybe twenty years from her teens – fourteen or fifteen – to the present. She'd always been a heartbreaker.

Male voices in the hall. They startled me even more than the phone had. If the cops were going to search the room they'd come up in a team of some kind.

I stood absolutely still. Listening as they got nearer, louder, until they started laughing and passed on down the hall. Flop sweat in my armpits and on my back. I took a deep, deep breath and went back to work.

By my watch I'd been in here six minutes. Way too long. When I eventually reached the elevator, my old buddy Earl Leonard appeared from around the corner. 'How'd it go, man?'

'Pretty good.'

'I won't rat you out, man.'

'No more money, Earl.'

'I wasn't asking for any more.' He sounded hurt.

'I know how bad you want to keep your job, Earl, so you won't rat me out, because if you do I'll say that this was your idea and then you'll not only lose your job, you'll be doing time in the same joint I am.'

'This is pretty bad shit, huh?'

'Real bad shit.' I stepped into the elevator and faced him. 'And you're right in the middle of it, Earl. Just like me.'

The doors closed. I actually liked Earl all right; I just didn't want him confiding anything to any of his friends after he'd had a few drinks. I had to scare him a little.

SEVEN

I spent the next half hour in my room with my laptop. Despite the world of Senator Logan collapsing into scandal, I had to check with my various campaign runners to see how their own work was doing. They filed email reports constantly through the days. Every internal poll I saw looked decent; even the ones that had been lagging were now closing slightly. There was still time to win the election.

Then I went to the websites of all the networks and cable news shows. As expected, the Logan story was getting the kind of play that Jack the Ripper would have gotten following those bloody long-ago nights in Whitechapel. All the sites except for Empire News showed at least some restraint. Not enough was known yet to come right out and say that Senator Logan had smashed the skull of his bimbo honey. Empire News had already placed him on the gurney where he would receive the injection that would take him to the depths of hell. They went heavy on his liberal politics and quoted one of their familiar talking heads, a so-called professor at a Christian college that had a white supremacist on the staff. He said, 'If you want to understand how liberalism corrupts all those who promote it, look at Senator Logan. He might have been a decent man at one time in his life. But if these charges are true – and I must say, things don't look good for the man – then his decadence speaks for itself.' This was the same man who reported sightings of Jesus even more often than a certain type of person reports seeing Big Foot eating French fries at McDonald's.

I had no doubt that if a polling company started questioning people the results would show that the majority would be certain that the senator was guilty. And the story was only a few hours old.

I found the number for the police station and called it.

'Police station.'

'My name is Dev Conrad. I'm Senator Logan's campaign consultant. I'd like to know if the senator is still there?'

'I'm going to connect you with Detective Roberts.'

'Thank you.'

A minute-long wait. 'Detective Roberts.'

I went through my introduction again.

'What can I do for you, Mr Conrad?'

'I'd like to know if Senator Logan is still there and if so when you expect him to be released.'

'He's still here but I can't tell you anything about when he'll be leaving. Detective Hammell is in charge of the investigation. That'll be up to him.'

'So I assume Jane Tyler is still there, too.'

'She's with Detective Hammell and Senator Logan, yes.'

'I'd appreciate it if you could give her my phone number and ask her to call me.'

'I'll do what I can. I'm plenty busy myself.'

'I understand.' I gave him the number of my cell. 'I appreciate your help, Detective.'

'If you're thinking of coming here, I'd recommend against it. The place is a zoo. We've never seen this many reporters.'

'I appreciate the tip. And I won't be coming. Thanks again.'

Just as I was hanging up my room phone rang. I was sure I knew who it would be. Somebody from Washington. I wondered why they hadn't called sooner. They were past masters at panicking and for once this was a time for it.

'Our phone here might be bugged. We haven't swept this room for two days. I just ducked in here because I don't want anybody eavesdropping.'

Both parties have what functions as a headquarters. Ours is a conduit for everything from gossip about an opponent to getting emergency campaign cash. The man on the line had been a congressman many years earlier but had stayed in Washington because he liked the nightlife there, as all of his wives would attest to. Some people disintegrate when they panic; he was the type who just got real pissed off when things went bad all of a sudden. The way he was clipping his words off I could tell he was pissed right now. I should also mention that we weren't what you call fond of each other. I thought he was smug and he thought I was ungrateful. We'd never actually met and that was, I suspected, a good thing.

'Did he or didn't he?'

'No.'

'A setup?'

'Yes. Howie Ruskin's out here.'

A pause. 'You sure of that?'

'Yes. As soon as we hang up I'm going to start looking for him.'

'We've probably lost the seat no matter what now.'

'Maybe.'

He had a nice, mellow whiskey laugh. A Jack Daniel's black label laugh. 'For such a cynical bastard, Dev, you're always surprisingly optimistic.' Then, 'This is such a mess I can't believe it.' He'd controlled his rage and now had let it dissipate. 'I'm getting calls from campaigns all over the country. They're afraid this'll hurt their candidates.'

'Poor babies.'

'It just might.'

'Maybe. But since we're still not four hours out I'd give it a little time.'

'There's supposed to be a big fundraiser tonight. This'll put a pall on it.'

'I wish you could see the tears in my eyes. I'm sorry but I couldn't give a shit about a fundraiser right now. I've got other things to worry about.'

'You think you and I will ever like each other?'

'Probably not.'

This time the Jack-blacked throat emitted a laugh. 'Me neither.'

I called Lee Sullivan in Chicago. He'd been a homicide detective who'd gone private and then started doing a lot of work for me and our candidates. He had a computer-wizard son who was also excellent at opposition research. Jason had picked up two opponent scandals that a big opposition firm had missed.

As soon as Lee came on the line, he said, 'It's all anybody's talking about.'

He didn't have to include a subject in that sentence. 'It's going to get a lot worse.'

'You have an opinion yet?'

'I believe he's innocent. I think he was set up by forces unknown. The woman's been hanging around his events for a while. She was a stunner. She was also a trap that he was stupid enough to walk into.'

'Pols should be eunuchs.'

'I'll pass that along.' Then, 'I need everything you and Jason can find on a woman called Tracy Cabot. And emphasize everything.'

'Of course.'

'I'm sure she was tracking Senator Logan on

someone else's dime.'

'We'll start right away.'

'I've got some interesting news for you, Lee.'

'Yeah?'

'Howie Ruskin's out here.'

'Wow. Now this is getting *really* interesting.'

'She may have been working directly with him. Or maybe she was hired separately and the third party put them together.'

'It figures that Ruskin would end up with a murder rap. He's such a creepy little bastard.'

'I thought about that, too, Lee. But as much as I hate Ruskin that's a real big step. Ruskin's never even gotten close to violence before.'

'OK, maybe not murder, but there's always a first time when the stakes are so high. By the way – and I hope this doesn't piss you off – you sure Logan didn't kill her?'

'I asked him and he said no. I have to believe him, Lee, because if I didn't I'd resign.'

'Yeah. I can see that all right.'

My only problem is that I still had to allow for the possibility that Robert had been lying his ass off.

'Oh, by the way,' Lee said just before we hung up, 'Jason says he's working on something hot for you. You know how superstitious he is, though. He won't even give me a hint till he's sure of it. Say your prayers, Dev.'

But I was way ahead of him on that one. Political consultants pray every waking moment.

When I walked into the Linton campaign headquarters the bright, ambitious volunteer staff I'd been told about had been reduced to two college-age girls in jeans and red and blue sweaters respectively, sitting at a table piled high with circulars to be delivered throughout the city.

I introduced myself and got a suspicious glance. The one who wore the Wendy name tag said, 'You're not another reporter, are you?'

From the back of a room packed with faxes and computers and two different phone banks a voice said, 'Hi, Dev.'

Connie Taylor had been recommended to me by another client. She'd run his hometown campaign office without a hitch, he'd said, and so I'd hired her for here. She was an African-American woman of thirty-two who was finishing her dissertation on the subject of unions in American politics. She was an attractive woman with a smile that was a boon no matter what kind of mood you were in. But there was no smile tonight. She couldn't summon it, and it wouldn't have helped me anyway.

She wore a russet-brown dress with a wide, dark brown belt and sensible heels. Running a campaign office for a senatorial election is a bitch. If you factored in sex and murder, the job got many times worse.

She had a dry, businesslike shake and signaled with a nod for us to walk to the back. Behind us, Wendy said, 'Sorry, I didn't know who you were.'

'No problem.'

'They're hard workers. Or were until about four hours ago. As soon as the news came on TV all the volunteers started drifting away. I imagine a lot of them are drunk by now.'

'I don't blame them, Connie.'

'Neither do I.'

There was a refreshment table with several kinds of nuts and candies and popcorn. A bubbling coffeepot and a Coke machine stood to the left of the table. She had coffee; I had a Diet Coke.

'Is there anything new, Dev?'

I'd been prepared to address as many as twenty or thirty people. Reassure them as much as I could. But I was glad I didn't have to do it. It would have all been bullshit and they would have known by the time I'd finished my second sentence.

'I'm waiting to hear from Jane Tyler. She's with the senator at the police station.'

'Jane's a good woman. She spends a lot of time working with us on the campaign.'

Maybe Connie knew. 'I was at the cabin talking to a Detective Hammell when she pulled up. They have some strange kind of animosity toward each other. She tries to be civil but he can't quite make himself be decent. You have any idea what that's all about?'

She had small hands. She made one into a brown fist and shook it. 'She was married to his son for three years. A very angry and jealous guy, as it turned out. He threatened her quite a bit and twice he beat her up. To his credit, Hammell tried to help her – his son's a cop, too, and he's warned him that he'll kick him off the force if he breaks the restraining order Jane got. But it's put a strain on his relationship with Jane and sometimes he takes it out on her.' Then, 'I need your advice, Dev. I don't know what to tell our volunteers. Should we be out on the street handing out information?'

They'd be facing at best curious citizens; at worst, hostility and angry humor. 'Just freeze everything until mid-morning tomorrow. This is too crazy right now.'

My cell phone chimed. 'Excuse me, Connie. I'd better take this.'

'I need to go back to my office anyway.' She nodded to a stairway leading to the second floor. 'There are a few people I should call to tell them what you said. They can help me spread the word to the other volunteers.'

Jane Tyler was the name on the display.

'Hello.'

'I'm sitting in the parking lot of the police station. James has just picked up his brother and they're headed back home. I'm going out there, too. James' orders.'

'I take it you're not a fan?'

'Is anybody? James has given his brother bad advice for years and unfortunately Robert has taken some of it. He's jealous of Robert even though he's let him fund three failed businesses for him. He's into him for well over two million dollars that Robert will never see. Now all of a sudden he's his big brother's protector. I wanted to drive Robert out there myself so I could talk to him in private. He didn't do well.' Jane sighed. 'Hammell's a pretty good interrogator. He tripped Robert up time and again and made him look bad. I had to keep interrupting and telling him not to answer. I don't know what he said to you but with Hammell I knew he was lying. He's holding something back.'

'And Hammell knew that, too?'

'Of course. He's not stupid. You can bet that right now Hammell's on the phone with the county attorney and they're setting up the inquest and a grand jury. This'll be a huge "get" for both of them. With all the media out here, they'll become celebrities. They'll be on all the cable news shows.'

I wasn't sure that somebody like Hammell would get his head turned by cooing news talkers but from what I knew about the county attorney – a shiny young man who peddled piety – this would be the official start of his run for governor. You'd begin hearing his name in the Chicago press more and more often now as a serious candidate. He'd be the latest version of Eliot Ness, crimebuster.

'I need you to talk to Robert alone tonight, Dev – if I may call you Dev.'

'Of course.'

'Hammell will drag him back in the morning and I don't want to sit through another session with Robert lying.'

'You're going out there right now?'

'Yes. Where are you?'

I told her.

'We could get there about the same time. I'm sure it won't be pleasant. I like Elise very much but sometimes she gets on my nerves. And I'm sure this has devastated her.'

I decided against telling her what Elise had done earlier. Jane had enough problems.

'I'll see you there,' I said.

EIGHT

When I got on the country road I wanted to keep driving. There was a gaudy gold full moon and with the radio off and the window partially down the air was sweet and the voices of owls and horses and night birds caught me up in a daydream of driving for a long time to a place where everybody was guaranteed a fair shake and there were no politics. And where the woman I'd been looking for would step up and claim me.

There were so many media trucks on the perimeter of the Logan estate it looked as if an army had amassed for an invasion. Dozens of lights of different sizes cast the night into a troubled brightness, that taint of emergency that so often meant death. At the gate to the property were two men in brown security uniforms with shotguns and mean faces. Three more of them were patrolling the ten-foot-high black iron security fence. These three had nightsticks and looked as if they were eager to use them. As I pulled up to the two with shotguns several reporters started shouting at me. By what right should I try to get past the two guards when they'd had no luck?

I stopped five feet away from them and put the car in neutral. One of the security guards stepped up. The night was cold enough for his breath to be silver. I put my window down. He stuck a middle-aged hard-ass face in and said, 'Who are you?'

'My name's Dev Conrad.'

He walked back to the other man. They had two chairs there, apparently in hopes that they could rest at some point. Unlikely. He picked up a clipboard and held the top page up to the light. He scanned it and then set it down.

'I need to see your license,' he said when he came back.

I was ready for him and handed it over.

He examined it with a flashlight he wore on his chock-full belt. Then he handed it back.

'Has a Jane Tyler been here yet?'

'I passed her through about five minutes ago.'

My daydreaming had slowed me down. 'Thanks.'

Windows on the ground floor gleamed in the cold night; the upstairs was dark. I pulled in next to where five other cars were parked and when I stopped and killed the engine I saw Jane Tyler step out of hers and walk toward me. She wore a flattering black double-breasted coat. With the collar up the pretty woman looked a bit glamorous.

'Hammell called me on my cell while I was driving out here. He wants the senator back in his office at nine o'clock.'

'Relentless.'

We started up the flat stone walk past the mullioned windows. 'This is my first experience with the big-time press.' She nodded to the army of lights, technology and people ranged across the line of iron fence. 'It's scary. I don't like them. And I'm supposed to be a liberal.'

Mrs Weiderman answered the door, looming in silhouette in the lighted vestibule. She was solemn instead of cordial. The day had worn even her down.

'Good evening. They're all in the living room, including Mr Zuckerman.'

'How bad is it?' I said softly as we followed her inside. She took our coats.

'Elise's doctor was here and sedated her just a little. She's sitting up but she mostly just stares into space. She refuses to lie down in the master bedroom.'

Before we reached the living room I could hear James Logan intoning.

'Uncle James, will you please sit down and shut up.'

'My favorite niece,' he said just as we entered the room.

'Your only niece,' Maddy said. 'You're not helping anybody and you're completely wrong about...'

She froze when she saw me. So I'd been the subject of conversation.

'Here he is now,' James said to Robert, Elise

and Maddy on the couch, 'and what's he been doing? Escorting your Ms Tyler around.'

'More than you can say, James,' Jane snapped. 'Since I'd never go out with you.'

Maddy laughed sharply. James glared at her. The way his body lurched I could tell he was well along with his drinks.

He was duded up tonight – jeans, black shirt, black leather jacket and enough mousse in his dark hair to give him the look of the oldest-living lounge lizard. 'In case you haven't noticed, Conrad, the press is killing us.'

I ignored him. 'Hi, Robert. Is Ben here yet?'

'Bathroom,' Robert said.

'Did you hear what I said? What the hell are you doing about the press?'

Ben Zuckerman came through the door, scowling. 'James, I thought I told you to sit down and shut up or get the hell out of here.' Ben was a short, tightly-wound man who did not suffer idiots well. He was by most accounts the single best criminal attorney in the Midwest. The number and variety of cases he'd won was astounding. He'd boxed in college and was now an amateur handball champion. His small, classic features gave him the mien of a gentle man. They were misleading.

'Who the hell d'you think you're talking to?' James said.

'Robert,' Ben said. 'He goes or I go.'

Robert nodded and stood up. He quickstepped to his brother, ripped the drink from his hand

and then took him by the arm. 'You need to lie down, James.'

'Zuckerman and Conrad are friends, Robert. They're both incompetent. You need to talk to that lawyer I know in Saint Louis.'

But Robert wasn't letting go of his arm or slowing their progress toward the hall. He'd set the drink down on an end table and was now prepared for anything James might do.

'I'm sorry, Mrs Logan,' Ben said to Elise.

Mrs Weiderman hadn't been exaggerating. Elise, clothed tonight in a mauve robe over a purple pajama set with matching purple slippers, glanced up at the mention of her name. But it was easy to see that she did not comprehend what Ben had just said to her. Maddy slid even closer. 'There's nothing to be sorry for, Mr Zuckerman—'

'Ben.'

'Ben, then. There really is nothing to be sorry for. My uncle is a horse's ass. Usually I'd be more polite but under the circumstances I don't care.'

Again, Elise's face showed no emotion.

'Ben, this is Jane Tyler,' I said.

He was a courtly man and he greeted Jane with a handshake and a warm smile. 'Robert's told me all about you. He said you did a great job at the police station. I hope you'll continue working with us.'

Ben Zuckerman, no less, was asking a local lawyer to assist in the defense. This happened most of the time but not always, and when it didn't it was a snub everybody – including the press – noticed.

Jane's smile made me smile. 'I'm very flattered, Mr Zuckerman.'

'I'm Ben and you're Jane, if that's all right.'

'That's fine.'

'Now, Mrs Weiderman said that you and I can use the study for as long as we need it, so why don't we fix ourselves a drink and carry them in there, and you can bring me up to date.'

'Sounds great.'

Ben went over to the dry bar. 'What would you like to drink?'

'Bourbon and 7UP, if they've got it.'

'They do.'

As Ben fixed the drinks, he looked at me. 'Do you like the hotel you're staying in, Dev?'

'Not bad at all.'

'Any kind of gym?'

'A small one.'

'That'll work for me.'

Ben brought the drinks over. 'Did you two come in separate cars?'

'Yes,' Jane said.

'We may be here a long time. You don't have to stick around if you don't want to, Dev.'

'I need to talk to Robert, then I'll head back.'

Ben tilted his head in the direction of the hall and followed Jane out of the room.

By now Elise's face had a porcelain sheen. She surprised me. 'Stop looking at me like that,

Dev. You're making me feel like a freak.'

'I apologize, Elise. I'm just worried about you.'

'Robert's the one you should be worried about.'

'Believe me, I am.'

'He doesn't deserve this.'

'I know he doesn't.'

'The second I saw that woman—' She didn't finish.

Maddy patted her mother's folded hands. 'You're exhausted, Mom. I can hear it in your voice.'

I heard the same thing. Maybe she'd be able to fight the sedative her doctor had given her but only for a time. Even when her words were emotional her voice was a monotone.

A long, weary sigh. 'I guess you're right, honey.' And then to me: 'I'm sorry James was such an ass, Dev. He thinks he's an expert on everything.'

'That's all right. Just about every candidate has a naysayer in his or her group. Somebody who thinks they know a better consultant or a better way to win the election. And sometimes they're even right. Nobody in my business has a perfect track record by a long shot. James probably thinks he's protecting his brother.'

'He's an asshole,' Maddy said. 'I hate him.'

'Honey, he's family.'

'You don't have to remind me, Mom. I never liked him, even when I was small. He was condescending even back then. Now, c'mon, let's go upstairs.'

Maddy was as careful with her mother as a nurse would be with a drastically sick patient. And Elise was uncertain on her feet, nearly falling back on the couch before Maddy and I grabbed her.

''Night, Dev. I guess I'll go to bed, too. I think I'll watch some lame movie with a happy ending. Maybe I can forget about everything for a while.'

'I hope it works,' I said.

'Thank you, Dev,' Elise said.

'Get some sleep, Elise. Hopefully things will be a little better in the morning.'

One of those lies that are embarrassing when you think about them. Things would be better in the morning? Really? How?

I walked over to the dry bar and opened the door of the small refrigerator hidden from sight. I found three Heinekens inside and took one. I'd just popped the cap when Robert came rushing into the room.

'I wrestled James upstairs and threw him on the bed in one of the guest rooms. Sorry he was such a dick. I didn't want to be here with Elise. Maddy told me she calms down when I'm not around. I don't know how the hell she can even function with the sedatives the doc gave her. But I suppose since she's had so many kinds of antidepressants over the years she's built up a resistance. Anyway, the best thing I can do is leave her alone.' He nodded to my beer. 'I'd take one of those.'

I dug one out and handed it to him.

'I won't even look out of any of the northern windows. This looks like the Michael Jackson trial. Or OJ. All these reporters from all over the world. I'm waiting for them to just overrun us and drag me away and lynch me. And I'm only half kidding. I tried to take a little nap a while ago to calm down and I had a dream of something like that.'

'Jane tells me you were holding something back from Hammell?'

Since he had a mouthful of beer he could have done a spit take and made both of us laugh. Instead the eyes bulged a little and color came up in the cheeks. 'She gave me the same bull-shit in the station parking lot. I like Jane but she's wrong as hell about me holding something back.'

'You said she was a good lawyer. And a good lawyer learns how to read clients.'

'You can be good without being invincible.'

'She's trying to help you and so am I. And so is Ben.'

'What'm I supposed to do? Make things up to satisfy you three? I told you the absolute truth.'

'Hammell may request a lie detector test.'

The gaze narrowed; a tooth bit the edge of an upper lip. In poker that would have been called a 'tell.' A hint of deception.

'So? I'm not worried about a lie detector.'

But he was and so much so that he turned away from me and walked back across the living room and sat in an armchair. He needed time to compose himself again. Maybe he hadn't even thought of a lie detector test until I'd brought it up. I sat down across from him.

'Did you hear what Shay had to say about it all?'

'I've been busy, Robert.'

'Enough to make you sick to your stomach. Such a goddamned Good Samaritan. A Chicago station had him in the studio and our worthy opponent claimed to be very sad for me and my family and that he was sure everything would turn out all right for me because I was a decent man and then we could get back to campaigning and talking about why it was a good thing that one percent of our population controlled eighty percent of the wealth. Some goddamned consultant wrote it for him, you can bet on that.'

I appreciated anything that made me laugh. 'I'm some goddamned consultant, Robert.'

'Oh, right. Sorry.'

'And I would've told him to say exactly what he said. Let everybody else play the bad guy. Make sure you look reasonable and civil – that's all that matters.'

He leaned forward, elbows on knees, the green bottle hanging from his folded hands. 'Say we wrap this thing up in a week or so. What're my chances of pulling it off – the election, I mean?'

I could have reminded him of how bad things were for him right now. I could have told him he was worrying for nothing because we were likely all done. I could have told him that the affair alone, in a tight race, could be fatal. But he was a politician – a good one and a major one – and they really don't think like you and me. They make moral compromises most people couldn't bring themselves to make and they almost never let go of the idea that some-how, some way they will be re-elected, even if they are caught in bed with a thirteen-year-old girl they've just given heroin to. If you don't believe me consider the true story of a well-known US politician. A tabloid breaks the story that a) he has a mistress, b) his cancer-dying wife knows about his mistress and is crushed and c) his mistress is now pregnant. His presi-dential aspirations have crashed completely but he still calls the president elect's people and offers himself as attorney general material. This is being disconnected from reality on a cosmic level. It's a drug, this sense of entitlement. I stayed silent.

When he sat back and focused on me I knew what was coming. He was going to lay a brother James on me. I was about to become the boogeyman. 'So what exactly are you doing to help me?'

'I've got the best private investigator and his oppo researcher son finding out everything they can about Tracy Cabot.'

'That's all?'

'And I brought Ben Zuckerman in.'

'I could have done that myself.'

'Yes, you could've. But you didn't.'

'In other words you're sitting here wasting time.'

'I'm sitting here because I wanted to see Ben.'

'And Jane. I saw the way you two looked at each other. If you want to get laid, Dev, do it on your own time.'

'Like you, you mean?'

'What's that supposed to mean? I told you we didn't have sex.'

'I've decided I don't believe you.' If he wanted pissy, pissy he'd get.

'So now I'm a liar?'

'So now you're cleaning up your story. There's something you're not telling me.'

'I could fire you right now and bring in James' man.'

'Be my guest. I can see the story on the news. Senator is person of interest in a murder with a sexy woman he might have been having an affair with – and his campaign consultant quits. Kind of a double whammy, Robert.'

'Ah, shit.' And he waved the subject off. And set his head back and closed his eyes.

'You all right, Robert?' I said after a time.

'Just ducky.'

'I wish you'd think over what I said.'

'About what?'

'About telling Ben and Hammell everything.'

'I already have.'

I set my beer on the coffee table and stood up. 'I'm going now.'

Still with his head back, eyes closed. 'What're you going to do?'

'Get some hookers up to my room and have a party.'

'Fuck yourself.'

'I'm working on something but I'm afraid to tell you because you'll have to give a live statement sometime and I don't want you blurting it out.'

Head up, eyes opened. 'You have a lot of faith in me.'

'Actually, I do, Robert. But I'd blurt it out, too, because this could turn the story in a whole new direction.'

'What the hell are you talking about, Dev?'

'Howie Ruskin's been in town for a while.'

There was a pause, then he said, 'Ruskin's behind this, he must be. Wait ... Ruskin and Tracy worked together?'

'Maybe.'

'Ruskin killed her!'

He was up on his feet like a man who'd just been saved at a religious event. He was even waving his hands in the air. He had seen the truth and the truth went by the name of Howie Ruskin. 'How the hell can you just stand there so calmly, Dev? This is the whole nine yards.

That prick set me up with Tracy and then killed her to make it look as if I'd done it.' I sensed the kind of relief that comes to those whom the Lord has singled out for salvation; the salvation only a grifter peddling solace from the ugliness of an unforgiving world can inspire. In my fantasy revolution I hang all TV ministers and ministerettes. Right after the deserving Wall Streeters.

'Proof, Robert. Proof. We don't have any as yet. But he's staying at the same hotel that I am and I've paid a bellman there to let me know the moment he sees him. The man's name is Earl and he's got my cell number.'

'You're awfully goddamned calm about this, Dev.'

'Maybe we should get James back down here and let him handle it.'

He made a face at me but then his entire body settled. The high had left him. 'Yeah, you're right. We don't have jack yet, do we?'

'No.'

'But I'd bet anything he's involved.'

'So would I.'

A half-smile. 'Well, my well-paid consultant finally agrees with me on something.'

'Ass-kissers charge even more.'

His long hands went to his face. He reminded me of Elise doing the same thing. 'God, I just can't believe this has happened to me. It's so insane.' The hands came down. He stared out the window. 'I can hear them down there.

They'll all be filing story after story, even though there's nothing new to report.'

'Some of them have probably been in town interviewing people.'

'Oh, sure. "I always figured that Logan for an ax-murderer. You know how those socialists are."'

I was walking to the vestibule where Mrs Weiderman had hung my coat. 'I'm going to look up Earl when I get back to my hotel. If I get any news I'll call you right away.'

'I'm sorry for dumping on you.'

'I'd be just as upset as you are, Robert. You got set up and I'm pretty sure we're both right about who's involved.'

The temperature had to be in the low forties when I walked outside. Maybe the high thirties. But the weather hadn't deterred the press. As I neared the checkpoint more than a dozen people with cameras and microphones ran toward the guards with the shotguns. A car leaving the Logan home? Maybe there was a story in it.

The guards watched me approach and had opened the gate by the time I reached them so I could drive straight through. The reporters screamed at me as if I were a rock star.

NINE

Halfway back to town – I knew it was halfway because I remembered an ancient abandoned school being roughly midway – my cell phone rang. I pulled over.

'It's me, Earl.'

'You got something?'

'Yeah. Strange. I had to help set up for this big event tonight because there's flu going around and we're short on people. So while I was doing that, this Ruskin guy calls in and says he's sending his assistant over to pay his bill and pick up his stuff. The kid at the desk told me she came in about five minutes after Ruskin called. She was real nervous and seemed scared, he said. Said she was kind of dumpy and looked sorta like a hippie. One of the other bellmen took her up to the room, she packed everything up and then left. The desk kid had his hour dinner break and the girl running the desk didn't know anything about it. She told me that she hadn't seen Ruskin so I assumed there was no problem. I got busy so I didn't get a chance to ask this kid until a few minutes ago.'

'What time does the kid get off?'

'Eleven.'

It was eight thirty-six.

'And there's somebody else here looking for Ruskin, too. And he's also looking for you.'

'Did you talk to him?'

'No, but the kid did. He said that right now the guy is in the hotel bar.'

'I should be there in fifteen minutes.'

'Sorry I wasn't more on top of things.'

'You did fine, Earl. I appreciate it.'

The sensible – or maybe the word should be lazy – reporters were hanging out in the hotel lobby. They stood around with drinks in their hands laughing and greeting new arrivals with shouts and verbal jabs. This had to be the second string. The ones freezing their asses off out at Robert's place were the ones who mattered. These knew they weren't important and were taking advantage of that fact.

A few of them eyed me with whiskey scorn. I was, after all, not one of Them. The first thing I did was check for messages. There were none. The 'kid' as Earl called him – his name was Kevin, according to his name tag – said, 'This is like Chicago tonight.' He was stoned on the excitement. 'Late in the afternoon four reporters I see on the evening news all the time checked in, all in less than an hour. I was going to ask for an autograph but I thought maybe I'd get in trouble.' I guessed Earl was right to call him the kid.

'Somebody told me that Mr Ruskin checked

out and a woman picked up all his stuff for him.'

He allowed himself a moment of surprise and then said, 'Gosh, word sure does get around. But that's right. A woman did pick up his things.'

'Can you describe her?'

'Describe her?'

'Yes. Describe her.'

'Oh.' Suspicion played across his bland face. 'Is something going on in the hotel I should know about, Mr Conrad?'

'I don't think so.'

'Pretty dumpy. Hippie-like. She looks real young until you see her close up.'

'So you took her up to his room?'

'Uh-huh.'

'Did you go in with her?'

'Uh-huh. She had me put all his stuff in garment bags and put them on the cart.'

'She say anything while you were helping her?'

'She just told me what to do and then she just sort of ignored me.'

Behind us the reporters started applauding for somebody or something.

'They like to have fun, don't they? I recognized one of them from Channel Eight from downstate. That's where I grew up.'

I was about five steps from the check-in when I saw Earl waving at me. He stood to the side of the door leading into the bar.

'This place is a zoo,' he said when I got to him. 'We should have murders more often. No offense, but I'm getting rich tonight.'

Earl didn't have much of a future in public relations. Good for him he was getting rich tonight. A man innocent of murder was getting lynched in the media and I was losing a vital campaign. But I needed Earl. 'I'll see what I can do for you. Pick out a couple of people and I'll off them for you. I mean, since murders are so good for your business.'

I'd tried keeping my irritation out of my little joke but he picked up on my anger.

'Hey, I said no offense, man. It was just a stupid joke, all right?'

'All right. Now tell me about the man in the bar.'

Basically he went through what he'd told me on the phone. But this time he added, 'He's an official of some kind.'

'How do you know?'

He touched his nose. 'I can smell them. Cops, politicians, narcs. You can't catch bells all the years I have and not be able to pick them off. All the guys can who've been at it for a while.'

'And you're sure he's still in there?'

'Unless he went out the back door, which almost nobody ever does.'

'How about you point him out to me?'

'Sure. And listen, it really was a joke I made.'

'I know, Earl. Believe it or not, I can be an asshole sometimes.'

He handled it just right. He did a fake double take and said, 'You be an asshole? I never woulda guessed.'

Earl was all right; he could put you down and make you smile about it.

We stood in the dark doorway of the crowded bar while he scanned the room. I didn't see how he could find anybody in the packed drunken crowd. But then he said: 'There. The tall guy talking to the little redhead.' Almost as soon as he said it the redhead disappeared behind a surge of bigger people. But the tall man with the rimless glasses and the gaunt face could still be seen. He must have been six-five, at least.

'He says his name is Michael Hawkins.'

'Thanks again, Earl.'

For the next three minutes I pushed, twisted and sidestepped my way through a crowd of resistant bodies that smelled of perfume, after-shave, sweat, cigarettes and most especially alcohol. Hawkins loomed like a lighthouse above this wreckage, almost serene in his indifference to all the clamor of the people who were talking at him. He was just taking it in, like a recorder. Some kind of law, he had to be.

He didn't hear me at first because I had to shout over the din. The third or fourth time I shouted, the green eyes behind the rimless glasses narrowed and then the gaze ran down his long, thin nose and settled on me. The briefest smile. He managed to say: 'The coffee shop. Five minutes.'

Grateful we weren't going to stay here, I turned and plowed and muscled my way back to the lobby. Earl wasn't anywhere in sight.

The coffee shop had red leather booths and a small spray of fresh flowers on every table. The food and the coffee smelled warm and inviting. I took a booth next to the window. I ordered coffee and a tuna sandwich and sat watching people stream from the parking lot into the hotel. The wind was knocking them around; a few of the slighter women resembled toys being scrambled by the invisible hand of a girl playing dolls.

'That bar is one hell of a place, isn't it?'

Hawkins seated himself in parts; he was that tall. Now that I got a good look at him I saw he was in his forties, graying of hair and decent-looking in a stern, Latin teacher way. He wore businesslike blue pinstripes. He had that kind of quiet authority the good ones have.

The waitress came so quickly I didn't even get a chance to tell him that I agreed – that the bar was indeed one hell of a place. He ordered coffee and a steak sandwich.

Long fingers then went inside his suit coat and retrieved the kind of small brown leather holder that contains badges. 'Just so you know who you're talking to, Mr Conrad. My name is Michael Hawkins and I'm an investigator for the US Attorney in this district.'

He showed me the badge and then the ID on the facing side. Since the ID contained not only his name but also his photograph, I had no doubt that he was who he said.

'I was looking for you because I'm trying to locate a man named Howard Ruskin. I've never worked a political case like this one before but I do read the newspapers. Ruskin has quite a reputation.'

'I'm not sure why you'd think I could help you locate him. I work the other side of the street politically.'

'We have a warrant out for his arrest. We believe he's been in our jurisdiction for over a month now but I haven't been able to find him. This morning our office got a tip that Ruskin was spotted in town here. I was on my way before anything about this murder broke.'

'Senator Logan did not murder her.'

He leaned back. 'Believe it or not, Mr Conrad, I'm only interested in Senator Logan's case as a spectator. I'm after Ruskin. I assumed that you might be assuming that Ruskin might be involved in your case in some way. I checked you out. Army intel and you've worked on criminal cases for a couple of your clients.'

Pretty impressive. He would assume that I would assume Ruskin was behind the murder – maybe even committed it himself – so I would be trying to track him down. So why not tap me for any information I'd already been able to pick up and save himself some time in trying to nail Ruskin?

'If I had anything, I'd share it with you. I want

to catch up with the bastard as badly as you do.'

He kept his elbow on the table until the waitress brought his coffee. The longer I watched, the more I saw a professor under the investigator. He was judicious in his words, almost ruminative. 'I can't tell you much about why we want him but I can say that it involves extortion.'

'I'm surprised that it took till now to catch him at it. He's made a lot of money and I always assumed he was shaking people down. But I still don't know why you'd think I'd know where he is.'

'As you say, Mr Conrad, you work a different side of the street. You may hear something I wouldn't be privy to. So I'd appreciate you sharing anything you have with me.'

'Of course. I want him caught.'

'Then we're on the same team.'

Our food arrived at the same time. Occasionally I glanced out the window at the men and women battling the invisible force of the wind, nearly getting knocked on their dressed-up asses for doing so.

The dialogue got rote – a little politics, a little sports and a little rote remorse about how pols so often went bad these days though, as I had to point out, we were living in a second Gilded Age and the first one had become the textbook the current plutocrats still used. In the 1880s and 1890s senators were so openly crooked some newspapers didn't identify them by state;

instead, they said, 'The Senator from Oil' and 'The Senator from Railroads.' These days we had public relations agencies working for senators to make them more palatable to the public.

Yes, Senator Gleason did indeed drunkenly run over an eighty-six-year-old woman in the crosswalk, but he was on his way to a cancer fundraiser. What a guy.

Toward the end of our conversation, he said, 'I try to stay as apolitical as I can in my job. You know the US Attorneys took a hit a while back when they fired some lawyers for political reasons. I don't want politics to get in the way.'

The Bush administration had fired a number of sitting US Attorneys because they wouldn't carry out his political schemes. They had mostly been replaced by young graduates of Holy Shit University who came on with not only a political agenda but a religious one as well. They pretty much destroyed the integrity of the whole operation. I wasn't the only one who was still skeptical. I wondered how many of them had actually been driven out.

'I appreciate that, Mr Hawkins.'

He nodded as he wiped his mouth with the paper napkin. The way he set the napkin down signaled that our meeting was over. He put a long hand across the table and we shook the way two guys do in used-car commercials where the sucker grins his pleasure at now owning a car that had been driven off a cliff six months earlier.

He picked up the tab and left a handsome tip for the waitress, and we walked back to the lobby together. He nodded to all the reporters who had divided up into small groups. Two or three of the better-looking female reporters were surrounded by eager collections of horny boozed-up admirers and seemed to be enjoying it.

'I would appreciate having your cell number, Mr Conrad. I'd be happy to give you mine.'

When we finished punching the numbers into our respective phones, he said, 'Good luck to both of us.'

TEN

In my room I dumped my clothes so I could sit in my shorts and T-shirt with a Blue Moon beer next to my laptop and get to work. The first thing I did was log on to the US Attorneys website and make sure Hawkins was legit.

It took a few minutes but finally there he was. He was so gaunt in his official photo he resembled one of those early New Englanders who enjoyed burning witches. DePaul University graduate, Cincinnati homicide detective five years and five years at Global, a giant security company that was as insular and mysterious as the Vatican. Four years working as an investigator for the Illinois Attorney General's office. This was his third year with the US Attorney's office in this jurisdiction. He was official all right.

I consulted the sacred Rolodex I had on my computer. I remembered an attorney I knew from the Chicago Democratic machine. Decent guy. He'd invited me and my woman of the moment to a party at his house a few years back. Tom Neil. I dialed his number and asked the young girl – maybe eight or nine – if her father was home. 'Yes, he is. May I tell him who's calling, please?'

I smiled and thought of my own daughter at that age. All the times I'd been on the road and her only contact with me was phone calls from afar. The kind of memory you hate yourself for till the day they plant you.

'My name's Dev Conrad.'

'Thank you.'

When he came on the phone, he said, 'This is a pleasant surprise, Dev. Great to hear from you. We never did have that drink. I'm sorry I had to cancel that time. A hysterical client, as I recall.'

'Happens all the time. No problem, Tom.'

He got quieter. 'I can't believe what's happening with Senator Logan.'

'I don't have any choice. I have to believe it.'

'They've already got him in the execution chamber.'

'That's one of the reasons I'm calling. There's a guy up here from your office. I just met him and I wanted your opinion of him.'

He hesitated. 'Everything is between us, of course. And I'm pretty sure you're talking about Michael Hawkins. One of the best. I hope that makes you feel better.'

'It does. And I apologize for calling. I just like to know who I'm dealing with. And Google doesn't tell you if he'd leak things to the press or anything like that.'

'Not Michael. On the contrary, he's very

competitive. Likes to take credit for everything. So he keeps everything close till he's ready to attack.'

'Good. He can have all the credit he wants if he can help us get the senator out of this disaster.'

'Think it's all over for Logan no matter what happens?'

'Fifty-fifty.'

'How about sixty-forty in favor of Empire News?'

'I try not to watch those bastards but every once in a while I'll catch a link and I can't resist.'

'This is like the biggest sexual thrill in recorded history for them. One of the bimbos hinted that Logan should do the honorable thing and eat a gun.'

'Yeah. I'm surprised she didn't offer to buy him the gun.'

'That'll be later tonight.'

'Well, thanks, Tom. Good to know about Hawkins.'

'I wish I was a praying man. I'd say a few for you and the senator. And let's have that drink sometime.'

After the call I opened up all the computer material from the Sullivans.

Tracy Cabot – real name Louise Tracy Cabot. Daughter of noted fanatical right-wing New England newspaper publisher. In constant trouble at Smith for interrupting her professors to imply they were Communists. Became icon of campus conservative movement. After graduation – 3.1 grade point – went to work for a shadowy ultra-reactionary think tank. Then for a few years she was listed as a 'political consultant.' But there was no record of a client. Surfaced on her twenty-ninth birthday as the woman Senator Peter Boggs, Democrat, was videotaped leaving a motel room with. In a tight race Boggs lost. Two years later she was revealed to be the paramour of a Dem congressman who went on to lose a third term. At this point a left-wing blogger named Daniel Marlowe, who had been tracking her, learned she worked for a virtually invisible group called The Alliance for Liberty. It was during this time that she began working with Howie Ruskin for the other side on everything from voter suppression to funneling illegal money to candidates.

Her taste in men seemed limited to a roster of married conservative movers and shakers. If she and Ruskin had ever been lovers that part of their relationship had been short-lived, because both of them were linked to numerous partners during their tenure as political saboteurs.

There was a page of thumbnail photos of her. Babe-o-Rama. Not difficult to understand how she had her way with so many men. Not one of them showed her in any kind of reflective mood. The images left the impression that she was always at her alluring best even when she was – as in one shot – standing in some kind of religious shrine. But always upper crust. Nothing downscale about her. You knew she didn't know how to sweat.

And Robert had gone for her.

All of it was useful information, but hardly the kind of bombshell we needed.

I had just about finished my beer – I'd been at it long enough for the bottle to be warm – when my cell phone rang. I was happy to hear Jane Tyler's voice.

'You missed the excitement.'

'Do I want to hear this?'

She laughed. 'Probably not. But I'm going to tell you anyway. James woke up and came back downstairs and started hassling Ben. And Ben knocked him out with one punch.'

Now I was the one laughing. 'I was hoping I'd get first crack at him. Ben's a pretty controlled guy. James must've pissed him off big time.'

'Ben was very controlled. He just kind of blew off all the insults until James grabbed him and that was that. Ben didn't even get a clear shot at him. But he knocked him out. Then Ben grabbed him and dragged him to the couch. He pulled over an ottoman and sat there until James came back and then he apologized for hitting him.'

'How'd James take it?'

'He was the perfect gentleman, of course. He started shouting that he was going to sue Ben for so much money Ben'd be declaring bankruptcy. I tried to help calm him down but then he started on me. He called me a whore and said that everybody knew that was why my husband beat me up.'

'I'm sorry you had to put up with that.'

'Robert had been on the phone the whole time. He came in on the end of it and got so mad that he tried to punch James himself. And then he said, "You can forget about me bailing you out this time." I don't know what he was talking about but it certainly calmed James down all of a sudden. He got all apologetic to everybody and begged – and I'm not exaggerating when I say begged – Robert to go to the study and talk to him.'

They must have been arguing about that damn loan, I thought. 'I've wanted to tell Robert to dump his brother but that's easy for me to say. Blood's blood.'

'I know. I still feel guilty about leaving my husband and I shouldn't. I used to feel superior to all those women who put up with abusive spouses. I didn't put up with it for long but I still think about the days when it was good.'

'You have a history with him. That'll be with you a long time. Maybe for life.'

'You sound as if you know what you're talking about.'

'I do. I was a terrible husband. I didn't abuse her physically or anything like that but I was always on the road as a consultant so in a real sense I deserted her. By the end she was a stranger to me. I'd forced her to be one. There's a part of me that can't let go of that. Can't ever forgive myself.'

'Are you in touch with her?'

'We have a beautiful daughter in common who lives in Boston and is about to marry the intern she's lived with the past few years.'

A yawn. 'Sorry.'

'Was that a comment on my life story?'

A giggle this time. 'Hardly. But aren't you as exhausted as I am?'

'Yeah. In fact, I'm probably going to hit the bed as soon as we hang up. And as soon as you agree to have dinner with me tomorrow.'

'I'd like that. Thanks. And by the way, Ben's press conference will be in front of the county courthouse at nine tomorrow. He said he likes early ones because the reporters are hungover and not as sharp as they'll be later in the day.'

'Ben's a genius.'

'And a very nice man. I like him.' Another yawn. 'God. Sorry.'

'See you tomorrow.'

For once the demons didn't come to wake me up. Usually I go through a list of those I'd done wrong and a list of those who'd wronged me. Sleep is at a premium on those nights.

Tonight I dropped off quickly.

ELEVEN

Ben Zuckerman appeared on TV promptly at nine a.m. looking well-rested, relaxed and well turned out in a boardroom gray suit. He wore a stony expression. *Don't fuck with me, buddy, or you'll regret it.* He stood in front of the courthouse without notes of any kind.

There were at least fifteen upright microphones in front of him and at least twice as many hand mikes being pointed at him. As the camera panned the press, familiar faces were seen. Network faces and recognizable ones. This was the big time. A US senator involved in the murder of a beautiful woman.

'I know we're all busy here so I'll keep my remarks brief and allow only five minutes for questions. I would ask you to remember that this situation is less than twenty-four hours old so despite all the rampant speculation nobody – and I repeat – nobody knows anything for certain yet. With one exception. Senator Robert Logan, my client, categorically denies having anything to do with the death of Tracy Cabot. And I emphasize the word "categorically." He is innocent of the charges some of the media have accused him of. I would ask the press to do their job responsibly. The senator and I are well aware of why this story has dominated every news cycle. But we do ask for you to be fair and wait for solid facts before making any implications about his role in this tragic event. Now I'll take questions.'

Then came the deluge.

Was Tracy Cabot his mistress? How long had the senator known her? Why would she be at his cabin if the senator didn't know about it? Did the senator have an alibi for the time of her death? How about the reports that the senator had a long-standing reputation as a womanizer? Had the senator taken a lie detector test? Would the senator step down in light of the suspicions the press had about him?

Ben answered each question forcefully but quickly. Yes and no were his favorite responses but when he had to go into detail, as in his answer to the query about the senator's rep as a chaser, he used his words to chide the press. 'I've known Senator Logan for ten years, going back to the time he was in the state legislature. In all that time I never once heard anyone refer to him as being any kind of ladies' man – which he definitely is not. This charge surfaced last night on the network whose sole purpose is to destroy every single member of my party. And their weapon of choice is always character assassination. When you make a habit of cheating on your spouse – and this goes for men and women both – people eventually know about it. And talk about it. Ask anybody who's known Senator Logan for any length of time and they'll tell you that that charge is ludicrous and false.'

He'd needed to vent and by God he'd vented.

'Now let's let the police do their work and I'm confident that they'll find that Senator Logan is innocent of all these suspicions. Thank you very much for your time.'

'He's really good,' Jane Tyler said.

We were sitting in the small conference room of her small office building that had room for Jane and three other lawyers. The walls were covered with historical photos of the area at the turn of the last century and the walnut conference table itself also seemed to be historical. Only the chairs and the dark blue carpeting and the plasma TV mounted on the east wall were recent. She aimed the remote dagger-like at the screen and it died.

'He's very good but he knows that what he said won't make any difference to most people. If you polled across the country now at least fifty percent of people would say he was guilty.'

'Have you ever considered the possibility that he *is* guilty?'

'Of course. But it's extremely unlikely.'

'He was definitely involved with her.'

'That we can't deny.'

'I mean, maybe more than he's letting on.'

She wore a burnished-yellow silk blouse and a black skirt revealing fetching legs and ankles. Her dark hair was slightly mussed from the rush we'd made from the car into the Hardee's where we'd grabbed our breakfast and dragged it to her office. I'd called her from my hotel room and asked if we could have breakfast and watch Ben together.

Now, the Hardee's sacks in front of us, she said, 'I called a friend of mine at the police department.'

'Hammell will probably fire whoever it is if he finds out you've got a confidant inside.'

'It's the one and only female patrol officer who's unhappy with how the boys' network treats her.'

'And she says what?'

'She says that when she signed in this morning the county attorney was just pulling into the lot and Hammell and his number one were standing outside to meet him. And then they all shook hands and hurried into the building. She said it was like watching a TV show. You know, everything so urgent and everything.'

'But she doesn't know what it's all about?'

'No. She says it always takes a while for news to filter down to her level. It doesn't sound good.'

'No, it doesn't.'

She sat down, finally, across the table from me. 'I need to get hold of Ben and tell him about this.'

A knock on the door. A middle-aged man peeked in and said, 'I just saw Mrs Havers' car in the parking lot.'

'Bob Raimi, this is Dev Conrad.'

'Nice to meet you, Dev. Want me to cover it for you?'

'No. She's eighty-two years old. She has her grandson drive her into town. That's a forty-mile trip one way. She's used to seeing me.'

'All right, then. Nice to meet you, Dev.'

When the door closed, she said, 'He's the first partner. A very nice guy.' Then, 'I hate to chase you out, Dev, but I need to get ready for this client. She's an old sweetie and I'm really trying to help her.'

As I was getting out of my chair she said, 'I'll call you as soon as I hear anything from my friend in the department. This has me worried.'

'Me, too. I just wish that Robert had been honest with us.'

A wry smile. 'You're trying to help them and they still lie. I've never understood that. Sometimes I feel that I'm the prosecutor when I talk to clients. I have to drag every bit of information out of them kicking and screaming. A few of them, anyway. Thank God most of them come in and lay everything out for you.'

I was on my feet and bagging up the debris from our breakfasts. 'You mean I forgot to mention running over those three nuns that time? I guess I thought you already knew about that.'

'God, you probably get it much worse than

we do. All the lies.' She swooped up her papers, her glasses and her coffee cup. 'I'm sure we'll talk sometime today. Thanks again for breakfast.'

She was gone before I got to the door.

The day was Midwestern gorgeous and cold as hell. Maybe high thirties. As I was climbing into my Jeep my cell phone rang and as I slid behind the wheel I punched in the call.

'Dev, this is Jackie.'

Our office receptionist. She only called when it was important.

'We watched Ben. Everybody in the office. He did a great job but that isn't why I'm calling. A woman who won't identify herself has called here twice this morning insisting that she needs to contact you right away.'

'Did she say what she wants?'

'She says she can put you in contact with Howard Ruskin.'

'It could be some kind of a prank.'

'I don't think so. And I don't think you would either if you heard her voice. She sounds terrified of something.'

'Is she going to call back?'

'No, the second time she called I asked for her number so you could call her.'

'All right.'

'But it isn't really her number.'

'What?'

'You're supposed to call this number and leave your number and whoever answers will call her with your number.'

'This is crazy.'

'She may be crazy, Dev, but I think she really believes she can put you in touch with Ruskin. That would be a pretty strange delusion for a crazy person to have.'

'I guess. You may as well give me her number.'

'I hope this amounts to something.'

'So do I.'

I wrote down the number she gave me.

'How is the senator holding up? It must be terrible for his family.'

'It is.'

'His wife is so ... fragile.'

'She is at that.' But I didn't have time to go on like this. 'Thanks, Jackie.'

I sat in the parking lot staring at my cell phone as if it might explode and envelop me in a glow that would imbue me with peace of mind and ultimate truth and more youthful stamina when younger ladies allowed me into their boudoirs.

Then I punched in the number and began what turned out to be the complicated process of talking to Howie Ruskin's lover.

TWELVE

The call I made to the mystery number where I was to leave my number turned out to be an auto repair shop. The man who answered had one of those cigarette rasps that should have scared the hell out of him but probably didn't.

'My name is Dev Conrad. I'm supposed to leave my cell phone number with a guy named Pop.'

'Pop ain't here. He had to step out. I'm Pop, Junior. But he told me to take the number.'

'I'd like to know something about who I'm dealing with.'

'My real name's Verne Andrews, Junior at Andrews' Auto Repair.'

'Sorry, I meant I'd like to know something about the woman who wants my number.'

'Pop said I wasn't to answer any questions in case you asked some. I'm just supposed to take the number down. And look, we're really stacked up here. I gotta go.'

I'd been in enough auto repair shops to know that when they were busy – or just working at all – there was considerable noise. Except for a muffled conversation somewhere behind him the place was quiet.

The too-busy-to-talk always worked. You couldn't call him a liar because you couldn't prove he *wasn't* busy. I'd once seen a woman who was not unduly fond of me in a super-market. When I approached her and started a conversation she said, 'I hate to run, Dev, but I left a repairman at my house working on my sink. You know how it is with them. You can't trust them. Sorry I can't talk more.' Really stunning bullshit and completely successful. He wasn't in her league but he did get my number so he was the winner of our little game.

Twenty minutes later I was on the road leading to Robert's cabin. I hadn't spent any time scouting the area itself. Autumn was having its way with the woods, the colors vivid in the cold sunlight. In a few places you could even see morning frost still bearding the ground. Frantic squirrels were everywhere shopping for the winter that would be here all too soon.

I was doing what the police would normally have done if they hadn't already decided that Robert was their man. They would say other-wise, of course – that they were considering all the possibilities – but we all knew that was just a press release to satisfy the public.

A bungalow of the Craftsman style was partially hidden by pine trees. I pulled into the gravel drive. The house was wood and stone with a low-pitched roof and stone porch sup-ports. Vines crawled over much of the house, lending it both a venerable aspect and to my eye a somewhat sinister one, as if the house itself held a terrible secret. It stood no more than thirty yards from the turn-off to Robert's cabin.

I stood outside the car listening to the natural sounds of the day: birds, dogs, a tan plump cat on the side of the house mewling at an escaping rabbit. The stuff of children's books I dimly recalled from ages three or four.

As I approached the house I saw, in the window to the right of the door, the face of what I guessed was a white-haired woman. I say guessed because she was only a flicker and then gone. I hadn't even reached the steps before she came out on to the porch, all five-two of her in a faded rose-patterned housedress. She'd been pretty a long time ago but age had not been kind; her head kept twitching and so did her arthritic right hand. What troubled me about the hand was that it held the kind of .45 used in World War Two.

And what surprised me, the closer I got, was that she wasn't as old as I'd first thought. Probably no more than late sixties.

'No need for a gun.'

'Don't tell me what I need and what I don't. And I've got a permit to carry this, don't worry. I inherited the gun and the permit when my husband Stan passed away seven years ago.'

I could have argued the point that while you might legally inherit a gun you could not legally inherit a permit to carry. But the way her hand jerked about so violently I decided it was best to let her have her fantasy.

'Who are you, anyway?'

Just then a breeze redolent of fall and pumpkins and Halloween stirred both the heavy piles of tumbled leaves and my own memory as well. At age nine I would have known enough not to pester this old lady for treats.

'My name is Dev Conrad. I work with Senator Logan.'

Her smile was so malicious it deserved scientific study. How could a smile convey this much hatred? 'So he finally got it, huh?'

'If you mean all the rumors—'

'Rumors my eye. Him and all his taxes and his apologizing to other countries – and saying it's all right for two men to get married. Maybe he didn't believe in God until yesterday but you can bet he does today. He knows that the Good Lord takes care of those that don't take care of Him.'

With no warning at all she raised her fragile head the way some breeds of hunting dogs do and then began sniffing at the autumn winds. 'She was back again last night.'

'Who was?' The chill I felt had nothing to do with the temperature; she was playing out a mad scene.

'Who? That harlot he married. I can still smell her perfume on him sometimes.' Then her blue eyes fixed on mine; she was terrifying. 'She told him once she was afraid I'd kill her some

141

night when she was asleep. She was right.'

He came around the west side of the house, a large, square, middle-aged man wearing a flannel shirt and jeans with a green John Deere cap stuck on his head. He limped so badly on his right leg that his entire body jerked when he moved. He didn't speak, just assessed me as he came close. I got the feeling he wasn't going to give me a very good review.

When he came even with the porch and glanced at the woman, he smiled. 'Mom, you don't need that gun.'

'What'll you do when the federal troops come to arrest us?'

He looked back at me. Embarrassment on his face.

After turning back to her, and in a gentle voice, he said, 'I wish you wouldn't listen to those radio shows, Mom. They put all that stuff in your head.'

Even as he put his arm around her, she said, 'I never thought my own son would be afraid to hear the truth. Your father wasn't afraid of it.'

'He didn't believe any of that stuff, Mom. And you didn't either until—' The gentle tone had become a sad one. He stood aside and held the door for her. 'You need to go lie down, Mom. You know what Doctor Williams said about getting too excited.'

'I told Doctor Williams about President Bush being behind 9/11 and he just smiled at me. He's afraid of the truth, too.'

He was tall enough that he had to half bow to reach the top of her head. 'Now you go lie down, Mom. I love you.'

She glanced all the way up at him. 'Mark, if you'd sit down and listen to my shows with me you'd change your mind. I guarantee it.'

'I'll give it a try, Mom. Sometime.'

I was surprised by how mollified she sounded. 'Good. We'll have a nice lunch and I'll turn on the radio. Just don't try to take my gun from me.'

She shuffled her way inside and he closed the door quietly, then made his pained way across the porch to talk to me.

'That probably scared the hell out of you and I apologize. It's not loaded anyway. My dad died seven years ago and she had a stroke. She's never been the same since. A form of dementia. I've got this uncle who got her to listen to all these crazy right-wing talk shows. He's a big conspiracy nut. And he's the one who gave her this gun.' He started down the stairs, then winced. 'I had enough guns in Iraq. That's where I got shot and got the misery.' He tapped his hip.

When he was on the ground he put out his hand. He could have crushed a ball bat with his grip. 'Mark Coleman's my name.'

'Dev Conrad. I work with Senator Logan.'

'You tell my mom that?' He was grinning.

'I did.'

'And I bet she gave you a speech.'

'Pretty much.' I smiled. 'I got the impression we couldn't count on her vote.'

He shook his head and glanced back at the house. 'The doc wants me to put her in a nursing home but every one I looked at ... I wouldn't do that to her. You walk in the door and they smell. I'm not even sure what it is. A mixture of things. But the stench is terrible. And half the people sit around tables all drugged up. I just couldn't do that to her.'

'I don't blame you.' He was an admirable guy. 'I'm trying to help Senator Logan.'

'Yeah, he needs some help. I voted for him, by the way. I'm pretty much an independent – but all these right-wingers ... My dad was a union man. He could never figure out why all his friends voted for the other side and neither could I. Which makes it so weird to me with my mother and all. If it wasn't so sad it'd be funny. Bush was behind 9/11. She really believes that.'

I wondered how often he went to the city. He had the lonely man's need to talk to somebody.

'You spend a lot of time on the yard lately?' I asked because of the rake that leaned against a plastic bag full of what appeared to be leaves. There were three bulky bags, in fact.

'Yeah. I keep busy. Since the wife left two years ago I've been remodeling the whole house inside. She used to like to work outside but after she left—' Unfinished sentences were often more eloquent than finished ones. 'Well, I do all the yard work myself now.'

'I ask because from your yard you can see the turnoff that leads to the senator's cabin.'

'Oh, sure. In fact, every once in a while, especially during the summer, I'd see him and he'd honk and I'd wave.'

'Have you seen the senator around here in the last couple days?'

'No, I guess I haven't.'

'Or how about anybody making that turn?'

He pursed his lips. 'Hmm. I guess I'd have to think about it.'

'But you have been out in the yard.'

'Oh, sure.'

'You ever walk down by the river?'

'Sometimes. When the weather's nice.'

'How about the last few days?'

'Don't think so. It rained a lot.' Then, 'Wait. I think I did see somebody.' His forehead was rutted in thought. 'Well, I heard them, I guess. Didn't see them. When I walk down the slope in back I get pretty close to the Logan cabin if I follow the river. I heard two voices. They were pretty mad. Two women, from what I heard.'

'Two women?'

'Right.'

'No men at all?'

'None I could hear. I was looking for a stray kitten. Our black one on the back porch had a litter a while back and the little ones are just learning to get around for themselves. The one I called Tootsie disappeared couple of days ago. Something's probably grabbed her and killed

her by now but I keep looking for her anyway.'
I wondered if he'd said something like this right
after his wife left him.

'Could you tell anything about the two
women?'

He had a wholesome big boy grin. 'You sound
like a cop.'

'I was an army investigator. I had to ask a lot
of questions.'

'Well, I'll be glad to help the senator any way
I can.'

'Did either of these women call the other by a
name?'

'No, I'm afraid not.'

'Any guess as to their ages?'

'No. Not really. Just two women.'

'Think about it. Younger or older?'

'There was this music playing. Some kind of
rock – the new stuff. I hate it. Anyway, it was
just loud enough so all I could tell was that they
were mad at each other.'

To my right I heard the front door open and I
looked in time to see his mother's return to the
stage. 'That man has a gun, honey. You be
careful of him.'

'He's fine, Mom. Nothing to worry about.'

'One of my programs said that a federal man
would come on my property with a gun and
take me away.'

'Not today, Mom.'

'You're young, honey. You don't know how
the world works. Your dad didn't either. If

you'd start listening to my programs I wouldn't have to worry about you so much.'

'You don't have to worry about me at all, Mom. Now you go back inside and sit down, and I'll come right in and fix you a cup of tea.'

His patience and tenderness made me wonder what had gone wrong with his marriage. But maybe he'd been shorn of both patience and tenderness in the days of his return from Iraq. At the rate troops were committing suicide, home was as frightening as the war had been. Maybe even more frightening.

He offered his hand and we shook. 'I better get inside.'

'Thanks. I appreciate your time.'

She was still on the porch waiting for him. He turned around and headed back into his more recent tour of duty.

I was a hundred yards from the green and white City Limits sign when I saw the unmarked black car behind me. Police. The landscape here was mostly light manufacturing or the remnants thereof. You had metal buildings but you didn't have people walking among the metal buildings. Instead you had large forbidding padlocks on gates and CLOSED signs on the perimeter fencing.

He gave me a burst of siren that had the proper effect on my heart rate and mind. I drove another hundred yards until I found a place wide enough to accommodate both cars. Then I sat there the way he wanted me to do. He sat there, too, letting me sweat it out some. At least, hoping I was sweating it out. Now that the annoyance of being pulled over had passed, all I was concerned about was how long he'd been following me. He knew the turf. He could make himself invisible.

From what I could see of him in my rearview he was a young-looking black man in a gray suit, white shirt and blue-and-red rep tie. A *Gentleman's Quarterly* cop? He was talking on his phone and I had no doubt he was talking about me. Hammell had set him on me for sure and now he was coordinating with Hammell just how hard he was to lean on me.

He was maybe six feet and slim and he walked with military crispness up to my car window. I hit the window button then handed him my wallet with the driver's license facing him.

'Thank you, Mr Conrad. That isn't necessary.' He wasn't going to play any games. He was here to deliver a message. He showed me his badge and ID. Detective William Farnsworth.

I withdrew the wallet.

'You are performing the activities of a licensed private investigator but as far as the police department can find, you don't have any license.' His short dark hair had touches of gray, Obama-style.

'I'm not sure what you're talking about.'

The smile was patronizing. 'Then you're

good friends with the man you just visited?'

'Is that any of your business?'

'You were asking him questions because you're working for Senator Logan. And you're not working as a consultant. You're working as a detective. You have a good record as an army investigator but that doesn't give you any authority to work as an investigator out here.'

They'd spent some time on Google.

'Detective Hammell would like you to limit your work here to your work as a consultant.' He had leaned in a little closer to talk to me. His aftershave had a spicy scent. 'I really need your word that you'll cooperate.'

'I'm afraid I can't give you my word.'

He stood up. His face disappeared. Cars passed by in opposing lanes. Gawkers gawked.

His hand came down with a business card in it. Followed by his head. 'Take this.'

'What is it?'

'The name and number of a reputable local investigator. Detective Hammell would like you to use him. That way you won't get into trouble.'

'That's not exactly a recommendation.'

'What's not?'

'That Hammell recommends him.'

'Detective Hammell is trying to do you a favor.' For the first time anger flashed through his words. The suit and button-down shirt and carefully cut hair might say corporate but the words were now pure cop.

'I'll take the card but I doubt I'll call him. And I suppose that means that you'll keep following me around.'

'Me or somebody else.'

'I have a right to—'

'You have no right. So give it a rest. You understand?'

I'd pressed the wrong button.

'Get out of the car.'

'Hey, shit, c'mon.'

'Out. Now.'

When I was standing next to the open door he said, 'You carrying a gun?'

'Not carrying. It's in the glove compartment.'

'Let's see it.'

'It's a Glock. You probably know what a Glock looks like.'

He held out his hand, palm up. 'The Glock. Now.'

So I leaned in and across to the glove compartment, dragged out the Glock and handed it to him.

'Let's see the permit to carry.'

'It's in my wallet.'

'Let's see the wallet.'

He watched me as if half expecting I was going to pull a second gun on him. I opened the wallet so the permit was visible and held it up for him to see.

'Uh-huh.'

'That enough for you?'

'Yeah.'

'I'd like to go.'

'So would I, actually. But I have to keep tailing you. And the next time I think you're asking questions only a licensed investigator should ask, I'm going to arrest you.'

'Bullshit. I have a right to talk to anybody I want to. A legal right.'

'Maybe and maybe not. But I'm going to arrest you. You've got the big fancy lawyer. If he's such a hotshot he'll probably be able to help you get out of our jail.'

A teenage boy in a passing car shouted something and then flipped us the bird. I flipped it right back.

'Very mature, Conrad.'

He pretty much had a good point.

'I'm going to make this official, Conrad. Detective Hammell, my immediate superior, wants to find the person who killed the Cabot woman. The medical examiner says she was killed around ten last night, by the way. Finding the killer is Hammell's only interest. He's an honest man. If Jane Tyler has told you otherwise then she's telling you lies. The problem they have is strictly personal and doesn't get in the way of the investigation. Detective Hammell is interested in Senator Logan for several obvious reasons. He knew the woman and she was found dead in his cabin. That's for starters. So don't think there's any kind of vendetta going on here. You can believe this or not, but both Detective Hammell and I voted for Senator Logan because the douche bag who ran against him wanted to cut the budget so much we'd have to lay off a third of the force. I want to make all this clear.'

He returned gun and wallet. 'I'm not harassing you. I'm trying to keep you out of trouble with the police. I'm doing you a favor.'

His buffed and shined black shoes kicked up some dust as he turned and started back toward his car, but then he stopped and walked back to me. 'You may not know this yet, but a woman came to the police station last night and testified that the night before the Cabot woman died she saw her having a very angry argument with a man she says was Senator Logan. This took place in the parking lot of the Regency hotel around midnight. The woman works in the kitchen of the hotel. If I were you I'd think about hiring a professional investigator.'

I sat in my Jeep for a long minute absorbing what he'd told me. He followed me all the way into the city and right up to the parking lot of Jane's office.

A woman testified that Robert and Tracy Cabot had been in an argument in the parking lot of the Regency.

What the hell else was Robert keeping from me?

THIRTEEN

'Did he give you his name?'

'Farnsworth.'

'Bill Farnsworth. Right. Great guy and very good cop.'

'I was hoping you'd tell me he was running drugs and pimping ten-year-olds.'

'Sorry, I can't help you there,' Jane said. 'He's a good man. Despite my argument with Hammell, most of his people are good. The chief here is mostly a figurehead. Country club connections. In fact, he and Hammell argue a lot about sending officers to night school to study criminology and keep up on the technology. Hammell knows how important that is. We had a very corrupt and stupid police force here for years. And I knew that firsthand. I had a somewhat wild older brother and one night when he was sixteen they caught him drinking a beer behind the fence at a football game. And they beat him up so badly they broke his nose and two of his ribs. The bastard who did the beating was later arrested for trying to run his wife down with the family car and burglarizing several stores. A real sweetie. Hammell's changed all that.'

'All right, you've convinced me Hammell's a good cop. But what if his son goes crazy some night and really tries to hurt you?'

'That's why I got my carry permit. He'll be sorry.'

We were in her private office. More historical photographs on the wall, an area with two bookcases filled with bulging legal tomes. And a desk as empty as George W. Bush's brain. The large window behind the desk overlooked a lovely asphalt parking lot where two men were unloading a furniture truck and eyeing the building next door – a medical supply house, according to the sign.

'Ben called me about fifteen minutes ago. He'd like you and I to go out to Senator Logan's place. He said he needs our support.'

'For what?'

'He wouldn't say but he sounded pretty upset.'

'This just keeps getting better, doesn't it?'

'Losing faith?'

'Not faith,' I said. 'Time. I don't believe Robert killed Tracy Cabot. But one other name keeps coming to mind as a possibility. The guy who set all this in motion.'

'You mean Howard Ruskin?'

'Yes.' Then I told her about Ruskin's lady friend trying to contact me.

'Why would she call you?'

'I don't know. Maybe she's afraid of him

now.'

'Of him?'

'I guess. Maybe he went crazy after he killed Tracy and he's coming unglued. Even for him, though, killing somebody is really a stretch.'

'Why wouldn't she just run away?'

Her phone buzzed. She picked up. 'I won't be available the rest of the day. Please apologize for me and see if we can reschedule.' After hanging up, she said, 'It's easy to forget there's a world out there that isn't all tied up with Senator Logan's problem.'

'What time are we supposed to be there?'

'Half an hour ago.'

'You want to ride with me?'

'Sure. Your Jeep looks pretty cool.'

I smiled. 'How old did you say you were?'

When Mrs Weiderman opened the door I saw how much Robert's troubles had damaged her usual indomitable spirit. The harsh circles under the eyes, the gray color of the face itself and the flat sound of the voice. 'They're all in the living room. It's a terrible day.'

As she stood back to let us pass I saw that Jane took the woman's hand and gave it a squeeze. Mrs Weiderman nodded in gratitude. She would usually lead us into the house but this time she disappeared somewhere behind us as we walked toward the living room.

And there they were. The colors of fall – trees, grass, small piles of leaves – were a seasonal portrait in the enormous window behind the grand piano. But the humans were the same zombie gray as Mrs Weiderman. Even brother James was restrained, sitting slouched in one of the comfortable armchairs with his eyes downcast and – for once – saying absolutely nothing. Of course, in his case it might be more to do with his hangover than Robert's dilemma.

Elise and Maddy sat almost exactly as they had yesterday. Both were dressed in sweaters and jeans. Ben and Robert stood next to the dry bar. Robert had a drink in his hand. Ben was too smart for that.

They gaped at us as if they didn't quite know who we were. No doubt they'd been going through some kind of psychodrama and were still trapped in its spider webs.

Finally Ben said, 'You can try and talk sense to him, Dev. I'm worn out.' Rarely did you hear Ben Zuckerman this frustrated.

Then the others awoke from their pod-people daze.

Maddy said, 'Daddy. Listen to Ben.'

James said, 'You're letting the media get to you, Robert.'

Elise said, 'Please listen to them, Robert.'

By now I knew what Robert wanted to do. Or thought he wanted to do. Or threatened to do.

'The worst thing you could do right now, Robert,' I said, 'is resign.'

'Damned right,' Ben said, finding his passion again. 'Dev's saying just what I did. Resignation now is as good as admitting you killed that woman.'

'I hate to agree with Dev,' James said, 'but listen to him, Robert.'

Robert wore a blue crew-neck sweater, jeans and a pair of tan moccasin slippers, no socks. When he raised the clear glass to his mouth I could see that he'd poured himself a mind-number. Not a good sign at this time of day.

He lurched away from the dry bar and walked quickly to the center of the room. Maybe we'd been summoned here for a recital and he was going to play his viola now.

'I'm here with the two women I love most in the world and with my brother and my other friends. I can't tell you what this means to me.'

The stilted language indicated he'd slipped into pol mode. He was going to give us a speech. I wondered if he'd had some kind of mental collapse. Or maybe when all politicians see the end is near they automatically start to declaim.

'And for all the tribulation we're experiencing, friendship is what matters most and—'

'Damn it, Robert. Did you tell these people you're planning to resign?'

His face showed not anger but pain. There was a hint of tears in his voice now. 'I was thanking my friends – and I include you in that, Dev – thanking them and—'

But he stopped. Dropped his head. Stood unmoving. Then a sob. And the glass slipped from his hand.

Maddy rushed across the room to him. 'Oh, Daddy, Daddy.'

We all watched silently as she led him like a child to an empty chair. The way she led her mother – also like a child – upstairs last night. She seated him with grave delicacy, as if he might shatter. Then he did what Elise had done yesterday. He laid his head back and closed his eyes.

I went over and picked up the glass and carried it to the dry bar. Ben still stood there. His grimace told me that he was as scared as I was. Our candidate was coming apart and we needed him to make a live statement in front of reporters.

Ben said, 'Dev and Jane and I will be in the study, Elise.'

All Elise did was nod; she kept her eyes on the chair with Maddy and Robert.

The study was sunny and smelled of furniture polish. The Persian rugs, the large antique desk with elaborate scrollwork and the walls of books invited an introspective mood, but we had no time for introspection.

Two brown leather armchairs faced a brown leather couch in front of a small brick fireplace. An elderly gray tomcat sat on the mantel watching us with cosmic indifference. Ben and Jane took the couch. I took one of the chairs.

The first thing I had to do was tell them both about the call from Ruskin's woman.

'Any sense that this might be some kind of trap, Dev?'

'It's crossed my mind. But my receptionist said she sounded desperate.'

'What if she doesn't call back?'

'Then she got scared off and backed out.'

'Leaving us nowhere.'

'Sure thing.'

'Shit.'

'But I have a feeling she'll call me.'

'I sure hope so.'

'Now I need to tell you about the man from the US Attorney's office.'

Ben liked the fact that Hawkins had a good track record with the US Attorney's office and had worked in security for private enterprise as well. Despite being a liberal on most issues, Ben, like me and many others, understood that if you succeeded in business there was a good chance you knew what you were doing.

'Sounds like you really checked him out,' Ben said.

'On Google. Didn't Cosmo Kramer on the old *Seinfeld* show say something about it being true if it's on the Internet?'

Ben had a laugh like a bark; Jane's was a half-giggle.

'Well, if a guy named Cosmo is satisfied then so am I,' Ben said.

The gag relaxed us briefly.

Ben put his arm along the top of the couch. 'When I woke up this morning I was thinking that today I'd start to get everything under control. So the first thing I hear is about this kitchen worker who saw Robert and the Cabot woman arguing in the parking lot. I wanted to call a news conference and have Robert speak this afternoon but that's out of the question now. I'll have to do it alone but that'll be suspicious.' Ben was cracking his knuckles. The sound was sharp in the library-like room. 'Left field. Totally unexpected. This is the kind of stuff that can kill you. The kitchen worker makes you wonder who else is out there.'

'Maybe that's what he was hiding from us,' Jane said. 'That he saw Tracy Cabot more than he let on.'

'Did you get anywhere with him telling you everything?' I asked Ben.

'His story is still the same – he didn't kill her and that's all that matters. A part of me wants to dump his ass. I won't, of course, but when you've got a client who won't help you—' He didn't have to finish his thought. 'I need to get back to the hotel and set up a press conference for later this afternoon. The media is killing us.'

He was on his feet, a prowling animal. To Jane, he said, 'Have you heard anything from your friend in the police department?'

'Nothing new.'

He prowled some more then turned back and said, 'Dev, have you thought about telling Detective Hammell about the call you got from

Ruskin's lady friend or whoever the hell she is?'

'Crossed my mind but I doubt it would do much good at this point. He's focused on Robert and I can't say I blame him.'

Ben's smile was grim. 'You didn't have to say that, did you?'

On our way back to the city Jane was quiet. Her fine, small hands were crossed on her lap and with her window partly open her hair was mussed most sweetly. I thought about going to bed with her, of course, but I was also interested in her as a cohort. I sensed a melancholy in her that was not unlike my own.

The kiss on the cheek surprised me and I appreciated the hell out of it. Sweet flesh, perfume, breath and intention. 'I hope I see you tonight. We deserve a good dinner.'

'You're on. I'll call you after a while.'

I watched her walk into her building. Been a while since I'd connected this way and I liked the feeling. In the past, one-night stands had been able to assuage my loneliness, but as I got older loneliness became preferable to a succession of strange, cold beds.

Twenty minutes later I walked into my hotel room. Three calls waiting on the hotel phone, all from Chicago reporters I knew were here now and hoping for favors. I didn't return any of the calls.

As much as I didn't want to, I turned on the big plasma screen, grabbed a diet Pepsi from the refrigerator and sat down to watch the boys and girls of cable news – just as I'd told Tom Neil I wouldn't – finish off the career of Senator Robert Logan.

Our network wasn't much better than the right-wing one. A couple of our senators managed to look embarrassed to say even a few supportive words about Robert, even though they were his long-time friends. They were up for re-election, too. And the so-called liberal journalists were saying there was no chance that Robert could win now, however this turned out. Thanks, guys.

Of course, the Empire News channel was unmatched in its virulence. As always they seemed to be parodying themselves with their innuendo, piety and outright lies. This particular panel contained a Southern minister to whom the others had ceded all moral authority. When he suggested that our party was one of 'atheists and whoremongers' they nodded in solemn television agreement despite the fact that their side was about eighty percent ahead of us in sex scandals.

But my favorite was a robotic blonde woman whose flesh seemed as lacquered as her hair and whose pitiless gaze would cause a Harlem pimp to wet himself in terror. 'I'm probably getting ahead of myself a little here but it does look as if Senator Logan is guilty of something. So I'd like to know if anybody on this panel knows if this is the first time in American history that a sitting senator might be found guilty of first-degree murder and possibly be executed?'

'That's a very interesting question, Poppy,' God's man at the table responded.

'Extremely interesting,' said a beefy pontificator. 'And his party would always be remembered for having a killer sitting in the Senate.'

I turned it off and went to work on my laptop. I checked out the internals on the various races my firm was involved in. There wasn't much change from yesterday, except for the race where we'd had so much trouble with white working-class men. In American politics that was the greatest of all mysteries. Our party had always championed their various causes and needs yet they voted against us. It's difficult to respect people who respect people who consider them little more than vermin.

My cell phone burred.

'Afternoon, Dev. This is Michael Hawkins. You have a few minutes to talk?'

'Sure. What's going on?'

'I managed to get hold of Ruskin's sister in Cheyenne. At first she told me to talk to her lawyer but I finally managed to convince her that her brother could be in serious trouble and we need to talk to him. I told her about Tracy Cabot being murdered but she already knew about it. I pushed her on that and she admitted that Ruskin had called her last night. She said that he was scared and that that was not like him; that he usually laughed things off. She said that he said, "I'm in over my head this time; I don't know what to do." There are a couple ways to interpret that.'

'That she wasn't supposed to die and he didn't have anything to do with her death or—'

'Or that he killed her.'

'You leaning one way or another on it?'

'I've been an investigator of one sort or another for a long time and I've learned that every time I make a wild guess it's wrong. So I keep my guesses to myself.'

'She didn't know where he was calling from?'

'If she did I couldn't get it from her.'

'I've got something, too.' Then I told him about the call from Ruskin's lover.

'You're thinking it's for real?'

'Now that you've told me what his sister said – about him being so desperate and everything – yeah, I think it's for real. He's in panic mode and scaring the hell out of her – she may be thinking about bailing out.'

'No offense, Dev. But why would she turn to you?'

'No idea.' Then, 'Hey, Ben Zuckerman's on TV. I need to watch this, Michael.'

'I'll catch a little of it myself. I'll be in touch later.'

'Great.'

FOURTEEN

The suit was a solid blue today. Gray button-down shirt. Dark blue tie. The narrowed eyes showed the stress. If the reporters had been hurling stones instead of questions, Ben would have been dead by now. He held up a hand for silence and did not take it down until most of the questions had stopped. 'This will be a brief one, ladies and gentlemen.'

Some of the reporters started shouting questions again; Ben's hand didn't do much good this time. Other reporters shouted back to their peers, 'Shut up!'

Ben stood in front of the police station this morning. Bright sunlight played off the front windows; a worker in jeans and a Bears sweat-shirt had just stopped mowing the lawn so Ben could speak. 'I've just finished meeting with Detective Hammell. Despite all the nonsense on TV and the Internet, Senator Logan has not been charged with anything. He is free to go about his business.'

'Can he leave the city?' a woman reporter shouted.

'That didn't come up in my discussion with

the detective, who was very cooperative and friendly, I should note. But the senator came home to rest between sessions. This is where he enjoys being and this is where he'll stay for two more weeks. He has no plans to leave whatsoever.'

More questions but Ben said, 'I mentioned that this would be brief. I want to stick to a few facts and not add to all the frenzy the press has created over this unfortunate situation. So let me get to my second point. The senator will make a live statement very soon.' He smiled. 'I suppose a few of you are interested in that.'

A Saturday afternoon football cheer went up. Ben was good with reporters and they liked him even though he took shots at them.

'So until then, my friends...'

The scramble. Approximately fifty people began squawking questions at him as he turned from the microphones and began his exit up the steps of the police station behind him.

I clicked the set dark. The same hand I'd used on the remote now hovered over my cell. Then I got to work.

'Wasn't Mr Zuckerman wonderful today?' Mrs Weiderman said after I'd identified myself.

'He certainly was.'

'He made me feel much better. This is just so ridiculous. The senator involved in anything like this.'

'I agree. But we've got to face it. And that's why I'm calling. I need to talk to the senator as

166

soon as I can.'

'Well, he's playing tennis right now.'

'That's a good sign.'

'It takes his mind off things. Even if James always beats him. It's the only thing that James is better at than his older brother.'

'And Robert doesn't mind?'

'No. He told me one time that it's good for James' frame of mind to have something he's better at than Robert. The senator is a very good man.'

'He is; he really is.'

'That's why this is all so stupid.'

'I'm coming out there right now. How long have they been playing?'

'Oh, I'd say maybe an hour. They usually play for ninety minutes or so.'

'Great. I'll see you soon.'

A fawn crossing the road with its mother was the only hindrance to me setting a speed record on my way to the Logan estate. Whenever I see an animal this delicate and this lovely I wonder why you'd want to kill it. I've never understood the thrill that comes from death. For me it's easier to understand the thrill of killing another human being. There's often psychosis and madness involved and those elements make the act rewarding for the killer. But killing an innocent animal? The one time I'd been forced to kill in army intelligence I hadn't felt any thrill at all. Just a kind of disgust with the dead man for forcing me to kill him and disgust with myself for not having figured out a way to take him in without taking his life.

I ran the gauntlet as usual. By now a few small vans from town were out here serving various kinds of food. The number of reporters was half of what it had been last night. Many of them had been in town for Ben's press conference.

The *thwock* of the tennis ball brought me around to the side of the formidable house. The double court was located on the west side. And there they were in their whites. Two brothers – Cain and Abel, if you like biblical shorthand. They didn't see me at first both because I stood far enough away, and because they played furiously. Robert wasn't giving anything away today. And James knew it, as his loud curses revealed. The reds and greens and golds of the surrounding trees provided a pastoral setting, the same kind of setting the swells of Victorian England would have enjoyed when they played the game on the sides of their castles; the ladies in their finery, the men drinking sherry and smoking cigars and betting on the players.

Robert had nearly put me to sleep one night exulting about his new courts and explaining to me at great labored length about the differences between clay and courts of acrylic and courts of grass. Or some damned thing.

James spotted me first. The way his long body lurched into defensive mode told me that he was, as always, delighted to see me. Then

168

Robert saw me and shouted hello and waved his racket over his head. *No problemo here; what murder are you talking about, amigo?*

'Your friend Conrad is here to spoil our fun, I see,' James said as I approached.

'Give it a rest, James,' Robert said. Then, 'Hey, Dev, I finally beat my younger brother.'

'It'll be in all the papers,' James said. 'Front page.' He was all sweat and tiny gasps. Years of carousing had begun to take their toll. The gym had kept his muscles in good shape for his age but alcohol takes your strength and your stamina.

Robert was sweaty, too, but his breathing was back to normal and, even with a small excess of belly and a fleshier face, his body signaled better health.

James touched his racket to his brother's arm and said, 'I'm going up to the house to let you two ladies talk.' He glared at me then brushed on by, ever the asshole.

Robert laughed. 'I have a feeling that sometime before this is all over you're going to flatten him.'

'If Ben doesn't beat me to it again.'

'Or even Maddy.'

'Maddy?'

'She couldn't, of course, but she wishes she could. She absolutely hates him.' He nodded to the house with a head full of graying wet hair. 'C'mon, I'll buy you a cup of coffee.' His relaxed manner had started to bother me. I wondered if the family doc had given him some kind of nirvana injection. From hysteria to bliss; we needed him somewhere in the sane middle.

I decided the best way to test his connection to reality was to simply tell him why I was here, but before I could say anything he said, 'How are you doing with Howie Ruskin? If we can find him we've got this whole thing resolved. We could even win the election if we can hang it on him fast enough. And we know he killed her.'

'Maybe.'

We'd started to walk toward the house but my single word stopped him.

'Maybe? You mean you can't find him or you aren't sure he killed her?' He was plugged back into reality now all right. He was implicitly accusing me of somehow betraying him.

'Both. I may have a lead on him and a good one, but I still think you're keeping something from us and I want to know what it is.' I hesitated. Then I just dropped it on him. 'I'm told everybody in the family has a key to the cabin.'

'Sure. The cabin's for the whole family.' It took him maybe four or five seconds. 'Man, you're not suggesting that somebody in my family—'

'Everything has to be considered here, Robert.'

'I can't believe that you think somebody in my family might have killed her. Do you know how insulting that is? You know who killed her.

Just because Hammell won't consider anybody else except me is no reason for you to start looking at my family, Dev. For God's sake, we're your friends. You know how much Elise and Maddy love you. And I do mean love. You know that. So please keep that in mind.'

'I do keep it in mind, Robert. But I don't want to make the same mistake Hammell is. Looking at just one person. Everybody in your family has a key to the cabin. Everybody in your family knows about your affair and is concerned about how Elise would respond to another one. What if one of them found out about Tracy Cabot being at the cabin?'

He took a different approach this time. No hurt feelings and anger again. Oh, no, this time he was going to evade any serious discussion by throwing a sweaty arm around my shoulder and saying, 'Dev, we're buddies. Look at all the ups and downs we've been through together. I was coming apart yesterday and I apologize for that. I'm sure I scared the shit out of you.' The arm came down. 'I'm ready for the battle now. Let's go have some of Mrs Weiderman's great coffee and talk about what we do next.'

'In other words, you're not going to tell me what you're hiding.'

He was pretty damned good, I'll give him that. Following a whoop of a laugh, he said, 'That's the Dev I love. One incorrigible sonofabitch!' Smiling as he said it.

I had not learned one thing.

FIFTEEN

The call came on my cell as I was nearing the city limits. When I heard the first ring I knew who it would be. Don't know how. I just knew.

'Mr Conrad?'

'Yes.'

'I'm calling from a pay phone so don't try and have this traced. It won't do you any good.'

'I appreciate the information.'

'I'm Howard Ruskin's girlfriend. My name is Sarah Potter. I have some information for you.'

'Information is always good.'

'But I'm pretty scared and so is Howard.'

The bellman who'd described her had said that she looked like a hippie. I kept trying to picture her.

'All right, Sarah.'

'This is very delicate, what we have to do.'

'Will Ruskin be joining us?'

'Not this time, I'm afraid.'

'Later?'

'That depends on how this works out. You and I.'

'So where do you and I meet?'

'There's a neighborhood bar named "Rick's"

at 3654 Fulmer Avenue. I'll be watching you from my car at eight thirty.' Then, 'I mean, would that be OK?'

The last line reminded me of my daughter when she'd been ten or so. She'd come over and stand in front of me and make a very adult presentation of what she wanted to do, and then she'd break my heart with, 'But I don't want you to be mad or anything.'

I liked this Sarah Potter a whole hell of a lot.

'That'll be just fine, Sarah. I'm easy to talk to and easy to deal with.'

The way she exhaled I could tell how tightly wound she was.

'Oh, God, that sounds so good. I looked you up on YouTube and saw a couple of your interviews. You have very kind eyes. So I was hoping you'd at least listen to me.'

'It'll be my pleasure, Sarah.'

Rick's was three blocks east of a large shopping center. It was painted a dark green with an outsize electrical sign on its roof and another one on its northern side. Both depicted the glowing golden profiles of a man and woman about to kiss. I'm sure somewhere there was a full-size version where they were making electrical love.

Since part of my business is working with both demographics and psychographics, I judged the customer base to be white, thirty to fifty, blue collar. There was a big screen that showed some sporting event – when all else failed there was always the Peruvian marble championship – but Rick or whoever had the grace to keep it low so the customers could shout at each other over the jukebox that played pickup truck music with a vengeance.

I ordered Bud in a bottle and a glass.

When she came in a few of the men along the bar gave her a quick glance then went back to their conversations or the TV set. She was entombed in this heavy, black, winter long coat – ready for a Russian winter – leaving her sweet, small, homely face seeming very small indeed. It was all wrapped up in a blue headscarf. She moved quickly toward me, the blue eyes frightened and fixed on me as if I was the star guiding her through a room full of monsters.

She slid into the booth, leaned toward me and said, 'I might have been followed.' Not till then did I realize she was out of breath.

'Who'd be following you?'

'That's just it. I can't be sure and neither can Howard.'

'Most people call him "Howie."'

'He's sick of that name. He said it makes him sound like a little boy.'

'Would you like something to drink?'

'No, thanks.'

The bartender was watching me. Waiting for an order. I shook my head.

She took her scarf off and let her scruffy blonde hair fall free. She was a tiny thing, a miniature. But the wrinkles spoke of long and troubled years.

'I know you probably hate Howard, Mr Conrad. I wouldn't blame you, either.'

'Well, I wouldn't say that I like him a lot.'

She had a tiny laugh that seemed to touch her eyes more than her lips. 'You're being kind.' Then, 'He needs your help.'

'Now that's a surprise. A hell of a surprise.'

She glanced around as if half-a-dozen men in fedoras had suddenly appeared. 'He said he can't trust anybody in his party because it's changed so much. The people he used to work with are out of favor. The new people scare him. They're so far right they're off the charts.'

Howard 'Howie' Ruskin afraid of his own people. Too good to be true. This could all be some kind of elaborate scam but I needed to follow wherever it led.

'Why me?'

'He said he's been aware of you for years. He says you're dirty but not dirty enough to be really bad. And that makes you clean enough for him to talk to.'

My laugh was loud enough to win the bartender's attention. 'I guess there's a compliment in there somewhere.'

'Well, if you knew Howard you'd know he talks like that all the time. So convoluted.'

'What's he afraid of?'

I'd flipped a switch. The playfulness of our conversation ended then and there. She pushed her little face toward me and said, 'I have no idea. But if he's this afraid – and I've never seen him this scared before – then I'm afraid, too, because whoever's after him will be after me as well. They'll think that I know something.'

'And you don't?'

She sat back. 'Oh, I know lots of things Howard has done. Fairly recent things. He usually tells me that so-and-so has hired him to do such-and-such. He did some dirty tricks for a few politicians during this past primary season and made a lot of money. But this thing, he'd never talk about it; not from the start and not now. That's why I'm so worried. He likes to brag about how well he's doing and most of the time it's fun to listen to. But it's only about the usual stuff. The really important stuff he keeps secret from everybody, including me.'

'When did you get into town?'

'Three nights ago.'

'Were you with him yesterday?'

'In the morning.'

'When was the next time you saw him?'

'Just after midnight last night. I knew something was wrong right away.'

'How?'

'He seemed upset.'

'Did you ask him about it?'

'I always ask him but it rarely does any good. He wouldn't tell me, of course. After all we've been through together. I'm planning to marry him. We've talked about it many times. And then he treats me like this. Something bad happened and he won't tell me what it was.'

Perhaps even for Howard 'Howie' Ruskin, killing somebody was too much of a burden. Maybe he was coming apart.

'What does he want to talk to me about?'

'I have no idea. He just wants me to set up a time and place to meet. There's a state park about six miles outside the northern city limits. Washburn is the name of it. He says if you pull in the entrance and then turn your headlights off, he'll come out. This would be at ten o'clock tonight. All of this – it's so insane. And he's so afraid. He's almost hysterical.'

I tried to puzzle through the setup. I couldn't see any danger for me. I wasn't important enough to be a player in Ruskin's games. I wasn't significant enough to bother with. But he was obviously in trouble and scared.

And so he wanted me to help him. Not because I mattered at all in the scheme of things, but because I was close by and because I had enough connections that I could lead him to the kind of protection he needed. What needed to be negotiated at this point was how much he was willing to tell me about his whole operation while I recorder-immortalized his every word.

'Please say you'll meet him. Please.'

'All right.'

'Oh, thank God.' Her relief brought tears. 'You don't know how happy you've made me. I am so afraid for him – for us.'

'Is he armed?'

She sniffled up tears. 'Yes. He's always armed. He has a Glock. I don't know anything about guns – I hate guns – but that's what he told me it is. But you don't have any reason to be afraid of him.'

'Why's that?'

Without any humor at all, she said, 'Because he wants something from you. That means he has to be nice.'

SIXTEEN

I sat in a near-deserted Burger King parking lot and made calls to Jane – who'd been wondering what had happened to our supposed dinner – and to Michael Hawkins. I didn't tell him much except that I was working on a strong lead and planned to call him with more information later. He suggested that we meet up and work on this lead together. I remembered what Tom Neil had told me: how Hawkins liked to be the star of all investigations. I told him it would go better if I worked alone. He didn't try very hard to keep the disappointment from his voice.

There wasn't much traffic on the highway to the state park. On the curves my headlights took snapshots of fall trees and farm fields and a lone isolated convenience store. But on the straight stretches there was just my beams piercing the night.

On the left side of the park entrance was a life-size bronze statue of a Native American and on the right a bronze life-size statue of a man in the uniform of the northern army during the Civil War. A splash of headlights revealed both to be covered heavily with bird shit. Then total darkness, the road into the park dark with only a few signs to guide me. I pulled over to the side and waited.

I unlocked my glove compartment and reached in for my Glock. I kept it in my hand as I sat there. There was no reason for Ruskin to try to hurt me that I could understand. But maybe he had a reason *he* could understand. And this could be a trap, after all.

I was far enough in that the occasional cars and trucks on the highway sounded remote, far enough in that when I clipped off my headlights and sat in silence the sound of my engine was enormous, as if it had the power of a racing vehicle. I kept checking my rearview as well as left and right windows. I gripped my Glock tighter.

I was impatient so my sense of time passing was exaggerated. I kept checking my watch, certain that ten, even fifteen minutes had passed. No such luck. Five, six, seven minutes only.

I resented being made this vulnerable. Sitting in this deep a darkness anything could come at me from anywhere and surprise me so completely my gun may be useless. Strong wind rattled the leafy trees now and somewhere ahead of me I could hear a car engine. Then I saw headlights through the trees as the vehicle made its way around curves toward me.

The highway patrol car appeared and when it reached me it stopped. Of course. A highway patrol car would check the park at least once a night. The darkness vibrated with the red and blue of his emergency lights.

And just as it did, way back at the entrance, I saw the headlights of another vehicle pull in and then quickly back up and start to disappear. Had that been Ruskin?

The officer, a tall and heavy man, stepped out of his vehicle. Tan uniform, campaign hat. The motor was still running. I'd already pulled my license out.

'The park is officially closed,' he said, taking my license. 'There's a sign right at the front.'

'I guess I didn't see it.'

'Any special reason you're sitting in the dark?'

I knew a number of variations on the standard shit-eating smile. I used number six-B. 'This is kind of embarrassing.'

'Oh, really?'

'Umm-hmm. I'm, uh, meeting someone here.'

'A woman?'

'Yes.'

'Married?'

'Do I have to answer that?'

'No.'

'Well, what the hell, I'll tell you. No, she's not married but she's got an ex-boyfriend who follows her everywhere she goes.'

'Tell her about this new invention called a restraining order.'

'She's had two of them.'

'Then somebody should bust his ass.'

181

'He's clever and has a good lawyer.'

'You're clever, too, or trying to be. I don't buy anything you just told me. I'd like you to step out of your vehicle.'

Shit.

He stepped back and to emphasize how serious he was, his left hand dropped to his holster.

Wind and the scent of coming rain. The first thing I did when I got out of the Jeep was look straight back at the highway. All I could do was try to hurry this along.

The first thing he did was shine his light inside the Jeep. 'That a Glock?' This close he smelled of pipe tobacco, which always reminds me of my father. Instant image: him sitting in his easy chair with a glass of Burgundy, his pipe and his British detective novels from the forties and fifties. He hated everything that came after that.

'Yes. A Glock.'

'You have a permit to carry?'

'Yes. You have my billfold. Look in where the folding money goes.'

He brought his small but intense light on the wallet and lifted the permit out. He studied it as if he was going to be quizzed on it in the morning. 'Why would you need to carry?'

'My business.'

'What kind of business?'

'I'm a political consultant. Things happen these days. I might have to protect my client.'

'You call them "clients"?'

'Yes. That's what they are. I do work for hire.'

'Who's your client around here?'

Here we go, I thought. He'd have a little fun at my expense. 'Senator Logan.' But instead of following up he said, 'Why do you keep looking at the highway?'

'To see if the woman I'm supposed to meet got here yet.'

'There is no woman. Not the kind you're talking about anyway.'

'What's that supposed to mean?'

He sighed deeply, then put everything back in the wallet and returned it to me. 'You're meeting somebody. That I buy. And maybe it's a woman. But what I don't buy is that this is about getting laid or anything. As soon as you said Senator Logan I knew this had something to do with politics. And if it's a woman that's why she's coming here. Now I'm ordering you out of this park. You're breaking the law. Do you understand?'

'I do, yes.'

'You pull out. I'll follow you.'

This was one highway patrolman who really didn't like Senator Logan.

'Next time read the sign before you come in here.'

'Will do.'

'I'd say the same thing if you were working for the guy I'm voting for.'

'I'm sure you would.' I tried to keep sarcasm from my voice. It wasn't easy.

Behind the wheel of my Jeep I waved to him. He was already in his car, waiting for me. His emergency lights were still on.

I swung the Jeep around and headed back up the road. When you have a law enforcement officer following you it's impossible to relax. Or to act natural. They can pull you over any time using any excuse they choose. They can even force you to get in the car and take you to the nearest police station. I was happy to see the highway no more than twenty yards ahead. I wasn't even thinking of Ruskin now. I just wanted to be away from the patrolman and his flashing lights.

But the game wasn't over. I supposed he would turn right. He was highway patrol, after all, and the greatest stretch of highway was to his right. Left would take him back to the city. But he turned left and for the first couple of hundred yards he kept his emergency lights on.

Irritation, agitation, fantasies of just tearing ass down the road ahead of him – I had to calm myself by force. And now I was back to thinking about Ruskin. What if the car that had pulled into the park entrance had been him? What if it had spooked him so much he'd no longer deal with me?

The highway patrolman took a right when we were about five minutes from town.

I needed coffee so I pulled into a Wendy's and went through the drive-up. I had a headache. I pulled into a slot on the lot and drank my coffee. I watched the teenage couples with great envy. In memory, lying memory, everything had been so passionate back then. And not just the sex. The feelings, too. It was all like driving a car that went six hundred miles an hour and you had no way to control it. New and startling and dangerous. There were in fact fates worse than death. The girl you loved could fall in love with somebody else. I knew men who never got over their first love; still talked about it even in their forties and fifties and sixties, partly in loss and partly in confusion. Why did they cling to those memories? Why couldn't they let go of them?

When my cell phone toned and I put it to my ear a male voice said, 'What the hell was with the highway patrol?'

'There's a sign that says you can't enter the park after ten o'clock. I guess he checks it every night. Or somebody does anyway.'

'This is Ruskin.'

'Yeah. I figured.'

'We still need to talk.'

'Where?'

'You know where the college is?'

'I can find it.'

'There's a small park on the west side of it. Twenty minutes.' He clicked off. It was a good thing I didn't have any objections.

I found the college and the heavily wooded park. An asphalt road twisted through it. Lights from the dorms pierced the tree tops. They were even stronger than the ornate lights used to illuminate the road here.

When I heard voices I angled around in the seat. Another young couple much like the ones I'd seen in the Wendy's parking lot. Could anybody possibly be as happy as these laughing people were? I hoped my daughter was, and my ex-wife, for that matter. I couldn't quite bring myself to extend that much happiness yet to my ex-wife's new husband. I wanted him to be happy, but exultant happy I reserved for my loved ones. Maybe in a year I would outgrow my pissiness. I'd been promising myself that in general ever since ninth grade.

Headlights filled my rearview mirror. A plain blue Ford pulled into the slot furthest from me. Then a motor died. A car door opened. A man mostly in silhouette emerged from the car and started walking toward me. He was round, walked like a duck and apparently tripped over his own feet because he stumbled as if he was going to go splat on the ground.

That was when the gunshots started.

PART THREE

SEVENTEEN

There is always that millisecond between the sound of the shots and your brain responding. Most people would take cover any way they could. Throwing yourself to the ground was always an option. But for a millisecond Ruskin froze. And that was why, when he was hit, he threw his arms up and danced like a puppet until he slammed into the asphalt about ten feet from my Jeep.

By now I had my Glock out and was working my way around the edge of the Jeep. Charged with adrenaline, crazed with both fear and anger, I hoped to be able to locate the shooter. Sarah Potter had mentioned somebody was after Howard 'Howie' Ruskin. I was now a believer. Capturing the shooter could lead to a lot of places few people knew about.

But then another millisecond decision came to me. Ruskin started calling out for help. *Shit*, I thought. I had to at least see him before I went after the person who'd tried to kill him. I had to move around the back of the Jeep now and put myself in a position to be shot at whatever I did. I might as well check on Ruskin first.

From what I could judge the shots had come directly from the area behind Ruskin's car. I had to worry about myself first. All I could do now was wait to see if there would be any more shooting before I pushed out into the open. I used my cell to call emergency and was told that somebody had reported the gunfire. I said we also needed an ambulance right away.

The shooter was gone. That was the bet I made with myself. No shooter would stay in place now that sirens could be heard.

Keeping my eyes and my Glock fixed on the point in the hardwoods where the shooter had stood, I moved carefully to Ruskin. He was impossible to miss and not only because he was rolling around on the ground. He made loud mewling sounds: fear. I couldn't blame him.

It's always disappointing to find that a major villain resembles a stereotypical Star Trek nerd, but that was Ruskin's curse. Writhing on the asphalt now, clutching the arm of his tan sport coat, his three-hundred-dollar jeans properly stressed, his glasses crooked on his pudgy face, his balding head shiny with sweat, the thick two-inch heels on his black boots jutting out, he might have been suffering the shame of having been shunned by other Trekkies. At least that was the noise he made – a sort of yelping. Not the sound of someone mortally wounded.

'You just gonna stand there, Conrad? I'm fucking dying here!'

I doubted he was fucking dying here, though

there was blood on the pavement and his fingers were splotched with red from where they'd touched his arm. I hunched down and examined the wound as best I could. 'Were you hit anywhere else?'

'Isn't this enough? I could die here.'

'Not if this is your only wound.'

'Oh, is that right, Mr Macho? What the hell do you know about it?'

I stood up. 'They'll take you to the ER and fix you up.'

'I knew they were after me.'

'Who?'

'Oh, no. I don't tell you anything until we make a pact.' He grimaced and rolled some more. I didn't mean to minimize his wound. Most people would have been in shock. He was certainly in pain and he certainly had a right to be afraid. Somebody *was* after him and somebody *was* trying to kill him. 'I'm in agony here, man.'

'You saved your own life when you stumbled.'

'What the hell're you talking about?'

'You stumbled just when the shots started.'

Apparently he wasn't listening. 'Where is the goddamned ambulance?' I was sure they could hear him in the distant dorms.

A police car with siren ripping the night jerked to a stop ten feet from my Jeep and two uniformed officers, a man and woman, lurched from the car and ran toward us.

'What happened here?' the female officer said.

'I've been shot!' Ruskin cried. 'What does it look like?'

The look she gave me said that they were inclined to give him another shot or two. The male officer walked over to Ruskin and said, with epic contempt, 'Who the hell are you?'

'If you read a goddamned newspaper once in a while you'd know who I was. Now get me the hell to a hospital before I die.'

Howie Ruskin made friends wherever he went.

To me, the officer said, 'Are you famous, too?'

I smiled at him. 'No. But believe it or not, in certain circles he's very famous.'

I don't know what Ruskin had said to the female officer who was hunched down next to him but she said with great scorn, 'What are you, five years old? You need to calm down. You're going to be all right.'

'You got some ID?' the male cop asked me. 'And while you're at it, tell me what the hell happened here.'

Now it was the white ambulance that arrived, blazing lights and blaring siren. We had already started to accumulate an audience. You could hear their feet slap-slap-slapping up the drive here toward all the fun. Students. In my college days an event like this would be as good as a movie; even better because it was real. There were already twenty or so of them, boys and girls mixed. None of them knew yet what had happened and from their vantage point they couldn't see past my Jeep so they couldn't know that Ruskin lay on the asphalt. But some of them had heard the gunshots. Who could resist gunshots? The ones who'd stayed away would be those who remembered all the campus killings that had shocked the country over the past decade.

The three men from the ambulance worked so hard and so fast I wondered if they were trying to set a Guinness record. These were the guys I'd want if I was the one needing emergency help.

'How about being careful, all right?' Ruskin shouted at one of the ER crew as they prepared to put him on the gurney.

I had no idea what he was talking about and was sure they didn't either. He was so used to bellering at people he probably couldn't control himself any longer. He was Howard 'Howie' Ruskin the Great, the Magnificent, the Most Wonderful of All. Neither the ER people nor the police found him wonderful tonight.

The first few drops of rain tamped my forehead.

'Just who the hell is this asshole?' the male cop asked me.

'He's in politics.'

'Big deal. Are you with him?'

'I know him. He was walking toward my Jeep

when somebody started shooting from the trees right behind him.'

'You wait right here. There'll be a detective along any minute.'

Meanwhile, they were guiding Ruskin into the ambulance. He was still yelling at them but not as loudly. Somewhere in the muddle of accusations he was hurling at them I heard my name. After they had him inside and closed the door, one of the ambulance men came over to me and said, 'Are you Conrad?'

'Yes.'

'He wants you to come to the ER.'

'I'll need directions and I can't leave until a detective talks to me.'

'He's quite a little fella.'

'You noticed that, huh?'

He snorted then grinned. 'Yeah, I noticed that.'

It was ten minutes before Detective Farnsworth arrived but only five minutes before the downpour began. I sat in my Jeep during my wait, listening to the rain on the roof.

Farnsworth opened the door of the Jeep and made himself comfortable. He wore a well-cut light brown overcoat that made him look even more like a stockbroker instead of a cop. Relentless, handsome young black man – TV series maybe? 'Too bad Hammell needed to pull me off following you. Something finally happens and I'm not there for it.'

'Why'd he pull you off?'

'Convenience store robbery. The robber beat the store clerk pretty badly. Sixty-three-year-old woman. Unarmed, of course.'

'They seem to get worse.'

'Meth, probably. Anyway, Hammell wants the bastard and so do I. But then I got pulled away out here. So who shot this Ruskin character?'

'I have no idea. And since you called him a character I take it you've met him?'

'Only what I could find about him online. So what happened?'

I told him everything I thought he should know. He was enough of a pro to understand that what I said I'd edited heavily. And I was enough of a pro to know he wanted to take a hammer and put a few dents in my skull.

When I walked into the ER reception area I saw a woman at the check-in desk sobbing so hard the woman behind the desk rushed around and took her in her arms. A nurse came rushing from somewhere in the back and took over, leading the woman to a seat then sitting down next to her. The nurse put an arm around the woman and started talking to her in a voice so low I couldn't pick up on what they were saying.

The ER reception area contained two couches and maybe twenty straight-backed chairs with cushioned backs and seats. End tables between some of the chairs held magazines and small toys for kids. We'd arrived during a lull. This time of night ERs are often crowded. This was when the victims of car accidents, domestic abuse, brawls and gunshots started showing up. But now, except for the sobbing woman, I was the only other visitor.

'I'm waiting to see Howie Ruskin.'

She typed in the name. 'Yes. Doctor Olsen is with him now.'

'Mr Ruskin asked me to be here.'

'I'll be sure to let you know when you can see him.'

'Thanks. Is there any coffee available anywhere?'

'Of course. There's a vending machine down the hall but I just got a pot going. Let me get you a fresh cup.' She was middle-aged and competent-looking. My demographic mind was fitting her into a pattern. She probably had kids and this was probably the only job she could get – the graveyard shift. She might have a husband but then she might not. This sketch would seem to make her a potential voter for us but I couldn't be sure. Though our side doesn't like to admit it, welfare has inspired some people who tend to rush to the ER for ills as minor as sore throats. They could wait and see their docs in the morning for eighty percent less but they don't. And when you talk to the workers who serve them you sometimes hear a great deal of resentment.

In the next twenty minutes I looked at three recent copies of news magazines, had a second cup of not-bad coffee and waited to be called to visit Ruskin. I also had time to think through everything that had happened. I'd assumed it was Ruskin who'd been followed, but if that was the case how had the shooter been able to get into position to shoot him so quickly? Ruskin had parked, cut his engine, stepped out of his car and started walking toward me. Then came the shots. That made no sense.

But what if someone had been following *me,* believing I would lead them to Ruskin? That made more sense, and was why I got up and walked down the hall where I was alone. I punched in the number for the hotel and asked for Earl the bellman. It took a few minutes to locate him.

'This is Earl.'

'Earl, it's Dev Conrad.'

'Hey, there, Mr Conrad.'

'Have you seen Michael Hawkins around tonight?'

'Hawkins?'

'Yes.'

'Well, I saw him come out of the restaurant about nine thirty and then go into the bar.'

'How long was he in the bar?'

'He's still in there. Something going on?'

'No. I was just curious, is all. There's a twenty in this for you if you don't mention this call to him.'

'No need to pay me, Mr Conrad. I keep secrets pretty good. It's part of my job.'

'Thanks, Earl.'

I hadn't given Hawkins any of the details about my meeting with Ruskin, but given his alleged competitiveness maybe that had been enough for him to follow me. Hard to imagine him being the shooter, but since Ruskin was certain 'they' were after him, 'they' could be anybody, including an investigator for a US Attorney's office. But maybe if Hawkins had been following me he'd gotten a look at the actual shooter.

At this time of night all the doctor/nurse calls over the hospital system were muted. As I walked back to my seat in the ER area the noise my phone made was ominous in its loud pitch.

'I told my friend in the police department about Howie Ruskin,' Jane said, 'and she recognized the name so she called me. Somebody shot him?'

'Yeah. In the arm. I'm at the ER. I'll get in to see him pretty soon here.'

'This is getting scary.'

'I just wish there was some angle in it that would help Robert.'

'Yes. But it must have something to do with Tracy Cabot, don't you think?'

'Absolutely. But right now that's *all* I know.'

'I'm still at the office working on a case. I've got an important court date tomorrow morning. I'm going to stop in about an hour. If you're up for a drink let me know.'

'I'd like that. I'll just have to see how it goes here.'

'Sure. Well, good luck.'

By the time I got back to my seat Detective Farnsworth was talking to the woman at the desk. When he saw me he excused himself and walked over. He took the chair next to me. 'When I was a kid I always liked horror films that were set in hospitals. You like horror films, Mr Conrad?'

'A few of them. But not the gory ones.'

'I'm the same way. The gory ones turn me off. My fourteen-year-old son talked me into going to see one recently and I barely got through it.'

'You don't look old enough to have a fourteen-year-old son.'

'I also have a sixteen-year-old daughter. I run a check on all her dates.'

I laughed. 'You tell her you do it?'

'Hell, no. She'd never speak to me again.'

Easy to know what we were doing. He was trying to make us momentary friends so I'd tell him more than I already had. Since I knew how these things worked – had worked a few of them myself – I wondered if he had a son and daughter at all.

He stretched long legs out in front of him. He still wore his overcoat.

'You working with Howie Ruskin now, Mr Conrad?'

'I thought we were talking about horror movies.'

'From what the ambulance crew told me, Ruskin is a horror movie.'

'I wouldn't argue with that.'

'When we were sitting in your Jeep you said he called you.'

'His girlfriend set it up. Just as I said.'

'Any particular reason he wanted to talk to you?'

'My favorite horror movie is still *Invasion of the Body Snatchers*. The one with Kevin McCarthy and Dana Wynter.'

He smiled with great tolerance. 'Too bad you're not a priest or a lawyer or even a private investigator, Mr Conrad. That way you could proclaim client privilege. This way you're shit out of luck. If I take you to the station and Hammell starts asking you questions, he won't be happy if you bring up a movie called *Invasion of the Body Snatchers*. He won't be happy if you bring up any movie at all, in fact. You'll actually have to answer his questions.'

But it was then that an angel in the form of a nurse appeared before us, backlit by the soft bluish light of the ER desk, and said, 'Detective Farnsworth, the doctor said you could talk to Mr Ruskin now. If you'd follow me, please.'

As he was pushing up from the chair, he said, 'I shouldn't be too long, Mr Conrad. I mean, if that's all right with you.'

The nurse, a middle-aged woman, caught his sarcasm and then glanced at me to see how I was reacting to it.

But I didn't give either of them the satisfaction they wanted. I just sat there expressionless and silent. Finally, seeming confused, she said, 'This way, Detective Farnsworth.'

Farnsworth was in a hurry when he reappeared. The brisk walk, the curt nod to me, the intense expression – there might have been a break in the beating of the convenience-store woman. He half-jogged the rest of the way until he disappeared through the doors down the hall.

It was another fifteen minutes before a redhaired woman in doctor whites came down the hall from the right and walked straight to me. About thirty, I guessed, trim, glasses with dark frames, not unattractive. 'Are you Mr Conrad?'

'Yes.'

'I'm Doctor Olsen. Mr Ruskin has asked to see you.'

'How's he doing?'

'We took the bullet out. He'll need rest but he should be fine.' A smile. 'He's quite the character.'

'You noticed that, huh?'

'He says you're a good friend of his.'

By now I was on my feet. After she said that I thought about sitting down again. I was afraid I'd pass out. 'That's strange.'

'Oh?'

'Actually, I hate him.'

She studied my face to see if I was joking. I think she gave up. 'Let's go see him.'

We didn't talk until we were in a large room where there were four other beds, all empty now. Curtains could be pulled for privacy.

He was propped up on pillows, studying a smart phone with the intensity of a bookie surveying the latest results from the track. He was doing this one-handed. His left arm was in a blue sling. He was in a light-green hospital gown. His hair was wilder than usual, the operatic tentacles of a madman. When he saw me, he said, 'Hey, dude. I bet you were scared. I wasn't.'

'Right. I noticed that being shot didn't bother you at all. You were screaming because you were so happy.'

'Can you believe this guy, Doc? His sarcasm?'

She was eager to leave. 'I'll leave you two alone for ten minutes. Then I'll be back.'

The metal sides on the bed were up. On the rolling table next to the bed was a 7UP and a glass full of ice. Then there was the rosary. Howie Ruskin had a rosary? But somehow that fit his reality. He was this thirty-eight-year-old near-genius who wanted to pay the world back for a lot of different reasons. The rosary surprised me because he always denied being associated with the right-wing religious nuts, claiming he was a non-believer. I didn't know many non-believers who carried rosaries.

I expected to hear more of his patter but instead he said, 'You have to hide me, Conrad. That's the first thing. You have to figure out where I'll be safe while we're setting everything up.'

'You're way ahead of me. First of all, why do *I* have to hide you? You're the one who knows all the bad guys.'

'Great. Somebody's trying to kill me and you're getting sanctimonious.'

'Back up a minute. Who's trying to kill you?'

'The people who hired me.'

'Why would they try to kill you?'

He winced – the first indication that he was in pain. 'Because there's already some jerk from the US Attorney's office on my case. He left a message on my phone. That's why I had to get the hell out of the hotel. They're afraid with him involved I might get indicted. And that if I get indicted I might talk. It'd be safer to get rid of me.'

So he knew Hawkins was on his case; that, at least, was true. 'This isn't just paranoid bull-shit?'

The childlike eyes. 'Does it *sound* like paranoid bullshit?'

'Yeah, it does.'

'I can deliver names and dates of a lot of things. And you're making shit out of me.'

The hell of it was the hurt feelings were sincere. A real grown-up would try to hide them, but then nobody had ever said that Howie was a real grown-up, had they?

He closed his eyes. Rested. I didn't blame him. I'd been surprised at how active he was.

'Howie.'

'What?'

'Why did you kill her?'

He lay still, but smiled. 'I knew you were trying to nail me for killing her. You're so fucking stupid maybe I shouldn't get involved with you after all.'

'That's not exactly a denial.'

His eyes opened and he bellered: 'Of course I didn't kill her, Conrad. Howie Ruskin doesn't kill people.'

Overlooking the fact that he was referring to himself in the third person, I found his resentment at my question believable. At least for now.

'How about this? I'm going to put you in my hotel room. There are two beds. Then I'm going to hire somebody with a gun to stand guard just inside the door.'

He was fading. 'They gave me ... a ... pill.'

I let him doze off and walked to the door. When I leaned out to look up and down the hall I saw Dr Olsen talking to a nurse who held a clipboard. Clipboards don't cost that much but in a hospital setting they can look imposing and important. Maybe the nurse was showing her some of the doodles she'd come up with tonight.

The doctor saw me, said goodbye to the nurse and walked up to me. 'Is everything all right?' she asked.

'He nodded off.'

'It's about time. He never quit talking. I was impressed.'

'What happens now?'

'Somebody needs to take him home with some pain meds and some instructions I have for his caregiver. He keeps talking about a woman. Sarah.'

'His girlfriend. She'll take care of him.'

'How does she put up with him?'

'One of the mysteries of life.'

'Can I give you his meds and the instructions? I'll have to get his permission.'

'That's fine.'

'He doesn't have a shirt, either.'

I remembered his sport coat. 'I'll warm up the car.'

'You'll have to sign some papers taking legal responsibility for seeing that he is taken care of.'

'I'll be happy to do that.'

She paused and gazes met. 'I still don't understand your relationship. I'm bothered by the fact that you said you hated him and you didn't seem to be kidding.'

'I wasn't kidding. But don't you work with patients you hate but you take good care of them anyway?'

'I wouldn't say "hate," but there are people who certainly piss me off.' I like it when docs swear. A human touch.

'Well, that's what I'm doing here. Howie is an old political enemy of mine. But now – for a reason I won't go into – I have given my word to Howie that I'm going to make sure that he's safe.'

'Safe from what?'

'Maybe you've forgotten, Doctor. Somebody shot him tonight.'

'I hardly forgot, Mr Conrad. I was the one who worked on him, remember? I'm simply asking why the police won't be keeping him safe.'

Speaking of people being pissed off, that was what she was doing to me. She was going to gnaw on this forever. 'Howie and I are now what you'd call circumstantial buddies. He'll be fine with me. If the police want to talk to him just tell them he's staying with me in my room at the Regency.' I put just enough irritation in my voice so she'd finally let it all go.

She nodded but her expression said she not only didn't like me, she didn't trust me either. 'I need to go see him now. Get his permission so you can take over.'

She left abruptly with no other words.

Jane was at the registration desk when I arrived there, looking smart and fresh in her blue Burberry coat, her hair slightly mussed by the winds. Her smile was the first thing I'd had to be happy about for a long, long time. When I walked over to her she touched my arm and it was like receiving a blessing from on high. 'You look exhausted, Dev. Are you all right?'

She said this quietly as we moved over to the chairs. She smelled of wind, rain, chill, perfume and woman. I wanted to dive into her.

I spent a few whispered moments bringing her up to date on the evening. She kept shaking her head as I described the shooting and the immediate aftermath.

But Jane was fixed on Ruskin. 'I don't understand. Who exactly is he afraid of?'

'From what I can tell, the people he's working for.'

'But why?'

'He knows the police'll keep on questioning him. And so will Hawkins from the US Attorney's office. Ruskin knows enough to put a pretty fair number of people in prison and to launch a lot of scandals. He's dangerous. He's under the impression that I can get him to the right people in the Administration and they can protect him in exchange for immunity if he tells them everything.'

'I doubt he'd ever get blanket immunity, and that's what he'd be after.'

'You know that and I know that but we're dealing with Ruskin here. He thinks he's got enough leverage to pull it off. By the way, he hasn't said much of this to me. But I'm pretty sure this is the general drift of what he's got in mind.'

'What are the chances he killed the Cabot woman?'

'I don't think so. He's not the type. And he'd know enough that his masters would have to have him killed if he did it. That's what he's fighting against now. They'll blame him for it going wrong anyway, even though he had nothing to do with it. But now I'm going out to get the car started. And I want to check on something.'

She nodded. 'So I'm going to meet the notorious Howie Ruskin.'

'If he's awake he'll undoubtedly put the moves on you.'

'Somehow I think I'll be able to resist him.'

I needed the cold air and the wind. I needed to be revived. I needed to think clearly. I passed a blue-suited security woman on my way out.

'I'm going to pull my Jeep up here. Warm it up for somebody I have to take home. Would you watch it for me?'

I took her hand and put a crisp twenty in it.

'Thanks. I appreciate it.'

The wind slapped me in the face and the rain soaked my head. I opened the Jeep remotely then climbed in and fired it up. Once I had it going for a couple of minutes, the heater going full tilt, I got out and locked it up again.

And then I went to the back of it and felt under the bumper.

As I'd suspected, a nice little tracking device had been planted there. Somebody had been following me all right.

EIGHTEEN

Ruskin didn't put the moves on Jane. He didn't do much of anything except slump down in the wheelchair that I stashed him in to get him to the Jeep. I used another wheelchair at the hotel to get him into an elevator, then the back door and a freight elevator in case a stray reporter who was staying there happened to notice who I was wheeling around. If we were spotted, we'd be the lead story on most of the morning cable news shows. Probably the network news shows, too, actually. *Who shot Howie Ruskin last night? What did the shooting have to do with Senator Logan? Why was Logan's consultant Dev Conrad pushing Ruskin around in a wheelchair and trying to sneak him into a hotel?* Political junkies would have tears of joy and gratitude streaming down their cheeks.

I'd given Jane the room card. She'd gone ahead to get the bed set up and to request an electric blanket. I'd called before we arrived to make sure that somebody would be at the back door with a wheelchair and that they would lead me to the proper elevator.

So now here I was, pushing the slumbering

Ruskin into my room.

'He's really out,' Jane said as we struggled to lift him out of the chair and sit him on the edge of the bed.

'Can you hold him there for just a minute?'

'Sure.'

My suitcase was on the other bed. I threw it open and grabbed a T-shirt, brought it up and slipped it over his head.

As she appraised my work as if it were a painting she was thinking of buying, her smile got wider and wider. 'It fits like Spanx.'

'We'll get his girlfriend to bring him some clothes.'

'Have you heard from her?'

'No. I have her cell number but she didn't answer.'

'That doesn't sound good.'

'It sure doesn't. But for right now let's get him comfortable.'

Jane grabbed the pillows from the other bed so we could prop him up. I tugged his black boots with the tall heels on them. They also had lifts. He didn't screw around when it came to making himself taller. Then came his jeans. He was in red boxer shorts and white socks. Those stayed on. We covered him up right away so he wouldn't get cold. There was a knock on the door.

'I'll get it.'

I was accompanied by my Glock. The shooting and the tracking device had changed everything. I eased open the door by inches. A young woman in a red blazer, white blouse and black skirt – the hotel's uniform – stood there with a blanket in her hands. The electric one. I had to take it with one hand. I kept my other one, the one with the Glock, behind my back. 'Thank you very much.'

When I got back to the bed Jane was talking to him. 'Are you comfortable?'

He sounded drunk. 'I told her but she would not listen.'

Jane put her hand to his forehead. 'He feels a little cold. Are you cold?'

'Am I ... cold?'

His eyes were open but I didn't think his eyes and mind were forming a coherent picture of Jane. 'Sleep...'

'All right. That's a good idea. Can you hear me?'

'Hear ... you?' The round face with the small, perfect nose was blanched white from the physical shock. The eyes tried to focus on Jane but I don't think they succeeded. 'I warned her...'

'You sleep now. If you want anything we're right here. You'll feel better in the morning and we'll get you a very nice breakfast.'

He said something I didn't understand and then his chunky body rolled over on its side. He yawned, and then he farted, and then rested like some machine that had abruptly run out of power. His breathing was ragged but steady.

She touched a finger to her lips and then led me over to the window where a small couch awaited. The midnight city was painted on the glass. Lights of red and green and yellow and white; the part of the main drag that passed through the downtown area still busy; the college toward the east lit from below; several large housing developments divided by a mall and other shopping areas; and the pulsing lights of the distant airport.

'I love this old town,' she said.

'You'd never move?'

'Probably not. I'm sort of a hometown girl and I know that probably sounds ridiculous. This isn't exactly a cultural center.'

'Neither are big cities except in certain places. They're just a lot of small towns sharing the same turf.'

She slid her arm through mine. Then kissed me on the cheek. 'I've never thought of big cities that way before. Or if I have I've forgotten it. Or maybe I'm such a hayseed I'm easily impressed by obvious ideas.'

'Well, if it's obvious ideas you want, baby, you've come to the right place.'

An easy-going laugh. 'Oh, God – I didn't mean it that way. I'm so sorry.'

'I know. I was just kidding you.'

'I hate to interrupt this fascinating conversation, but can I have some water here? You may not have noticed, but I'm dehydrated.'

Less than two minutes ago he'd looked unconscious. Now he was not only awake, he was his usual spoiled-brat insulting self, and being ridiculous on top of it.

I walked back to him and pointed to the pitcher on the nightstand. 'Jane thought of everything. Believe it or not, we're trying to keep you comfortable.'

'Only because you think I'm going to rat some people out for you.'

I lifted the pitcher and picked up an empty glass. 'True enough, Howie. Otherwise I'd throw this in your face.'

'Huh-uh,' Ruskin said.

'Huh-uh what?'

'Huh-uh, I don't want you to handle the water. I want her to.'

She stood next to me now. 'I told her you'd try and put the moves on her.'

'Normally I'd try but in case you haven't noticed I came close to dying a couple of hours ago and I'm kind of laid up as a result.'

'"Close to dying,"' I mumbled as I handed Jane the empty glass.

'I heard that,' Howie said. 'You ever think that maybe I have a heart condition and that the trauma of being shot might kill me?'

'You have a heart condition like I have this big eye on the back of my head.'

'I saw that episode of *The Twilight Zone*, too,' Ruskin said. 'That big eye was pretty cool.'

'Now you just lie back and I'll pour you some water,' Jane said. The maternal softness of her

213

voice would have struck me as endearingly sweet if it hadn't been wasted on a slug like 'Howie' Howard Ruskin.

Around dawn – my travel alarm clock said 5:30 a.m. – I was awakened by a strange voice intruding on a dream that vanished instantly.

'You bastard. Wake up and help me, Conrad.'

My brain slipped from Park into Drive. Ruskin. Summoning me. I sat up, nudging against the Glock I'd kept next to me.

'You're supposed to be watching over me, remember, asshole?'

Good to know he was still as obnoxious as ever. I swung around and sat on the edge of my bed in my boxers. 'Oh. Right. What's going on?'

'I need to piss but every time I try to sit up I get dizzy. So I need some help to get to the john.'

'All right. Just a second.'

As I came around the far side of his bed to help him he said, 'You didn't plank her. I sure as hell would've.'

'What the hell're you talking about?'

'The chick. That lady lawyer. I woulda banged her.'

'You were supposed to be unconscious.'

'Oh, right. It was in my contract. I was supposed to be unconscious while you and the lady lawyer got to second base. A guy as old as you are, second base is pretty pathetic.'

'Good to know you're back to normal.'

'Some of the dialogue was pretty corny, let me tell you.'

'We'll work on it for the next time.'

By now I was easing him out of the bed. Well, not exactly easing. In fact, I pretty much tore him out of the bed and he yelped when I did it.

'Hey, asshole, take it easy. I'm wounded, remember? Just because you couldn't close the deal with the chick, don't take it out on me.'

Funny, I was under the impression I'd more than closed the deal. When everything was wrapped up here she was going to visit me for a three-day weekend in Chicago. I wasn't about to sully my anticipation of that by sharing it with him.

'Somebody's trying to kill you, Ruskin. I'd be more concerned with that than with my love life.'

His hyena laugh. 'Man, you don't got no love life. Not from what I heard last night. You don't know jack about chicks.'

I shoved him into the john and pulled the door shut.

'Hey, easy, man!'

I walked over to the nightstand between the beds, picked up the remote and clicked on the tube.

The supposedly liberal channel had a talking head who said – the newsreader said this was a sound bite from yesterday – 'Right now, we have to face the facts. A senator on our side is not only fighting for his political life. He's fighting the suspicion that he may have murdered his mistress.' The man speaking was a rough-hewn fifty with gray hair and a pock-marked face. He was a reporter for a large Midwestern daily and was usually able to use facts to argue our case. But now he was calling Tracy Cabot Robert's 'mistress' and in so doing sounded as if he was auditioning for a slot on Empire News.

I clicked it off immediately. And in the silence that followed I heard faint sounds coming from the bathroom. Voice sounds. I walked over there and listened. I couldn't catch the exact words but Ruskin was definitely talking to somebody. I tried the knob but the door was locked.

'You wanna see me naked you'll have to wait in line!'

No point in standing here. I went over and made myself some coffee in the microwave. While it was becoming radioactive I grabbed my trousers and stepped into them. I was just retrieving my cup from the microwave when Ruskin came out of the john.

'Hey, dude, you gotta help me.'

He did look bad. Pale and weak and sweaty. And wobbly. I reached him in time to keep him from slumping to the floor. I got my arm underneath him and walked him carefully to his bed. I sat him down and then turned him around and helped him settle into his sleeping position.

'You need to take it easy, Ruskin.'

'I'm not some pussy. I can handle it.'

I wasn't rude enough to remind him that two minutes ago he'd called out for my help. 'Just lie there and relax and tell me who you were talking to.'

He was too wasted to call me a name. He just said, 'Sarah.'

'I've been trying her phone but she never answers.'

'Two phones.' Out of breath now.

'She has two cell phones?'

'Yeah.'

'Clever.'

He didn't speak for two or three minutes. Eyes closed, breathing starting to settle down. Sleeping already?

'She has a place for us.'

'Where?'

'Oh, no. That'll be our secret.' He waved me off. 'Sleep,' he said. Then he muttered: 'Sleep.' A few seconds later he had gone off. Or did a good imitation of going off anyway.

Now it was my turn in the john. A quick shave and shower and when I came back out he was snoring. I put on a gray button-down shirt, my charcoal sport coat and black pants, black ribbed socks and black loafers.

I spent twenty minutes on my laptop checking up on all the internals of our campaigns, plus I looked at all the messages. All my employees hoped that the Robert matter would turn out well and soon.

It was then I looked at my travel alarm again and realized that it was six forty-three a.m. What the hell could I do at six forty-three a.m.?

But an answer came soon after in the form of a knock and in the person of the little waif Sarah. Her face froze when she saw the Glock I held in my hand. It was pointed down and pressed flat against my leg. 'Howard has one of those and it terrifies me.'

A blue knit bag large enough to contain a small refrigerator was slung over her left shoulder. Whatever was inside bulged against the sides of the bag.

I stepped back to let her in. Without another word she went to him. He still seemed pretty groggy but that didn't deter her careful hugs and kisses and declarations of worry and love. I wondered if, even if she encouraged it, he would be strong enough to get to second base.

Then he started declaring his own worry and love.

It went on until I said, 'I hate to mention it to you people, but somebody's trying to kill him. And, Sarah, you're trying to take him away from here.'

She whipped around and that wan little face was just this side of nasty. 'We don't know anything about you!'

'He called *me*, remember?'

'So? We're desperate. We don't know who to trust. But that doesn't mean you won't turn us over to—' She caught herself.

'Turn you over to who? Or whom, if you prefer?'

'We're not sure. That's the big problem.'

I tried to play the reassuring father role. Acting 101. The voice a little deeper, the tone a little softer, the pace a little slower, the plea for understanding the most important part of it all. 'I have a vested interest in keeping him safe, Sarah.'

'I know, but I don't see what this has to do with me taking him now. I've picked out a good hiding place for us. And I've got a plan for sneaking us out of town.'

'What if they've been watching you?'

All the time we'd been talking, Howie had lain in place with his eyes closed. The way his mouth moved, his head jerked left and right sometimes and his lips made motions as if he was trying to speak, let me know that he was not only listening but also forming opinions about all this.

'Oh, God. I hadn't thought of any of this stuff.' She took his hand in hers and brought it to her face. Touched it to her cheek. Her eyes were bright with tears. 'I'm just trying to protect him, is all.'

'I know you are, Sarah. But he's better off here. I'm going to hire somebody to sit in here and watch the door.'

'Like a bodyguard?'

'Basically, yes.'

'Do we know we can trust him?'

'Or her.'

'I don't know about a "her." Howard has too many "hers" around him.' Her possessiveness made me wonder about her relationship with Tracy Cabot. She would have had the opportunity to pay a visit to the cabin.

'All right. I'll make sure it's a man.'

'But I already told this guy we'd rent his little house.'

'Tell him something came up.'

She still had her hand in his. 'What do you think, Howard?'

'I like the idea of a bodyguard.'

Before she could say anything else, I said, 'Let me make a call.' For this I went over to the window. The streets of the small city were crowded now. The workday was beginning. Suddenly, being in my Jeep and soaring along the Dan Ryan to my offices sounded comfortable. I was almost sentimental about the idea. It was a much more enjoyable notion than spending the day trying to clear a senator of a possible murder charge and hiring bodyguards and trying to keep a guy I despised alive.

'This is a great way to start the day. Hearing from you. Let me shut off my hairdryer. There.'

'Nice to hear your voice, too. But I'm afraid I've got to ask you a favor before you even have your breakfast.'

'Sure. Is everything all right?'

As Jane and I talked Sarah emptied the contents of her knit bag onto the bed. Two sweaters, two shirts, two pairs of pants, as well as socks and underwear. I wondered if Howie had any idea how lucky he was that she loved him.

'I think so. But to make sure I need to hire somebody like a bodyguard. Do you know anybody like that?'

'In fact, I do. I mean, we do at the office. His name is Leo Guild. He's a former detective who took early retirement to start doing investigations for law offices and individuals who can afford him. He does so much work for us we have him on a monthly retainer. We're by far his biggest client.'

'Has he ever done anything like being a bodyguard?'

'A few times, yes. And he also has a brother who was in a security detail in the Marines. We used both of them as bodyguards last year. We had a client who'd gotten crosswise with the mob downstate. He was terrified they were going to kill him before we could get him to the FBI. He wanted us to evaluate his connection and see how much he could be liable for. We all felt that the FBI would make a deal if he told them what he knew. So Leo put him in a hotel room and traded shifts with his brother for two days. There wasn't any problem.'

'Think we could get him over here right away?'

'We can try. I'll see what he says.'

'Thanks.'

Sarah was sitting him up now. Carefully. Lovingly. 'He's starving. Would you call room service, Mr Conrad?'

'I will if you'll call me Dev.'

'Dev, then.'

'Are you hungry?'

'Now that I think about it.'

'Like bacon and eggs and hash browns and coffee?'

Ruskin said, 'Yeah, God, get it up here right away.'

I went to the room phone and punched in the room service number. The clatter in the background signified that numerous guests were firing in their orders. Bacon, eggs, hash browns – I was making myself hungry just saying the words. Plus two pots of coffee.

In the meantime I used the remote. Rage would wake me up for sure so I turned on Empire News and there were the Three Witches, as they'd come to be called by people on our side. Between plastic surgery and Botox they were as close to being cyborgs as science had yet gotten.

My day had officially started. Within thirty seconds I was *muy* pissed.

NINETEEN

The redhead, a recent 'honors' graduate from Holy Shit University, was saying, 'I hope this makes people look at Senator Logan's party and what it really stands for. If you don't have respect for capitalism and if you're not willing to use force to demonstrate that the United States is still the dominant force in this world – except for God, of course – you see the slippery slope this puts you on. You have a mistress, which is sinful enough, but then you go even further and take her life.'

'Allegedly, Candy. You have to say "allegedly."'

'Well, all right, then, I'll say "allegedly" but I think everybody listening has made up his or her mind because the facts are already in.'

'I hate to keep saying this, Candy, but to be honest the facts aren't all in. We need to be careful here.'

Candy did not look happy. 'I take your point, Brooke, but I'm speaking to a greater truth than just the justice system.'

Brooke glanced at Gabrielle. Concern in their eyes. To their credit they were being reasonably honest brokers this morning. The single word that was taped inside their heads was LAWSUIT.

Gabrielle, a former runway model, said, 'The best point you're making, Candy, is that senators are role models whether they want to be or not.'

Enough.

The other channels I checked were more subdued but two of them had adapted the same theme. Robert, it was said, was 'in hiding.' People 'close to him' were saying that both he and his family were 'coming apart.' Someone in his Washington office 'would not rule out' resignation. This was likely all bullshit. There are always go-to people in Washington who pretend to know everything. The press always goes to them because they can be counted on to give inflammatory statements. By tonight these same people would be talking about Robert's forthcoming sex-change operation and also his forthcoming admission that he'd been selling some of America's most secret information to Venusian agents.

Ben Zuckerman was busy with his electric shaver when I called. I knew this because it was humming away when he clicked on. 'Lemme turn this damned thing off.'

'The news gets juicier every couple of hours.'

'They're killing us. I've got to get him in front of some cameras, Dev, and you've got to help me. When was the last time you talked to him?'

'Last night.'

'Well, he called me in the middle of the night. He's back to resigning.'

'When I heard that on the news this morning I thought it was bullshit.'

'Just a lucky guess. But if we ever have to go to court a resignation will look like hell. Juries will wonder why somebody as powerful as a United States senator wouldn't stand tall and defend himself. And keep his job.'

'How did you end the conversation?'

'I said I wanted him to talk to you about it.'

'He can be stubborn.'

'I believe he's innocent, Dev. And I think you do, too. Are you learning anything that might interest Hammell?'

He'd heard about last night and Ruskin being shot at. But he was shocked to hear that Ruskin was in my hotel room with his lover and a bodyguard on the way.

At the mention of his name, Ruskin tried to shout but didn't have the energy so he just said, 'Who you talking to?'

'Ben Zuckerman.'

'He's a jerk-off. What'd he say about me?'

'That you're a jerk-off.'

'Tell that putz he's a candy-ass punk.'

'He says you're a candy-ass punk, Ruskin.'

Sarah had no trouble shouting. 'Are you all little boys? I don't know what the hell you think you're doing, Dev.'

'Having a little fun. We need it.' But she was

right. How easy and mindless it is sometimes to slip back to fourth grade and the playground. 'I'm sorry, Sarah.'

'Thank you.'

'I'll get out to Robert's as soon as I can, Ben.'

'I'd really appreciate it. I've got another press conference scheduled at nine. I'm dying out there. I have absolutely nothing to say. All I can do is try and knock down the worst of the rumors. They're all over the place. I'm told one of the radio boys hinted that Robert is planning to flee the country. That'll be on Empire News very soon. They'll be demanding that he turn in his passport.'

'Where's my food?' Ruskin wanted to know as soon as I'd clicked off.

'It'll be here very soon.'

'I don't know why I decided to hook up with you, Conrad.'

I walked over to his bedside. 'We have a little bit of time to talk. I can't be any help at all unless I know what's going on.'

'I've been shot and now I'm starving to death. Why should I talk?'

'Howard, you promised me you'd be co-operative with Dev.'

'What's he done for me so far?'

'What I need to know from you, Howard, is who hired you for the job on the senator.'

'No way, Conrad. Not until I get guaranteed protection and immunity. Then I tell every-thing.'

He couldn't come right out and help me.

'If I talk now I have nothing to barter with.'

'Please tell him, Howard. I'll leave the room if you want me to.'

For once there was no bravado. 'I can't tell him, Sarah. If I do, I got nothing.'

'I keep forgetting you're actually a grown man. You keep sounding like a twelve-year-old.'

'I don't care if I sound like a twelve-year-old. I'm scared.'

His candor startled me; I think it startled Sarah, too.

'You'll notice there are no tears in my eyes. You destroyed at least four political careers that I know of and probably broke the law a couple dozen times, Howard. But I'm willing to help you get protection if you help the feds – feds we can trust – get the bad guys.'

I couldn't tell if the moan was from physical pain or from knowing that his career was coming to an end. 'How long before it'll be safe again?'

'It could be a long time.'

'How will they protect him?' Sarah asked.

'I'm not sure. They could relocate him deep cover in Europe. Or they could put him in some witness protection program here. New name, new address, maybe even a little plastic surgery.'

'Plastic surgery? Are you nuts?'

I couldn't resist. 'You don't want to look like

Justin Bieber?'

Sarah laughed. He sulked and said, 'Where's my goddamned food?' Interesting that only when he was angry did his voice work full volume.

'He'll tell you everything, Dev. We both will. I promise you.'

At the knock on the door, I slid over to the table where my Glock lay next to the laptop. Hiding it behind my back, I went to the door.

The cart was piled high with goodies. 'Morning,' said the smiling, uniformed young woman pushing the feast into the room.

I followed her in. The aromas were seductive. Who wanted sex when actual food was here?

As she went about plucking various shiny food covers off the dishes and setting them on the table, Howie said, 'I'm glad they sent a pretty one.'

When Sarah realized I was watching her, she just shrugged. Combat fatigue, most likely. She'd heard Howie's moronic man-of-the-world routine so many times it no longer mattered.

After she was gone, Howie shouted, 'Can I have some food over here? I'm dying of malnutrition!'

She had a winsome smile for me. 'I really do love him. At least, most of the time.'

'I heard that!'

She turned and looked at him. 'I wanted you to.'

She then picked up a plate and started piling goodies on it. I'd been under the impression that she was going to spoon-feed him while he lay in bed. But now he was on his feet and headed with surprising speed and confidence toward the plate she was making for him. He grabbed it from her with his good hand and then dropped into a chair at the table. 'I need some jelly for the toast. And a fork would come in real handy.'

'Yessir, Lord and Master.'

'Aw, shit, I'm sorry, Sarah. I'm being an asshole.'

I was closer. I handed him the fork. He ripped it from my fingers and mumbled something. I preferred to think he was expressing his undying gratitude.

We dined.

He was a noisy bastard but she was apparently used to it. She sat at the table next to him and didn't seem to notice the lip-smacking, mouth-full yakking and belching that went on constantly.

I just kept thinking ... *This is the guy who's tormented my party for a decade?*

Fifteen minutes after there was no more food – though the front of Ruskin's shirt bore traces of the slaughter – jelly-coffee-egg – there was another knock on the door.

The Glock in my hand, I went there to find Jane standing next to a tall man in a black leather jacket, a blue dress shirt and dark

229

trousers. He was maybe sixty with white hair and cunning blue eyes. The nose suggested he was not unacquainted with trouble.

'May we come in?' Jane said.

'Be my guest.'

Jane wore her blue Burberry, beneath which was a navy pencil skirt with a ruffled white blouse. When we got the door closed she made introductions.

From the table, Ruskin said, 'No offense, sir, but how old are you?'

'Old enough to do the job.'

'I have a right to ask that question. It's my ass on the line.'

'I'm sixty-one.'

Ruskin made a face in Sarah's direction. To Jane he said, 'No offense, but is this the youngest guy you could get?'

Leo Guild waved him off and stalked back to the door. I wondered if Howie noticed how quickly and deftly Guild moved.

Sarah jumped up and said, 'No, please wait.' Then, turning on Ruskin: 'You don't know anything about him, Howard. At least, let's talk to him.'

'Doesn't matter. Thank you for asking me, Jane. But I'm going to pass on this one.'

'Hey, Gramps, *you're* not passing, *I'm* passing!'

I wasn't sure Guild heard that one because it came just as he was closing the door behind him. He'd moved damned fast and I didn't blame him.

Jane moved just as fast and it was right to the table and Ruskin. Her face only inches from his, she said, 'You're a jerk, you know that? A stupid little-boy jerk. Leo Guild is an experienced security man in every respect. Last month the governor's security men hired him to help guard the governor; and whenever anybody important comes to town they always check him out on Google and then hire him. And you treated him like dirt!'

I enjoyed seeing him intimidated. When a man shouts in your face you have the option of shoving him away or even punching him. But when a woman shouts in your face you have to sit there and take it. And it's especially bad when you know you've got it coming.

The problem with Ruskin – no surprise – was that he didn't seem to understand he had it coming. 'Didn't you see him, Sarah? Did you see how *old* he was?'

'Did you see how tough he looked, Howard? Did you see how alert he looked? He would have protected us just fine. And you owe him an apology.'

'Apology? What the hell are you—?'

'I'm going to see if he's still in the hall,' Jane said.

'Apology,' Howie said as we waited for Jane to search for Guild. I picked up a piece of toast and jammed it into my mouth. I would have preferred jamming my fist into Howie's face.

A few minutes later Jane reappeared. Behind her came Leo Guild. Tensed up the way he was, he looked ready for payback.

'I want you to apologize to Leo,' Jane snapped at Ruskin.

'For what? I had the right to—'

Sarah's words stung with real nastiness. 'I'm sick of this clown show, Howard. Now apologize.'

'Forget it,' Guild said, his body angling once again toward the door.

'Please, Mr Guild,' Sarah said. 'Please do it for me. I need protection, too. I apologize for both of us. Please stay, for my sake.'

The waif face, the wounded voice – what's a man going to say?

'Please, Leo,' Jane said quietly.

Guild looked at Jane, then me, then back to Sarah. He did not look at Ruskin.

'Please,' Sarah said again.

'All right.' Now he stared right at Ruskin. 'But if he starts in on me again, I walk. Right out the door. No warning.' He addressed Jane now. 'That's my condition. He mouths off one more time and that's it.'

'Can you handle him?' Jane asked Sarah.

'He's going to handle himself,' Sarah said. 'Aren't you, Howard?'

'I'm wounded.' He pointed to his sling as if none of us had any idea of what it was. 'Somebody shot me last night. And now I'm the bad guy?'

'Yeah, you're the bad guy. Guild here could crush you with one hand and you're calling him out? Now you apologize to him and start treating him like the professional he is. You told me how afraid you were and how you wanted my help. Well, here's your help and you'd damned well better appreciate it,' I said.

The unthinkable happened. Howie Ruskin blushed. Blushed. Mr Jerk-Off himself knew enough to be embarrassed. And it wasn't just because of me. It was because of what Sarah and Jane and Guild had said, too. His eyes scanned the table as if a supernatural message only he could see had been scribbled across its surface.

'Shit,' he said, still not looking at us. 'I'm sorry. I guess I can be sort of an ass sometimes.'

You, Howard? An ass? Aw, c'mon old buddy, that's impossible.

I clapped Guild on the arm and said, 'I can't say I envy you.'

He laughed. 'Yeah? Why's that?'

'Oh, I don't know.'

'I've dealt with worse. I was a cop, remember. Try getting a three-hundred-and-fifty-pound drunk guy who's also strung out on meth into a car sometime.'

'I think I'll save that for when I'm reincarnated the next time. Something to look forward to.'

'I need to get to the office.' Jane drew her Burberry coat tight around her. 'It's really cold this morning. Brrr.'

'I'm headed to Robert's. Now's a good time. Most of the press'll be downtown. Ben's got another news conference.'

'Poor Ben. I don't know how he gets through those things.'

'I think he secretly likes them. He likes confrontation. Thrives on it.'

'I do, too. But I've never had to face a mob like the one Ben's dealing with.'

As she buttoned her coat, I said, 'I'll walk out with you.'

We said our goodbyes. Sarah thanked us just under thirty-two times, Leo Guild dragged a straight-backed chair over next to the door and sat down and Ruskin said to him, 'I'm giving you permission right now to kill anybody who comes through that door.'

Guild took this in good humor. 'I'll be sure to have my lawyer mention that to the jury when I'm on trial for first-degree murder. That you gave me that permission thing.'

Sarah's laughter was high and girly and delighted and delightful.

Ruskin sulked.

TWENTY

A sparse crowd of reporters. And only one security man at the gate. I drove on up to the house, parked and got out just in time to see Robert coming from somewhere in the back of the house on a racing bicycle. His way of relaxing. He'd gotten me to join him a few times, but two hours of ball-jarring monotony was more than enough for me. Pedaling didn't resolve my anger issues the way handball did. It's hard to pretend you're killing somebody with a Schwinn.

But his was no Schwinn. He'd told me once that it had cost eight thousand dollars and was aerodynamically designed. It was so lightweight he'd picked it up and turned it back and forth with one hand. Then he'd thrown it at me and when I grabbed it I saw what he was talking about. A few pounds was all. He went into how the materials were lighter than aluminum and then into this ratio and that ratio, but by then my eyes had glazed over.

He pulled up next to my Jeep just as I was getting out of it. He wore a blue track suit with white piping. He looked ten years older. A soul-sapping, suicide-inspiring ten years.

The temperature was twenty-seven according to the radio. I could see his tire tracks on the frosted ground. We spoke in smoke signals.

'C'mon in and have some breakfast with me. We can watch Ben try to defend me. The poor bastard. Nobody should have *that* job.'

A light sheen of sweat covered his face as he walked along next to me, pushing his bike as he moved. I wondered if he looked at the looming house as I did now. In happier times for both of us there'd been long and lively parties here. My wife had loved Elise and had always said that the only parties she enjoyed were the ones here because she got to spend time with her. As much as I enjoyed the company, too, I liked even more the number of important guests Robert always invited. My firm was able to pick up five or six elite clients because of my contacts here. But now not even the sunshine could make the house seem bright and welcoming; it was as if the turmoil within had sucked some of the color from the exterior.

'I've prepared my resignation address,' he said when we were within ten feet of the front steps. 'I'd like you to schedule time for me this afternoon with the local radio station of your choice. No TV. I'll read it from my den.'

I went through all the points against resigning. He listened, his eyes never leaving me, but when I finished he said, 'I know Ben sent you out here to talk me out of it. And I know that

236

you both think you're helping me by trying to stop me. But you're not. I need to do this for the sake of my family. They didn't do anything wrong but they're prisoners now. I want to resign and I want to find a home in the mountains somewhere. Maybe Colorado or Wyoming. I'll get involved in a few of the family businesses again. I'm rich. I can do that, and I need to do that. I owe it to Elise and Maddy for all that I've put them through. For my being so arrogant and stupid. You were right, Dev, about me. How could I not see that I was being set up? The Cabot woman knew how to make me feel young again. I wanted to be a teenager, I guess. And look where it led me.'

He leaned the eight-thousand-dollar bike against the stone front wall of the house and then faced me. 'This has been hard enough on them, Dev. I'm especially worried about Elise. How she'll get through this. I was so selfish. The least I can do is save her from any more turmoil.'

The house was quiet. While he went to take a shower I sat in the living room where someone had left the large plasma screen on. The face of the man who'd just told me to get some coffee in the kitchen as we'd entered the house was right there on the screen. A photo from ten years ago playing tennis in his whites. Full screen one moment and replaced the next by the smarmiest of TV shrinks, a Southern gentleman who always struck me as being a secret serial killer. A reptilian smile and predatory eyes played off against his marble-mouthed Southern charm – alleged Southern charm. I was glad the sound was off. I had no intention of turning it on.

It was fifteen minutes before Maddy walked in.

'Hi, Dev. It's good to see you.'

'Good to see *you*.'

'Mom finally got some sleep last night and she didn't even take that killer pill the doctor gave her.'

Yellow sweater, short black skirt, black tights and black flats. A very pretty suburban grade-school teacher sort of look. All the little boys would have these almost painful crushes on her. They'd daydream that she was – in some bizzaro world, in some bizzaro way – their girl-friend.

She gave me a quick peck on the cheek. 'Let's go to the kitchen so we can sit in the nook and watch the birds.' Then she paused and leaned her head back as if she were considering me the way a doctor would. 'Are you all right, Dev?'

'A lot of things on my mind, I guess.'

'If you mean my father, absolutely. He can dig his heels in sometimes and it infuriates my mom. And me, too.'

'He's holding something back from both Ben and me. Not telling us something.'

Now it was my turn to lean back and study her the way a doctor would. The lovely cheeks were faintly red now and the glistening brown gaze averted mine for a moment.

But she was good at recovering. She slid her arm through mine and steered me toward the kitchen. 'We can sit in the nook and look out the window. It's my favorite spot in the world. And I know I sound like a seven-year-old when I say that, but I mean it. I love how the backyard sweeps up into the woods and all the birds and the other animals that I can see back there.'

Mrs Weiderman fussed over us as if we were the children she hadn't seen for thirty years. There was an antique and heavily scrolled breakfast nook that overlooked the backyard. It was apparently Salute to Bunnies day because there were a lot of them, in all sizes, hopping around the browning grass in industrious innocence. Mrs Weiderman brought us mugs of steaming coffee and pastries I was pretty sure she'd made herself.

While I had the pleasure of disappearing my cherry tart and agreeing to a second cup of coffee, Mrs Weiderman went through a list of well-wishers who'd called to support Robert. She went all swoony when she mentioned the name of a Hollywood hunk. She likely would have cut some of her breaking news short or at least shorter but Maddy, ever the clever one, kept asking questions and making comments. Her blushing was still on my mind. Did she know what her father was hiding? She apparently didn't want me to pursue her for the answer.

By then Robert strode into the kitchen, blue V-neck, white T-shirt, Levi's and Reeboks with no socks. He slid in next to his daughter. He was favored with coffee and a cinnamon roll within forty-five seconds of joining us.

Partly because I needed her help and partly because I was irritated with both of them, I decided to make them unhappy. 'I take it you know your father is going to resign.'

'What're you talking about, Dev? Resign? Who told you that?'

'He did. The man you're sitting next to.'

'Damn you, Dev.'

Maybe we'd reached our end; maybe he would fire me now.

'Well, you won't listen to Ben and you won't listen to me, so I thought maybe you'd listen to your daughter.'

'You can't resign, Dad. Do you know how that would look to everybody?'

'That's what we've been telling him, Maddy. But he won't listen.'

'You and Ben are so damned clever, aren't you?' Glowering. 'Dragging my poor daughter into it.'

'There you go again. "My poor daughter." Dad, I'm a grown woman. And there's no way you can resign now.'

'What about your mother? How much more can she take, Maddy? She's my wife and I owe her—'

But Maddy was shaking her head and interrupted him. 'You were stupid about the Cabot woman. Very stupid and very selfish. Don't be the same way all over again about this. You know damned well that Mother and I will support you. What we want is for you to be proved innocent and to finish the race. Even if you lose. Do it the right way, Dad. For all our sakes, including your own.'

I was glad I'd brought her into it. Her words had a visible effect on Robert. The anger at me faded from his eyes, the tension in his jaw line relaxed and the voice was softer now. He even smiled. 'You always could talk me into anything.'

'Not "anything." You wouldn't buy me a car until I was eighteen.'

'Oh, that's right. You had to ride a burro back and forth to school. I forgot.'

She joined in the fun. 'Other kids had cars at sixteen. But then...' And she struck a dramatic pose. 'That was when I learned all about suffering.' That smile had doubtless broken several young hearts.

I eased out of the booth. 'I need to get back to town. I appreciate your help, Maddy. And Robert, Ben'll be calling you after talking to the press this morning.'

'I still should be mad at you, Dev.' He wasn't making a joke. 'Sometimes your cynicism really gets me down. I've talked to a few of your other clients. We all think that deep down you hate politicians.'

'Sometimes I do. But I hate consultants – myself included – just as much, Robert. We're all guilty.'

Genuine surprise in his eyes and voice. 'You really believe that?'

'Yeah, I do.'

'Oh, Dev, that's so sad,' Maddy said.

'Not as much as you might think.' I laughed. 'Because I love playing the game.'

I was about halfway back to town again when my old friend Detective Farnsworth appeared behind me and honked me over to the side of the two-lane blacktop.

He came up to the Jeep with a smile on his face and I wondered why. Through the open window he said, 'Have you seen the news in the past ten minutes?'

'Haven't had the chance.'

'Detective Hammell turned up a witness who claims that the Cabot woman told him she was afraid Senator Logan was going to kill her.'

'Oh? I notice you used the word "claims." If you had something for sure you wouldn't use a word like that.'

'She rushed into her hotel one night and asked if she could get a different room. The clerk there helped her. She swore him to secrecy about where she was hiding. That was when she told him about being afraid of Logan.'

All I could do was counterpunch. 'Did you put a tracking device on my Jeep?'

He managed to look curious. 'Somebody do

242

that?'

'Yeah.'

'It wasn't me. Or anybody in the department.'

'You speak for the whole department, do you?'

'In this case, yes. Two years ago we did it to a guy we suspected had murdered his wife. He figured it out and his lawyer got a judge to issue an injunction against us using one. The guy is suing us for two million dollars now. The mayor is pissed because we have to spend so much of the taxpayers' money on the case. So he gave the order. No more tracking devices till this is resolved. Does that answer your question?'

'Guess it'll have to do.'

He put a hand on the edge of the roof and leaned forward. This early in the morning and he was already tired. But then so was I.

'You managed to change the subject, Conrad. But now we're going back to it. I was headed out to Logan's with a search warrant to take a look around his house.'

'He didn't do it. He's not the killing kind.'

'Most people are the killing kind in the right circumstances.'

'Maybe. But he still didn't kill her.'

'So just as I'm about to pull up to where the security guards are on his property I see you about half a block away headed back to town. I followed you to give you the courtesy of being there when I hand him the search warrant. I'm told his wife is very highly strung.'

Maybe he was right. Maybe I'd have a minor calming effect on the family by being there. This hotel witness was one more reason Detective Hammell had to put a formal charge of murder on Robert.

'How about following me back?' His tone had changed considerably.

'Sure. But I've got a question.'

'What?' Guarded again now.

'Has the press gotten the news about the hotel desk clerk?'

'Probably by now. We've got a whole department full of leakers.'

I'd have to talk to Ben as soon as I could. The news just kept getting worse. The press would hang this around our necks like a noose. I felt sorry for Maddy and Elise. And I allowed myself the pleasure of getting pissed off at Robert again for setting all of this in motion. And then I had the most troubling thought of all – what if he was the killer?

The guards just waved us through. At the moment there were only around eight or nine reporters and camera people waiting around. That would change quickly when the first reporter got the news about what Tracy Cabot had told the hotel clerk.

As we walked up to the door, Farnsworth, dressed this morning in a gray tweed sport coat and black trousers and cordovan wing tips, said, 'I'll need you to help me keep everyone as calm as possible. That's why I didn't bring a crew with me. I'll call for them after I've had a chance to talk to Logan. I know his wife has had some mental issues. There's no point making things any worse than they need to be.'

'She was playing the hotel clerk.'

'Who was?'

'Cabot. This whole thing was a setup to destroy Logan's career. When she ratted him out to the press she'd drag the hotel clerk in on it and he'd testify that she'd told him how she feared for her life. So you'd have the affair, which never happened – he never slept with her – and for the cherry on top you'd have this bullshit about how she was afraid he'd kill her.'

'And you can prove all this?'

'Yeah, I can.' I wasn't happy about the irony of having Howie Ruskin save our ass. The strange bedfellows cliché had never been more apt. I took a few more hits of the chill, clean Midwestern air and then said, 'You'll be surprised.'

'You trying to talk me out of serving this search warrant?'

'Not at all. Right now at least three or four people in a city of your size are committing felonies of one kind or another. If you'd rather waste your time hounding an innocent man, be my guest.'

'C'mon,' he smiled, nodding to the front door, 'let's go waste some time.' Halfway up the stairs, he said, 'Every political op I've ever met is a bullshit artist. I thought maybe you were different. But you're all alike. And you get paid so much money for it. That's the part that amazes me.'

'Hell, if you want more money move to Chicago. I know cops there who make a couple hundred grand a year and they don't have to report any of it to the IRS.'

'To protect and serve,' he said and knocked on the door.

Mrs Weiderman answered, looked first at him and then at me. She didn't need to be told that something serious was going on here.

Farnsworth had his ID ready. Her eyes went from it to me. Beseeching me. *I don't know what's going on, Dev. But you need to protect us. These are the people I love. This is the only family I have left. They took me in when I lost everything. Please help us.*

But there was nothing I could say or do.

'We'd like to speak to the senator alone if we could, please.'

'Dev,' her eyes on me, 'do you know what's going on here?' Accusation.

'It'll be all right, Mrs Weiderman.'

'Do you know how much this family has been through in the past day and a half?'

'He's innocent, Mrs Weiderman. You and I know that. And Detective Farnsworth here will know it very soon now. I'll have a surprise for him. The best thing we can do now is cooperate.'

She wore a dark blue dress with an old-fashioned white embroidered collar and a large ivory brooch in the center. She touched the brooch now as if it was the only source of salvation she knew of. 'I still don't know why you'd help him make everybody here even more miserable, Dev.' Then to Farnsworth, 'Follow me, please.'

The den was sunny and smelled comfortably of Robert's pipe tobacco. Just as she was about to leave us, Mrs Weiderman said, 'I should have more sympathy – I consider myself a Christian – but I know she was a whore and meant to destroy the senator. I don't see why you'd waste any time trying to figure out who killed her, Detective Farnsworth. The world is better off just forgetting all about her.'

After the door was closed, Farnsworth said, 'She might be worth looking into. Motive and opportunity. And means.'

'Forget her, Farnsworth. Forget everybody in this house.'

'Oh, yeah? You really believe that?'

I didn't but I wasn't going to give him the satisfaction of telling him so. And I didn't have to worry about that anyway because Robert came bursting through the door with his face and eyes burning. I'd seen him handle himself in a few situations where the hecklers got threatening. The way he came at Farnsworth I wondered if he might shove him or something.

'You could have called first, Farnsworth. And

you could have saved yourself a trip. I just heard that story about what Tracy Cabot said – or supposedly said – to that hotel clerk. She made it up. She was framing me for the press. I would've denied it the same way I'm denying it now and you wouldn't have had to come all the way out here.' He was seething but restraining himself. The way his facial muscles bunched I could see how much physical and psychic energy the restraint was costing him.

'I'm not here for that, Senator,' Farnsworth said and slipped the search warrant from the inner pocket of his sport jacket. He handed it over.

Robert accepted it, but before he opened it he looked at me. Confused, angry. As if I was responsible somehow. The same way Mrs Weiderman had looked at me.

'What the hell's this?'

'A search warrant.'

'Are you serious?'

'I'm afraid I am serious.'

As I reached for my cell phone – in the Old West it would have been a six-shooter – I said, 'I'll call Ben.'

'Don't bother. He's on his way out here. He heard the desk clerk story and said he was on his way. What the hell are you looking for?'

'I'm afraid I can't tell you that right now; we'll talk about that a little bit later.'

'Are you hearing this, Dev? Are you hearing this bullshit?'

'Let them look, Senator.' In public he was always Senator. 'They won't find anything.'

'Senator,' Farnsworth said, 'listen to Conrad here. And for what it's worth, I hope we don't find what we're looking for. Nothing would make me happier than if this turns out to be a wild-goose chase.'

But Robert wasn't having any of that. 'Well, isn't that nice? It'd make you happy if I turned out to be innocent?' Then, 'Where the hell is Ben when you need him?'

Farnsworth said, 'I'll wait in my car. I have some things I need to work on anyway. I'm sorry about the intrusion, Senator.'

'Sure you are.'

Farnsworth nodded and left.

'Just dandy,' Robert said when the den door had been closed.

'You need to stay calm.'

'All the money I pay you, you can't come up with something better than that? I'm sick of hearing it.'

'I hate saying it and you hate hearing it, but it's the truth. This is probably nothing more than a fishing expedition. Hammell is squeezing you, hoping for a confession.'

'Well, he's sure as hell not getting one.'

'You're innocent. Of course he's not getting one.'

The word 'innocent' had its desired effect. Robert took a deep breath, shoved his hands in his pockets and said, 'I am innocent. I get so

worked up I actually forget that sometimes.'
Then, 'You really think this is a fishing expedition?'

'Yeah, I really do.'

'You learning anything?'

'I think I was about to when I heard about the hotel clerk and came out here. Ruskin and his girlfriend are still in my room and he's eager to talk. He wants FBI protection. I have a Bureau friend in Chicago. As soon as Ruskin starts telling me things I'll bring him in.'

He went around and sat behind his desk. 'You want to hear something stupid?'

'The stupider the better.'

That old Robert buddy-boy smile. It made both of us feel better. 'You're so full of shit sometimes, Conrad.'

'You're not the first person to tell me that, you know. I seem to recall a few thousand other people saying it before you did.'

'I had this dream last night that I was re-elected. You think there's any way that's still possible?'

'If we can wrap all this up fast enough.'

'You know, Elise is into astrology and all that bullshit. Always has been. I don't kid her about it. Or religion. They comfort her. But maybe she's on to something. She always tells me that sometimes dreams show you the future.'

Right now I didn't give a damn about him being foolish. The law was still after us – it was about to enter his house, in fact – but if it gave him a brief respite from what he'd been facing, fine.

'You think maybe I should go to the front door and be cooperative?'

'Good idea. That'll surprise them in a good way.'

Before we could say anything else the door was thrown open by a tornado in the form of Ben, who didn't enter the room – he invaded it.

'I want to see this search warrant.'

'Farnsworth is outside in his car,' I said.

'On his phone.'

'Oh.'

Ben was in a white button-down shirt, dark gray suit pants and a black cashmere winter coat. 'Farnsworth didn't ask you any questions, did he, Senator?'

'No, and if he had I wouldn't have been stupid enough to answer them.'

'Good, good.'

Mrs Weiderman appeared in the doorway bearing one of the family's coffee mugs. She called Ben's name. 'Oh, thank you so much, Mrs Weiderman. I tell you, come to Chicago and I'll set you up in business. I mean that. I don't know what you do to coffee but yours tastes better than any other coffee I've ever had.'

For just a few movie frames there Mrs Weiderman was a seventeen-year-old receiving a compliment from a boy she liked. Shy but eye-shiningly happy.

She closed the door behind her. As the den mother she knew when all doors were to be left open and when they were to be closed.

'What do we know about this hotel clerk?' Ben said.

Robert said, 'Tracy called me from the cabin. She told me she'd changed hotel rooms because she was having some trouble.'

'What kind of trouble?' I said.

'She didn't say. Maybe with Ruskin. I heard her talking to him on her cell phone one night and she was really pissed about something. Maybe about his girlfriend. They hated each other.'

'This is when we need you to speak up, Senator,' Ben said. 'We'll do it late in the afternoon so we get plenty of play as breaking news. Unless the police find something here – and I'm sure they won't – all you're guilty of at worst is cheating on your wife.'

'Ben. I explained – to *both* of you – that we didn't actually have sex.'

An exasperated glance at me from Ben. To Robert, 'Do you want to get into your inability to have an erection that night? You probably would have had sex if you could have.'

'You're making an assumption that isn't necessarily true,' Robert said.

'It doesn't matter, does it, Dev? Tell him.'

'Robert, later on we can go into all the details if you want to. Right now we have to stay on one message. You didn't kill her. You didn't threaten her, either. If she was afraid of somebody the night she asked the desk clerk for help, it wasn't you. You didn't see her that night and you swear to it.'

'Who the hell is going to believe anything I say?' Robert broke into one of his circular paces. The den was wide enough to give him some room. Sometimes he talked more to himself than to us. 'You see these guys on TV denying everything and you know they're guilty. They just make it worse for themselves. Then the comedians pick it up and you're really finished.'

'Then all we – all *you* do – is make your denial. I'm sure Dev can write something dignified that people will listen to seriously. You're a serious man, Senator. Even your enemies say that. Nobody has ever questioned your intelligence or your integrity.'

If Ben kept pushing we'd soon enough be watching Robert ascend into heaven and sit at the right hand of God. Robert's last election had gotten so dirty on both sides that both candidates came away roughed up. It became known that Robert had made close to half a million on a couple of sweetheart deals that only US senators hear about and that – whispered but never exactly proved – he'd had an affair that his distressed wife had heard about. There'd also been the guy who gave a TV interview about the time Robert had been so drunk he hadn't been able to drive his car out of an overnight parking lot where the guy worked. He'd been so drunk, in fact, that he fell out of the driver's seat and spent the night on the asphalt next to his car sleeping it off. Fortunately he'd been twenty-four at the time. The follies of youth.

'I need to get this set up,' Ben said. 'Can you write something while you're here?'

'Sure,' I said. 'But I want input from both of you.'

'If I don't like it, I won't say it. You two understand that, don't you?'

'Sure,' Ben said.

'Of course,' I said.

A good time was had by all.

If you're looking for help in writing for your candidate, just remember there is a political cliché for every situation.

In a political world of verbal excess and ten lies per minute, simple heartfelt sincerity gets lost. In fact, it looks suspicious. In Robert's case just saying that he was innocent would make him look as if he was hiding something. *He knows he's guilty, that's why he couldn't even come up with a defense.* So as I sat down to write I had to look up on my imaginary shelf of political clichés to find one that might work.

I ran a number of them through and settled on the old 'political enemies' routine. Yes, the one and only Dick Nixon (or Nick Dixon as Eisenhower once allegedly called him by mistake). Yes, Bill Clinton, feeling his own pain after being outed for his dalliance with Monica Lewinsky, used it too. But we had a specific person with a specific political hit woman background to point to. And point to it we would – though carefully; people tend to dislike you when you suggest that the still-warm corpse might be less than perfect when upright and ambulatory.

In the rush to find Robert guilty only one reporter (that I had been able to find online) had spent any serious time writing about Tracy Cabot's background. It was known that she was a political operative sometimes associated with Ruskin, but nobody had fed Ruskin to the public. There was a connection we could explore. Briefly. I wanted to keep everything under ninety seconds max. Plenty of time for claiming innocence, citing concern for family, thanking voters for their outpouring of support (he must have received at least one email cheering him on) and then offering condolences to the Cabot family over the untimely death of their 'troubled daughter who had been led into a dangerous lifestyle by people who had no concern for her well-being.' She wouldn't have been a treacherous whore if only she'd continued to hang with those two girls who became nuns.

Fire away, Empire News channel!

Three hours and two deliveries of sandwiches and coffee by Mrs Weiderman later, I had my draft and asked Mrs Weiderman if she would please round up Robert and Ben.

'They're playing blackjack in the kitchen. Ben has lost two hundred dollars.'

Blackjack was Robert's favorite card game. When there were two players you changed dealers every ten hands. I'd lost maybe a couple of grand to him over the years.

Ben saw me when I was one footstep inside the kitchen and roared: 'You got it? Is it finished? C'mon, get over here!'

'I got to remember to bring the tranquilizer gun I used on that bear that time,' I said, walking to the nook.

'Very funny,' he said.

I'd printed three copies so we could all peruse my brilliance at the same time.

As they started to read, Ben said, 'I'm not crazy about the first sentence.'

'I don't like the second one much better,' Robert said.

Nothing new here, not with these two. They couldn't get their engines started without grinding you up a little at the start, then they generally settled down and got serious. I've never known what they expected to find in the first five hundred words. Opening remarks that surpassed the Gettysburg Address?

I sat next to Robert. Mrs Weiderman slipped me a cup of her elixir-like coffee and I sat there quietly waiting for them to read it through a couple of times. I watched a squirrel next to a tree digging up some goodies to store for impending winter. He or she was putting in an honest day's work the way all of nature's animals do except the human animal. While a good share of humanity works hard with its hands and minds in clean, productive and honest ways, there is another segment, growing larger every year, that sits behind desks and contrives ways to bamboozle and coerce all those whose work is clean and productive into submission.

Ben said, 'I like it. A few tweaks but I like it.'

Robert said, 'I like it, too. A few tweaks but nothing serious. I knew you'd come through for us, Dev. You always do.'

Ben said, 'Now we head to Channel Four. We're way behind schedule. We can still hit the network news.' He was out of the booth and going somewhere. When he hit the door he said, 'I left my coat in the den. C'mon, you two. Hurry up.'

'Shit,' Robert said, 'I'd better run an electric razor over my face again.'

'Bring it along. You can do it in the car.'

'I'll grab a shirt and tie and jacket and be ready in two minutes.'

'I really appreciate the job you did, Dev. I really do.'

I followed him out of the kitchen. I went to the hallway and he went to the den.

I was just taking my jacket down from the coat tree when my cell phone rang.

The voice on the other end stabbed into my

ear with three words: 'They're gone, Dev.'

Not panic, not hysteria. But stunned disbelief.

'Who's gone?'

'Ruskin and Sarah,' Jane said. 'They drugged Guild's coffee with something so he'd pass out and then they picked up all their things and ran out. Guild just called me now when he woke up. I want to get him to the ER to make sure he's all right since we don't know what they put in him.'

'Does he remember what time it was when he passed out?'

'The last thing he remembers it was an hour and ten minutes ago.'

'What was going on then?'

'He said that everything had gone fine until this Michael Hawkins showed up and started asking Ruskin some questions. Guild said that Hawkins asked him to leave so that he could interview Ruskin and Sarah but that he didn't want to leave until he'd talked to you. He finally agreed to wait in the hall for twenty minutes.'

'And then what?'

'Hawkins came out exactly twenty minutes later and thanked him, and then rolled his eyes and made a joke about Ruskin and Sarah. Something about how he hoped his own kids never turned out like them. Then he apologized for leaning on Guild in the first place. The trouble came when he went back inside.'

Robert and Ben walked quickly toward me. Seeing me on my cell phone, Ben shot his right sleeve and pointed to his watch. He then stepped past me and opened the door and the two of them went through it. I followed them, still on the phone.

Jane continued her story. 'When he got inside he needed to visit the bathroom. When he came out he said Ruskin and Sarah had a cup of coffee ready for him. He thanked them. As he drank it he started noticing how agitated both of them looked. He said Ruskin was up and wearing shoes. His Glock was jammed down the front of his pants. He asked them if something was wrong. Sarah blurted out that they didn't want to talk to any federal agent you hadn't approved of in advance. They didn't trust anybody.'

By now we were outside. Robert was getting into Ben's bronze rental Buick. Ben shouted to me, 'See you at Channel Four!'

I waved back.

'Guild said he tried to calm them down but that they acted "crazy." His word. He said whatever they'd put in his coffee hit him around this time. He was kind of woozy for a few minutes and then he passed out entirely. That was when they escaped. He's really embarrassed, Dev. He plans to apologize as soon as he sees you. He says he should've been suspicious when she had a cup of coffee ready to hand him right away since he sensed that they were acting strange. He couldn't see why they were so agitated when it had been clear that Hawkins had just been interviewing them the way any kind of government investigator would have. He said their paranoia should have alerted him.'

'Tell him he doesn't have anything to apologize for. We're dealing with two very unstable people here. Now I need to find them all over again before they do something really stupid. The idea of Ruskin toting that Glock around bothers me more than anything.'

'Isn't his arm broken? How could he shoot?'

'Unfortunately his "shooting arm," as he calls it, is fine. But right now I need to go. Robert's going to make a statement on TV.'

'I'll be watching. Be sure to call me when you get a chance.'

'I will. It helps me just to hear your voice.'

'You say the nicest things.'

'Come to think of it, I do, don't I?'

TWENTY-ONE

Channel 4 was housed in a refurbished two-story red brick building on the edge of a recently built collection of business buildings. I knew they were recent because they all had the same awkward science fiction look architects seem to prefer these days. A lot of glass and a lot of metal creating sharp edges and a zoo-like peek into the daily lives of their bustling workers. Now in an early dusk of mauve and salmon, in the stingy light of a half-moon, with the lower floors splashed with the headlights of cars rushing to get out of the parking lot and back to places where the overlords couldn't get to them – not yet, anyway – the sense of frantic escape was unmistakable. Who could blame them?

As we approached the station, I could see a group of maybe thirty reporters and camera people packed in front of the Channel 4 doors. Ben's arm shot out from the driver's side of the Buick. He waved me on. We'd keep going right past them. I assumed – and was proven correct – that we'd go around the block and try the back door.

When we reached the rear lot a half-dozen

reporters and four camera people bolted toward our cars. I needed to do what I could to make it safe for Robert and Ben.

I whipped my car into a spot on the back edge of the small lot and then waited for them to lurch toward me.

'The senator is on his way into the station to make a statement. Right now that's all I'm at liberty to say.'

Only two pairs of them tore after Robert and Ben. The rest of them stayed with me.

'Is he going to resign?'

'Is he going to admit that he killed her?'

'Is he going to resign?'

'Is he going to admit he killed her?'

The shouted mantra kept going as I rushed to the door. The otherwise dark lot was now being attacked by the alien eyes of the cameras and the unsettling bellers in the relative quiet. I guess they had to get something on tape so my retreating back was as good as anything. I could write the copy for Empire News: 'Senator Logan's political consultant refused to talk to the press but instead raced to the door, giving the impression – the same impression the senator has been giving since Tracy Cabot's murder was first announced – that he's hiding something.'

A man inside the building had been watching for me and opened the door so I could run inside with the pack of reporters only a few feet behind me. Safely inside, I would have turned and given them the finger except, as you might expect, I was far too mature to do something that juvenile. And I didn't want to give the supermarket tabloids a juicy side story. 'Killer Senator's Consultant Flips Off Hard-Working Reporters Convincing Some That Murdering Senator May Have More Victims Buried Elsewhere! Aliens Involved?'

The man said, 'You ever get sick of them?'

'Never. They're like family to me.'

He was slow to realize that I was joking but when he got it a grin broke his moon face in half. 'If they're anything like the ones here they're pretty hard to take. But you didn't hear me say that, of course.' He was probably in his fifties, gone to flesh and weary humor. He wore one of those fish pins marking him as a born-again Christian. Despite that he seemed likable. 'C'mon. I'll take you to the senator.'

The makeup room was larger than I expected. There were three small tables with mirrors and bottles of makeup. The room was pungent with the sharp scent of hairspray. A fortyish woman so thin and gaunt I wondered if she'd been sick was daubing Robert up then standing back to appraise her work. Ben had fitted himself into a far corner and was talking low into his cell phone.

'Are they putting your golden words on the Teleprompter?' Robert said.

'Yes, they are. I just hope there's time for your country-western song, too,' I said.

The makeup lady's head swung around to me. 'He's going to *sing*?'

'Don't pay any attention to him,' Robert said. 'He thinks he'll keep my spirits up by making these stupid jokes.'

She touched a bony hand to her chest. The fragility of the motion and the hand made me feel sorry for her. But the smile was full on and she looked appreciative that I'd made her happy. 'Gosh, I was thinking how important this is for you, Senator. I voted for you, by the way, and I don't believe any of this stuff. But when he said you were going to sing—' She laughed. To me, she said, 'I have an older brother like you. I was supposed to be the smart one but he'd tell me these stories and I'd always believe them. It was just the way he told them. Real low-key, the way you did.' She shook her head then picked up a long black comb from the table and went to work on Robert's hair. In the round mirror encircled in small light bulbs he'd begun to look TV ready.

When she finished, she stood back for a final time and said, 'You look very nice, Senator. Very nice. And I've already said a few prayers for you.'

'I really appreciate that, Angela.'

'Now I need to get out of here so you can change clothes.'

When we were alone, Robert said, 'I should-'ve taken some Pepto. My stomach and my bowels are in bad shape.'

'I'll spare you the stupid jokes.' Though I was laughing.

'I actually appreciate them. They remind me of my life before I became a vicious killer.' He got up and started changing into his blue button-down shirt, red-and-blue rep tie and blue tweed sport coat. He left his jeans on. 'You know, I really don't give a shit if I lose. All I care about is getting out of this mess. And Elise would be delighted if we went to our house in the Hamptons and said goodbye to all this. Does that surprise you?'

'That giving up your seat looks good to you now? Of course not, Robert. I'd be thinking the same thing you are. You've been working the press for sixteen years and now they're working you. But I believe that everything you're feeling is temporary. We'll find the killer and then in a day or two you'll wake up and think how good it would be to be back in Washington. You like the game the same as I do. And buried somewhere inside the game are one or two actual ideals you've held on to while peddling your ass to survive. You care about average people, Robert. You've got a good understanding of how they live and what they need and how to appeal to the good parts of their nature. There aren't many on either side who can say that.'

'Hell.' Sad smile. 'That was so eloquent I'd vote for myself.'

Ben retreated from the wall. 'Sorry. Chicago

business. I'll have to fly back there tomorrow morning to be in court in the afternoon.' He raised blocky fists. Then dropped to a boxer's crouch and swung hard and fast at an invisible opponent. 'You ready, Senator? We're going to kick some ass, right?'

'I'll try.' He nodded to me. 'Dev says it's all right if I say "fuck" twice.'

Ben picked up the line easily. 'That's right, two fucks but only one cocksucker.'

'Got it,' Robert said. But the fun in his voice was waning, waning just as the knock came. 'Senator, we need to get going. Are you about ready?'

'We're ready now,' I said as I made my way to the door.

The same guy who didn't think much of the Channel 4 Action News Team (I was waiting for the *In*Action News Team to show up somewhere) waited for us to file out and then we followed him down a corridor to a door marked Studio B.

In small cities, Studio B's, or whatever they're called, always look the same. You have a desk with a picture of something on the wall behind the person in the chair – here we had a nature shot – and cheap bookcases filled with hardcover books brought from the homes of various Channel 4 employees.

When the young woman came into the studio, talking to somebody on her headset, I signaled that I wanted to talk to her. Her tight red blouse and tight jeans loved her overweight body a bit too much, but the face was intelligent and pleasant. When she finished talking on her headset she came over to me. 'I'm Mary O'Brien.'

'Dev Conrad. I work with the senator.'

As we shook hands, I said, 'Is there any chance we could lose that photo on the wall?'

'Sure. What did you have in mind?'

'Solid background. And shoot everything in medium close except when we open. Then we're out a little wider.'

'I was thinking along the same lines. I guess we must both be geniuses.'

'Speak for yourself. That's one of the few names I've never been called. And for good reason.'

It helps everybody to get along with the local crew. You generally get a better product. I've watched too many Chicago hotshots snap out orders to local people as if they were idiots. Once in a while they are idiots. But then so are some of the Chicago hotshots. And more times than they seem to realize.

There wasn't much to do except set Robert in the chair, spend a few minutes lighting him and then running through the words on the Teleprompter. Ben and I reassured him that he'd do fine and that this was the right thing to do.

The middle-aged gentleman operating the camera was either having an upset stomach episode or he didn't much like our senator. I caught him rolling his eyes when Robert got to the part about his enemies. And he caught me catching him. The apologetic smile confirmed my read of his political opinion.

The same gentleman gave the countdown. 'Senator – in five, four, three, two, one – in!'

I listened as carefully as I could. Nuance could kill you just as much as an outright mistake. Even though he insisted on his innocence and apologized to his constituents for putting them through this ordeal, and even though he offered his condolences to the family and loved ones of Tracy Cabot, he could undercut himself with an expression that could be misread or a passage he seemed to hurry through. Every breath he took would be parsed.

Ninety seconds isn't much in real life but in TV life it can be an agonizing year or two. I stood next to Ben as Robert started in. There was a monitor close by. I kept looking from Robert in the studio to Robert on the tube. He'd managed to relax some and that helped establish an intimacy with the public. He wasn't this treacherous beast. He was a guy – admittedly wealthy, admittedly a Washington insider and player – who wasn't all that different from most folks after all. And who had been falsely accused. He was especially good with that part of our response.

At the one-minute mark I realized I was sweating. Cold sweat; flop sweat. If he could just get through the next thirty seconds without screwing up...

And he did.

'And we're out!' the cameraman said.

Ben and I rushed to the desk and started telling him how well he'd done. We didn't have to hype it; he'd done damned well. I resented the fact that the cameraman was still in the studio wrapping things up. I wanted only true believers around for this little celebration.

'I wish I felt as good as you two,' Robert said. But he had allowed himself a tentative smile.

'That's the first step back, Senator, and a good one. You've faced your public. That's got to help.'

I put my finger to my lips. Robert and Ben glanced at me then understood when I nodded in the direction of the cameraman. He'd no doubt made an agreement with somebody to report on everything he'd seen and heard when we were here.

He pretended to be intensely interested in pulling a piece of cable a few feet along a baseboard.

'You about done over there?' I said. I didn't bother to sound friendly.

'I work here, remember?'

'Great. But we'd like a little privacy, if you don't mind.' I realized I likely sounded like one of those Chicago hotshots who pushed around local TV people. At the moment I didn't give a shit.

He dropped the snaky black cable to the floor and rolled his eyes again. We weren't in danger of becoming buddies. Then he sort of flounced – yes, flounced – toward the door and let himself out.

'Friend of yours?' Ben smiled.

I returned the smile and then said, 'OK, now we make a run for our cars. I'll do what I can but they'll be moving in a pack and that'll make it even tougher.'

'This is like a commando raid on our own cars,' Robert said. 'As long as I've been in public office I've never seen anything like this.' Then he understood what he was *really* saying. 'Of course, nobody ever thought I'd killed anybody before, either.'

Ben had brought all of Robert's other clothes along so we were ready to go, out of the studio, down the short hall, down the long hall and to the back door. I was the one who peeked out. Dark, wintry air and a blast of camera light that hid the mob behind in shadow. They could have been anything, vampires or werewolves or creatures up from the bowels of the earth as in all those wonderful old late-night horror movies I cherished enough to never watch again. The most I could see of any of them was the way some of the camera light illuminated their eyes, which only enhanced the feeling of inhuman beings.

I looked back at them. 'You ready?'

'As we'll ever be,' Ben said.

I pushed the door open only wide enough for me to step through. If their words had been bullets I would have been in ragged pieces on the ground. They pushed, lurched, lunged and surrounded me. I raised both arms as if I was about to bestow a papal blessing. 'My name is Dev Conrad. I'm here to see if all you sensitive, caring people will do Senator Logan the kindness of letting him get to his car and go back to his home. I can assure you that everything you want to hear him say you'll hear in the ninety-second statement he made on tape just now inside Channel Four.'

'Did he admit he killed her?'

'Why would he do that? He had nothing to do with her death.'

'Does he have any idea of who did kill her then?'

'No.'

'If he's innocent why does he need a high-powered attorney like Ben Zuckerman?'

'Is that supposed to be a serious question?'

'Yes.'

'He brought in Mr Zuckerman because before the police forensics team had even left the cabin where Ms Cabot's body was found parts of the media – especially the TV media – had already found him guilty.'

'Is there any truth to the rumors that he may resign?'

'No.'

'How is his family dealing with all this?'

'How would any family deal with it?'

I didn't have to look behind me to know that Ben had appeared. The group of thirty-plus with all their equipment started to lean in his direction as he ran toward his Buick. He was playing football again. Doing some broken field running and not looking back. But most of them stayed in place.

'Was he having an affair with the Cabot woman?'

'I don't mean to be rude but these are the same questions you've been asking Mr Zuckerman. He was not having an affair with the Cabot woman.'

I watched Ben swing the Buick around behind the reporters and honk his horn. Robert came rushing out. They were on him like leeches. He did a football run, too. Far to their right and then straight on to the car. Ben had tracked him so that before they could stop him he was diving into the open door and Ben was screeching away before that door was closed.

In most circumstances, all this would have been funny. Everybody from the lowliest and most incompetent of TV writers to the great Federico Fellini had parodied the press trying to overwhelm and lynch its prey. But tonight it held no charm; no charm at all.

The ones who'd strayed returned to the coven so they could join in yelling at me. I answered a few more questions and then said, 'I'm afraid that's it for tonight, friends. Now you know as much as I do about the whole story.'

They didn't believe me and kept shouting at me. I didn't try an end run. I just started walking toward them and enough of them parted to let me continue my journey until I was clear of them. They stayed behind, a thundering herd, but I guess that by now they were as tired of it as I was. Bars and restaurants sounded much warmer and fuzzier than trying to browbeat a minor player into giving you something you knew he wasn't going to give you anyway.

I got in my Jeep and gave it the gas before clipping on the headlights, turning on the heat and strapping on my seat belt. I just wanted to get away from here. I did all these things in the next few blocks. I headed by pure instinct toward the same kind of refuge the press sought. My hotel and its restaurant.

There was no escaping the reporters, of course. They were all over the lobby. For the most part these were the A-list boys and girls. Lesser lights would be on less generous expense accounts so would be staying where you had to do a lot of things for yourself, a constant reminder that you weren't successful enough to deserve A-list treatment.

I thought about going up to my room first but was led by a cosmic force into the restaurant where I asked for a table for two. It was warm in here and the candlelight had a nurturing effect on me, and when I speed-dialed and got Jane a great good peace settled on me as soon as she said she'd join me within ten minutes. There's a kind of loneliness that only comes with being on the road. Not so much in your twenties and thirties, maybe, but for me my forties were starting to make the road seem bleak and endless.

Jane seated herself with a smile and scents of woman, rain and, more faintly, perfume. The middle-aged waiter's blue eyes very much approved of her looks.

I'd waited until she was here to order. We decided on Scotch and waters and mushrooms stuffed with lobster meat as appetizers.

'Channel Four led with it,' she said. 'The senator really did well. I'm prejudiced on his behalf so I did my best to be objective. He looked good, he sounded sincere and what he said made sense.'

'He told the truth. The one thing I expect the right to jump on is the reference to his "enemies." People always have a problem with that. But in this case I'm pretty sure it's true. There's a group called The Alliance for Liberty. That's the only point of contact we have. Tracy Cabot's old man was involved with them. But they may not be part of this at all so that's why we can't talk about them publicly. There are secret groups working twenty-four/seven and they get bolder all the time. Bring down enough senators on our side and they can take over the government.'

'That sounds like a science fiction movie.'

'Something like it happened before.'

'Really?'

'You can Google it – 'The White House Putsch.' I read about it a few times before but I needed to read up on it again. A retired Marine Corps major general named Smedley Butler claimed that a secret group of millionaires and billionaires were plotting to take over a veterans' organization – those organizations were powerful back in the thirties – to use as the leading edge of a *coup d'état* that would overthrow FDR and seize control of the federal government.'

'Was that really true?'

'Well, historians are still arguing about it. The consensus seems to be that the plot was true and that a number of very, very rich men were involved. The debate seems to be over how close they came to actually acting on the plot. It's the same today. I don't know if anybody could pull it off but maybe they'd try it. There are a lot of true believers with a lot of money. There's one big problem.'

'What?'

'Now I sound like every conspiracy nut I've ever made fun of.'

The waiter appeared again and Jane ordered a large Caesar salad. I ordered the salmon.

After the waiter left, Jane said, 'The idea of a coup is really scary. Most people wouldn't think it was possible.'

'There's this movie I've seen a number of

times where this actor named Kevin McCarthy is running down a road pounding on car windows and warning everyone that they're coming.'

'I love that movie. The first time I saw it I was eight. I was convinced that half the people I knew were pod people. I just wish it had a different title. You tell most people *Invasion of the Body Snatchers* is a great movie and they think you're an idiot.'

'It's their loss. They're the idiots. Anyway, I'm not even sure that's what Ruskin is talking about. And he's such a bullshit artist, who knows what he's going to tell me when we finally catch up with him. The only thing I know is that he's convinced whoever hired him has sent somebody to kill him.'

'Do you believe him?'

'I believe he believes that. Which doesn't mean it's actually true.'

'And you have no idea where he's hiding?'

'None. But he also seems to believe that I'm the only one he can trust. He thinks a number of people on his side are involved. He can't be sure which ones. That would go along with the conspiracy, of course. So I expect to hear from him.'

She sat back; a melancholy smile. 'I really am a small-town girl. I thought it was a big deal to have a sitting senator from here and go to parties at his house occasionally where other sitting senators and well-connected political people were hanging out. But all this intrigue – I have to slow it down every couple of hours just to take it all in. And now Ruskin insisting somebody's trying to kill him.'

'Robert was set up. Nothing illegal was done on either side so there's no case against it. A senator made a fool of himself over a pretty woman. In an election cycle that can make a difference between winning and losing. What they'd planned was simple. They'd leak some incriminating photos of the Cabot woman and Robert together – they'd have the hotel clerk testify that she was afraid of him; they'd have testimony that Robert was there in the parking lot clearly angry with her – and that would be that. Robert would be finished. The Cabot woman's murder changed everything.'

The food was served and the aromas reminded me of how hungry I was.

The salmon and Caesar salad were both tasty and the second Scotch and water so good I knew I needed to cut myself off. Be pretty easy to sit here and get hammered, especially with Jane framed in the candlelight.

'It's just so nice to sit and relax for a while,' Jane said. Then laughed. 'I keep sounding older every year. More like my mom. She worked hard all her life – she raised my brother and me after my father decided he wanted to stay in the Navy and have a girl in every port – in a place that was a forerunner of Walmart. By the time I was a sophomore in high school I was an activist because I saw how big business treated people like my mother. Long hours, no health insurance, the threat of firing if the word got out that you even mentioned anything about unionizing. So several times a week after ten-to-twelve-hour days she'd sit at our little dinner table and let one of her shoes drop off so she could rub her foot and say, "It's just so nice to sit here and relax for a while." I'd been doing ninety percent of the housework and washing and ironing all the clothes since seventh grade to help her out. And my younger brother always had jobs. Thank God I got scholarships for college.' She used her fork to point to her salad. 'Sometimes when I eat at a good restaurant I feel guilty because my mom could never afford it. She died of heart disease. I wish there was time travel so I could take her to Chicago and buy her a nice dress and take her to a fancy restaurant and get her a good car. The old Chevy she drove was almost twenty years old.' For a few moments she was a little girl again doting on the woman who bore her and loved her and raised her. And obviously raised her well. 'She was a wonderful woman.'

'I'm getting the same feeling about you.'

Too much. I'd embarrassed her; I couldn't tell if she was blushing but her expression portrayed her discomfort. 'I'm selfish and self-centered and have a bad temper. My mom was none of those things, Dev.' I'd also managed to irritate her. She'd mythologized her mother into a perfect creature. Now I knew better than to try and argue with her.

My cell phone toned. It was Sarah, but at a speed and decibel that defied comprehension. All I was able to get on the first pass were the words 'scared' and 'screaming.'

'Sarah, Sarah. You have to slow down. I can't understand you.'

Jane's eyes were fixed on mine. She'd picked up on the alarm in my voice.

Sarah was sobbing now. 'He ran out the door. I can't believe he had the strength to do it.'

'I assume you mean Howie?'

'Yes! And Hawkins went after him.'

'Hawkins? How did he know where you were?'

'That's just it. Howard said you told him. He said you sold us out so Hawkins could kill him.' Everything she said was between sobs.

'I couldn't have told him. I don't *know* where you are.'

'The Sleep Tight. A motel out by the airport. If you didn't tell him, I don't know who did.'

But I knew. It wasn't a person, it was a thing. A tracking device. Hawkins had slapped it on their rental just as he'd slapped one on mine. Where it had been the other night when he shot at but failed to kill Ruskin. That good ole buddy of mine, the finest bellman money could buy, Earl Leonard, had lied to me, of course. And Hawkins had paid him to lie, to provide him with an alibi so I wouldn't think an investigator for a US Attorney, a patriotic cuss and a man among men, could possibly lie under any circumstances.

'Sarah, Sarah, listen to me. Howard is right. Hawkins may be trying to kill him. I'm on my way. You just sit tight and wait for me.'

Now she was crying so hard she couldn't even form words. I thumbed the phone off.

'What's going on?'

'I can explain on the way, if you want to ride along.'

That smile of hers could get her into Top Secret rooms without a pass. 'Of *course* I want to ride along.'

I waved the waiter over. 'I'll leave you a fifty-dollar tip if you can get us out of here in under three minutes.'

He needed fifteen seconds to compute what I'd said then he jerked the card so hard he almost took my hand off with it. And then he was running, yes, running, toward the cash register area.

We were a little more leisurely in our sojourn to the front of the restaurant. We merely jogged there.

The well-dressed middle-aged woman who would normally have processed our card had been pushed aside by the waiter. I knew this from the way her eyes and mouth were set in a Ted-Bundy-spots-his-prey look. Later she would see to it that the manager would take care of the matter for her. Castration with a butter knife would be only the beginning.

I had no idea if he'd made the three minutes or not, but I added fifty dollars to the bill and we rushed out of there.

I spotted our bellman Earl over by the elevators, but like the restaurant manager I'd have to wait until later for my vengeance. Jane and I raced to the hall that would take us to the side door and then the parking lot.

I shot out of the parking lot and into the dark, cold night. Suddenly Howie's conspiracy theory sounded a lot more believable.

TWENTY-TWO

The red and blue emergency lights bouncing off low-hanging rain clouds told a story I didn't want to hear. And we were still three blocks away from the motel.

The parking lot on the west side of the motel was set up for making a movie. All the props and people in place. You had your three police vehicles, your four uniformed coppers, your ambulance with the back door open and you had your crowd of motel guests all bundled up against the low thirties temp. It wasn't even quite eight o'clock but a few of the women had nightgowns showing under the hems of their winter coats. And screeching into place seconds before I turned into the lot a van with CHANNEL 6 NEWS NOW! splashed across the side in red and yellow action colors.

No problem finding a parking space. The thing was you had to park way back because that was where the police officer, a large man with a flashlight you could club a black bear to death with, directed us. Something terrible had happened in this lot not very long ago.

The official perimeter was at least fifty yards

from the motel itself and another squad car pulled in to reinforce the way these officers had decided to mark off the crime scene. Jane shivered next to me. It felt twenty instead of thirty.

We walked up to a slender African-American woman in a dark blue police uniform who was reminding people about the perimeter.

'Excuse me, Officer.'

She did not seem unduly charmed by my presence. 'Uh-huh.'

'Can you fill me in a little on what happened?'

'Fill you in? Are you with the press?'

'No.'

'Then why would I fill you in?'

Since I couldn't give her a quick answer – I certainly didn't want to bring up Robert's name – she walked away.

Jane said, 'I was going to talk to her but she left so quickly.'

'You know her?'

'Well, not *know* her know her, but I met her once or twice at police charity functions. Just wait here. It's worth a try.'

She left as fast as the cop had.

I eased closer to the crowd itself. A number of them were walking in place and rubbing their hands together or covering their ears with their hands. A prairie wind was streaking across the lot rattling signage and some of those tiny new two-seater cars.

More TV station vans arrived and reporters and camera people were deployed to the front lines where they positioned themselves like snipers.

The crowd members offered conflicting stories. There'd been a shooting or a knifing or a bludgeoning. It had been a lovers' argument or a robbery or a drug deal. There was one dead, there were two dead, there were three dead. Real, real helpful. And by this time my entire face felt as if it had been Botoxed by the cold night winds.

The crowd swelled and so did my sinuses.

And that was when I saw a familiar figure stepping out of the backseat of one of the unmarked police cars. And it was none other than my old friend Detective Farnsworth. I broke into a run.

And as I was running toward him, Sarah slid out of the backseat and joined him. I could hear her sobbing from here. Head down, her shoulders shaking so hard Farnsworth slid his arm around her protectively as he moved her past the demarcation line and toward the open motel room where light lasered across the lot.

No point in yelling. Farnsworth wasn't about to let me join them and it would just upset Sarah all the more anyway.

Several steps and I was behind the crowd and headed back toward my previous position. The number of press vehicles had doubled now. Network and cable news directors were dispatching reporters the way Hannibal had dispatched troops.

I got a glimpse of Jane and the cop. They were deep in conversation.

By now I was stamping my feet, rubbing my hands together, covering my ears. As soon as Jane got back and told me what she'd found out I planned to do the unthinkable and walk back to my Jeep and get my hat, gloves and scarf, something in my haste I'd forgotten to do.

'Oh, God, Dev, what a terrible night.'

'What'd you find out?'

Her shudder might have been in response to the winds but I doubted it. More likely it had to do with what she was about to relate to me. 'Howie Ruskin was shot to death by Hawkins. His story is that he'd had Ruskin under surveillance for several hours. When Ruskin came out of his room to go somewhere, Hawkins told him to stop. Ruskin tried to run and when Hawkins came after him Ruskin pulled his gun, but before he could fire, Hawkins shot him twice. Head and chest.' She paused. Then, 'And Sarah came out screaming and knelt beside Ruskin, who was dead. She picked up his gun and aimed it at Hawkins but he convinced her to put it down. And now you're going to ask me if there were any witnesses to Hawkins and Ruskin and from what Connie knows, no. There were witnesses to Sarah and Hawkins, though. God, I feel so bad for poor Sarah.'

'So Hawkins could be lying about Ruskin

pulling a gun?'

Her voice was a whisper. I was sure her mind was still on Sarah. 'Could be. That's what Sarah says anyway. It's just hard to believe that somebody from the US Attorney's office could be—'

'Easy way to kill off the one person who could link Howie to the bad guys.'

She still sounded disturbed about Hawkins. 'What about Sarah?'

'No. Ruskin never shared the secret stuff with her, she told me. He was afraid a beautiful woman would carry him off to Paradise, leaving Sarah behind with all this "info" as he called it that she could kill him with, so he kept it to himself.'

Then I saw my chance with Hawkins. From the backseat of the car he'd been in stepped a heavyset detective in a gray topcoat. The man wore a fedora and gaped around as if he was worried about an assassin. Then he stepped back from the car and from the open back door Hawkins emerged.

The two men shook hands and said some words, their breath pluming, the detective jamming a cigarette into his mouth, Hawkins digging his cell phone out and checking it as soon as the detective started walking away from him.

'I need to catch Hawkins. Why don't you wait in the Jeep and run the heater.' I pitched her the keys and took off.

As I moved I realized I'd probably have to get

past the police blockade; otherwise Hawkins could just walk away safe inside the zone. But he surprised me. He talked to Officer Connie briefly and then headed toward his rental. The one he'd likely used when he'd first tried to kill Ruskin.

He was unlocking the door to his rental when I caught up with him. He'd looked up when I was about twenty feet away from him. He finished with the door but didn't open it. 'I was going to call you before I left the parking lot.'

'Tell me what it feels like to kill a guy, you mean?'

'You forget. I checked you out; that's an experience you've had yourself.'

'You had to kill him.'

He was pretty good at it, not great. I'd seen much better, but he wasn't bad. Tall guy like him with that gaunt face expressing the unique sorrow of a man who'd just taken the life of another man. Hands shoved deep in the pockets of his tweed topcoat. Green eyes tired, mouth broken by a frown, timbre of voice pitched low. Not horse shit, no; a couple of levels up from horse shit, his acting skills. A deep sigh. 'Of course I had to kill him and I resent the implication that I didn't. He pulled a gun on me; I didn't have any choice.'

'Poor baby.'

His acting got a lot better when he covered the distance between us in four steps, got in my face and said, 'You don't want to push me tonight, Conrad. Not in any way. I can make your life real miserable if I want to.'

'I believe it, Hawkins. You made Ruskin's life pretty miserable, I'd say.'

'Keep that in mind.' Then, abruptly, he was walking back to his car.

'The people you really work for going to give you a bonus, are they?'

He stopped moving. Stood still for maybe thirty, forty seconds. 'I don't know what you're talking about.'

'Sure you do.' I was winging it now. 'The first plan was you locate Ruskin so you could see how it was going with Tracy Cabot and Senator Logan. Ruskin must have made your real bosses nervous about something in the setup. But then Cabot got herself murdered and your people got scared and panicked. A lot of law enforcement people were going to snoop around and it was problematic how long Ruskin could stand up to the pressure before he cut a deal and started talking. So your job changed. You not only had to locate him; you also had to take him out. I doubt this was the first time you'd killed somebody for them. You almost nailed him in that little park near the college; if he hadn't tripped you would've had him. When you came up to his room this morning he must have suspected what you were really up to. I was too stupid to catch on. I bought your act.'

There were just the two of us. All the clamor of the cops and the emergency team and the crowd had faded, leaving just me and Hawkins. He'd listened to my accusations without moving but now he was facing me again. And smiling.

'I hope you invite me to be in the room when you pitch your conspiracy theory to somebody. I want to watch their faces as your story gets wilder and wilder.'

'It's happened before. A group of billionaires plotted a coup to seize control of our government and get rid of FDR.'

'Good. A history lesson. That'll make your presentation even better. And I happen to know about that attempted coup, by the way. I'm a history buff. They weren't very good at it. They needed to involve key generals and bungled it. But if you make a study of what they did then you can learn from their mistakes and not make those mistakes again. And today you have more generals who might be interested. Generals who don't like what's happened to this country.' Something in my expression must have alarmed him; he was saying too much. 'But that's all theoretical. And crazy.'

He opened the car door now. 'I'm due at the police station.' The smile was back. 'Maybe you can start with them – with Hammell, maybe. I'm told he likes a good story. And you've *got* a good one. It'd make a helluva good movie, in fact.'

He started his car, gave me a kind of half-salute and drove away. This time with a tiny smirk and look of superiority and mischief on his long, New-Englander face.

I was walking back to the Jeep where Jane was waiting when my cell phone interrupted my scattered thoughts. I connected to hear Ben's voice. 'Where are you?'

'At the motel where Ruskin was killed.'

'So it is Ruskin. Sonofabitch. I had something like that in the back of my mind. All we're getting from TV is that there was trouble at this motel. Maybe a homicide. I'm at the senator's. Naturally, we were curious. I doubt a town this size gets many murders. Is this something that could help us?'

'Yes. But I don't want to go into it on the phone.'

'That's all right. We want you to come out here anyway.'

'See you soon.'

'I saw you talking to Hawkins,' Jane said when I got into the driver's seat. 'Any luck?'

'He claims self-defense.'

'Of course. Think he can get away with it?'

'With Ruskin's reputation for going armed and waving guns in people's faces, Hawkins should have an easy go. Especially with no witnesses. Then there's Ruskin drugging the bodyguard you got him.'

'Oh, sure. In a trial the jury would see how unbalanced Ruskin was the day he was killed. And he was armed.'

'Exactly. And Sarah herself told me that he

ran out the door away from Hawkins. Hawkins is a federal investigator. He has a right to detain him and ask questions.'

'Slick.'

'How about going out to Robert's with me?'

'Fine.'

I was glad to get away from it all. I still didn't have any warm feelings for the little prick but I was sorry for Sarah.

And speaking of Sarah...

Just as we were starting to pull out of the parking lot Detective Farnsworth appeared in my headlights, waving his arms for me to stop.

'What the hell,' I said, hitting the brakes.

He strode over to my Jeep. I had the window down waiting for him. When he leaned over and looked in, he said, 'Evening, Jane.' But he didn't wait for a response. 'Conrad, I'm going to pull my car around here so you can talk to Sarah. I promised her I'd set it up. I want to calm her down. I actually like her; that's why I agreed. I don't know what she saw in a scumbag like Ruskin.'

So Farnsworth was on our side after all. I pushed my luck. 'Are you sure yet that Hawkins was justified in killing Ruskin?'

Surprise played on his face, then curiosity. 'You have any particular reason to say that?'

'No witnesses. Anything could have happened.'

'You're getting ahead of yourself, Conrad. We've got a whole investigation to go before we make any judgments. But he's an investigator for a US Attorney and he had a right to find Ruskin and to ask him questions. Ruskin was a clown but he always made a big deal of carrying a gun and being so good with it.'

Between the lines of those sentences were two words: 'Case closed.'

'So wait here. You can get in the backseat with her. 'Night, Jane.'

''Night, William.'

After he was gone, I said, 'See how fast he bought my story about how Hawkins maybe killed Ruskin in cold blood.'

She snapped her fingers. 'Like that. You'll get tired of telling your story, Dev.'

'How about you? Do *you* believe it?'

'I don't *not* believe it. I'd like to learn more about it. You know, do the due diligence.'

'Now there's a vote of confidence.' But I was smiling when I said it.

Farnsworth's unmarked car pulled around and parked about fifteen feet from my Jeep. He pulled the emergency brake on and stepped outside.

'Tell Sarah I said hello,' Jane said.

'Will do.'

I got out and walked over to Farnsworth.

'Ten minutes. Detective Hammell is waiting for us.'

I nodded and walked to the door. As I slid in I saw that Sarah was huddled in the opposite corner as if she was trying to hide. I'd expected tears and panic. Maybe she'd run out of both.

After I had slammed the door and sat there for an interminable silent minute – I wondered if she'd gone into some kind of shock – she said, in a voice I barely recognized as hers, 'He lied and exaggerated so much it was hard to know what was real sometimes. Until last night when somebody shot at him, I didn't really believe any of this. And even then—' For the first time she really looked at me; for the first time her eyes showed the warmth I usually found there. 'It's a terrible thing to admit, Dev, but when we were at the hospital I half wondered if he'd set this all up. You know, hired somebody to shoot at him. Every once in a while he'd do things that got him "press" as he always called it. Usually a few months before he had a book coming out or before he was giving a big speech somewhere. He knew how to promote himself. But this wasn't one of those times.' No tears, not even now. 'So I'm alone and I don't have any idea what to do, Dev. In a weird way I always thought of us as one person. He hated me saying that. We'd have big fights about it. Especially if he was having one of his little affairs. But I really do feel like half of me is gone now.'

'You're a whole person, Sarah. And a good person.' I moved much closer to her.

'They're going to be rough on me, aren't they? The police and the press, I mean.'

'I doubt the police will be. I never read any of

his books but I saw him say on TV one night that he never gave you the details about any of his activities. That he was the only one who knew them. That you only found out what they were after they'd happened. I think the police will believe that sooner than later. But the press is another matter. They'll be after you for a couple of years. So will the supermarket tabloids and a few of the papers of note. Some people will write books about him. And you. And they'll make up outlandish stories that the American press will take as fact. There'll be absolutely no evidence whatsoever for them. But the people who write them will make a lot of money doing it. And now it's fact quote unquote. So you can expect stories like that somewhere along the line about Howard.'

A childlike smile. 'You can call him Howie. He was definitely more of a "Howie."' Then, her body relaxing for the first time, 'Is it all right if I start calling you sometimes? Just telling you how I'm doing and maybe asking for advice.'

'Of course you can.'

'I'm even thinking of moving to Atlanta. I've got a cousin there who's about my age. She's divorced and has plenty of room in her house.' Then, 'He didn't have to kill him.'

'I know.'

'I said that to Detective Farnsworth and he just sort of mumbled something. He's been very nice. I was hysterical and he sat with his arm around me the whole time and told me that his little daughter had died from cancer when she was three and that he knew how hard it was to lose somebody, but that eventually things get better. But he still didn't believe me – about Hawkins, I mean.'

'I believe you.'

'You do? Thank God. Thank God.' She reached out and took my hand.

'But nobody else will believe us unless I can find more evidence and that'll be tough.'

She squeezed my hand. 'But you believe it. That's the main thing for me right now. That you believe it.'

The way she leaned forward I think she was going to kiss my cheek but just then Farnsworth knocked on the back window.

'Oh, God, I'm so glad we got to talk, Dev. This means so much to me, you can't imagine.'

I was the one who kissed *her* on the cheek. 'Any time, night or day, you call me, to catch up or if you have a question, all right?'

'I will, Dev. I will.'

When I got out of the car I looked into the eyes of a man who'd lost a three-year-old to cancer. Unimaginable. We just stared at each other and then he walked away and got into his car with Sarah in the backseat. They drove away. Neither of them waved.

TWENTY-THREE

Mrs Weiderman was smiling when she let me and Jane in and behind her, in the living room most likely, there was the kind of laughter you hear when people are just sitting around getting stiff on good drinks and saying screw it to everything else. Considering everything he was up against, Robert had done damned well tonight.

Mrs Weiderman led us there then stood aside as if ushering us into a temple of pure delight. 'Just go in and have some fun, you two.' I wasn't going to spoil anybody's fun by bringing up the possibility that one of them might be the person who had done Tracy Cabot wrong.

Maddy flung herself off a divan and tore across the room and gave me the kind of hug a man of less probity and wisdom might mistake for more than a simple excited greeting. But I knew Maddy and I knew better. 'Sorry, Jane. I couldn't resist. And by the way, you two make a very cute couple.'

Jane and I realized, about the same second, that little Maddy was a wee bit tipsy. And all the cuter for it. We smiled knowingly at each other and stood there while Robert and Ben and Elise all toasted us. James just stood there trapped in his prison of being James.

I can't tell you much about the next twenty minutes or so because it was just chatter. Robert and Ben were at least half bombed and filled with the kind of radiant optimism only alcohol can inspire. Or, as Robert put it, 'Now we know that Ruskin killed the Cabot woman.'

'And how do we know that?' I said.

'Suicide by cop. Or in this case federal investigator. He intentionally ran away from Hawkins so Hawkins would be forced to kill him.'

Ben, who never played along with anything, played along. 'You have to admit there's some logic to it.'

Who was I to parse that sentence? 'Some logic' can only be used when your blood alcohol reaches a certain illegal limit.

But for all the underpinning of fantasy and desperate hope it was pleasant to see Robert again. The old Robert, the one I liked if not exactly admired, the one who could often be bought for the going rate but who tried not to let his whoring get in the way of taking a stand when the oligarch party (as well as too many members on our side) tried to make life even easier for people who had yachts to worry about and even tougher for people who had impoverished little ones to worry about.

Somebody decided to check on how the

talking heads were assessing Robert's perform-
ance. The giant TV screen bloomed to colorful
life, presenting us with three dolorous men and
one preening woman. Ostensibly this was 'our'
cable network but with a few exceptions the
yakkers were just the usual Beltway boys and
girls who bathed in their own imagined im-
portance. But tonight they were pretty good,
actually.

They liked the way he'd handled himself but
sensibly enough didn't make any claims about
his innocence. I gave them points for that. I also
gave them points for having some fun with
some of the nastier comments made by the
other side, comments I hadn't caught up with
until now.

'My favorite,' said the attractive blonde, 'was
when Sheila St Germaine said that Senator
Logan should have to hand over his passport
because he's a flight risk.'

'Yeah and then Lawrence Todd said Logan
would head for Cuba where Castro would let
him stay.' The man had everybody laughing
with this; even a crew member or two could be
heard chortling.

'And don't forget,' the always-breathless host
said, 'the body language expert who said that
Logan reminded him of Ted Bundy based on
how his right shoulder moves when he changes
the subject.'

Even Elise, not the most demonstrative of
people, was laughing. She had to lean against

Maddy in order to keep from falling off the divan. Maddy had switched to coffee, which was probably a good idea. With her mother finishing an entire wine cooler by herself, somebody had to protect her from destroying the known world with that sweet-sad smile and that small Monet face. If she had another wine cooler she'd probably sign up to be a NASCAR driver or enter a tractor pull. A drinker she was not.

Soon enough an angel appeared in the person of Mrs Weiderman with a tray of hot deli-style sandwiches and two pots of coffee that she rolled in on a hotel-style cart. I wasn't hungry for food but I was for coffee.

I enjoyed sitting on one of the couches next to Jane and watching Robert and Ben and Maddy making all the smart-ass remarks about the various jabs and counter-jabs going on in television land. None of it mattered, of course. That kind of speculative talk vaporized as soon as it was uttered. But sometimes it was fun, as it was tonight.

Jane sighed and whispered, 'I could put my head on your shoulder and go to sleep.'

'Be my guest.'

'Really?'

'Sure. Why not? I don't see how you can sleep with all this noise going on but if you can, do it.'

'I can sleep anywhere.'

I doubted it but I was wrong. Within ten

minutes she was gently snoring on my right shoulder. I was a bit muzzy now so I held her hand, and if anyone found that smarmy I couldn't give a rat's ass.

James' official job was to glower. He hit the bar three or four times to get more of the devil juice then moved back to an armchair where he disappeared inside his iPad. Porno, probably.

Elise had eaten half a sandwich and consumed two cups of coffee, and her earlier ebullience was now slipping into the melancholy we were all familiar with. Ben and Robert had gone to the billiard room and Maddy had disappeared somewhere. Jane, who was obviously not any more of a drinker than Elise, still slept soundly. I eased her into a corner of the divan, slid a throw pillow under her head and stretched her legs out. I pulled my V-neck sweater over my head and laid it across her chest. Better than nothing.

Behind me I heard Elise say, 'Oh, God.'

I went over to her and sat down. 'Everything all right?'

'You— That was so touching. Robert and I haven't had a moment like that in years.'

'Young love, I guess.'

'You really care for her, Dev. You have to be manly and make a joke of it.'

'All right, Mom. I like her quite a bit. Is that enough?'

She had that fragile smile. 'It is for now.' Then she put her head back. Her neck was a masterpiece. 'I shouldn't drink. I've got a head-ache already. But maybe I'll sleep better tonight. I've started having dreams again about Gretchen Cain. I was up every two hours. I'm so sick of the sleeping pills I take – I'm always so groggy the next day – that I didn't take them yesterday, and so last night it was good old Gretchen again. And I suppose it will be again tonight. You remember Gretchen, of course.'

'Oh, yes.'

'You should. Robert made you tell me about her.'

'That's a little overstated. I just said that Robert had confided in me that he'd done something stupid.'

She yawned and that brought her head down. The wan child in her looked at me through a rainy March window. 'You did his dirty work. I'm naïve sometimes but rarely outright dumb, Dev. When you said he'd been "stupid," I knew what you were really saying. That there'd been a woman. What else could it have been? And in this case it was Gretchen Cain. Her husband and I commiserated. Did you know that?'

'No.'

'We even talked about sleeping together to pay them back. There's a term for that.'

'Grudge fucking.'

'Oh, right. We got very drunk one night and made out like ninth graders but then gave it up.' Mischief in her smile. 'He was a very good kisser, I might add. I shouldn't say this but he

301

was a much better kisser than Robert, and I would appreciate it if you'd never tell Robert that.'

I drew an imaginary zipper across my mouth.

'But she still comes back to me, Gretchen does. I always catch them in bed. Our bed. I can even smell her somehow. She wore the most God-awful cologne. I thought she did, anyway. We had several dinners with them. That's how it started. I plead with her to leave him alone but she just sits up in my bed covering herself with my sheets and smirking at me. Robert, at least, is nice enough to look embarrassed. But she's very blunt. She speaks for him – for them. She says that Robert will be moving out – that in fact he'll go with her tonight and he'll send for some of his clothes in the morning. And by then I'm sobbing and pleading. And by the time I wake up I'm afraid they'll put me back in the psych hospital again. I hate it there so much, Dev. I can't tell you.'

No tears. Just talk. Just sorrow and fear.

The sound of my cell phone affected Elise physically. She frowned as if it were a person who'd interrupted us.

'Excuse me, Elise.' Then, 'Hello.'

'Do you know where my bedroom is?' Maddy. Sounding sober now.

'Yes.'

'I'm out on the little porch. I'd appreciate it if you'd come up here now.'

'All right.'

302

'Anything serious?' Elise said.

'My office telling me to check out an internal poll they just sent me. Excuse me. I think I'll go in the kitchen and have a cup of coffee while I read it. Bring you back anything?'

'No, I'm fine. Thanks for listening to me. You're not only less expensive than a shrink, you're a lot better.' She squeezed my hand.

Maddy's bedroom was next to the guest room in which I'd spent some restless nights. I generally didn't stay over unless there was trouble. It was such a comfortable and decorous room I wanted to stay in it once when I could enjoy it.

When I opened Maddy's door I wished I'd worn my snowsuit with the snowmen and Santa Clauses decorating it. Given the winds tonight and that the door leading to the tiny porch was wide open, the room was cold enough to make snowballs out of gin.

'You like it a little nippy, huh?' I said, shivering for effect.

'I thought it would help get me sober faster.' She'd made no concession to the temperature. No extra sweater, no jacket, no hat. Then, 'Hardy pioneer stock.'

'I wish I could say the same,' I said. 'Brr.'

She hadn't faced me yet. She stared out at the forest and the glowing half-moon above it. You could taste and feel and smell the snow that would soon be here. Her small hands were wrapped tight around the black iron porch railing. The only item on the porch was a rattan chair.

And it was kind of funny. As soon as she started talking I no longer noticed how plugged-up I was already feeling. I was too engrossed.

'The afternoon before she was killed I rode my bike to the cabin. I had no idea anybody would be there. I recognized her right away. I asked her as politely as I could – which probably wasn't all that politely, I'll admit – how she'd gotten in and exactly what she was doing there. She said she was a friend of my dad's. But the way she said it – very smirky. You know, implying they were a lot more than friends. And I got mad and I started yelling at her. All I could think of was how my mother would react if she knew that bitch was at our family's cabin.

'She started yelling right back at me. Told me to grow up. I told her to leave but she said she was there at my father's invitation and didn't care whether I liked it or not. I was so angry I decided the best thing to do was get out of there, find my father and confront him about this. So I left.

'But I wasn't able to find Dad until after dinner, and even then I had to wait until late because we were never alone. When we finally had our talk he told me everything and told me how sorry he was and assured me that there had been nothing between them. And then, when the news came about her being found dead, he was afraid the police would bring my name into it and I'd be implicated. He begged me not to tell anybody. But I think you deserve to know.'

So this was what Robert had been hiding from me.

She raised her head, looked up at the stingy moon and laughed abruptly. 'I just kept thinking how intimidated I would be if I were in her position. But she wasn't at all. She was just such a bitch...'

And then she went on to give me another example of Cabot's nastiness, and in so doing reminded me of somebody I should have been thinking about all along.

Ben and Robert came charging in excited as two teenage boys on their first drunken spree. Robert grabbed the remote and shouted with grand and outright glee, 'I hope he's still on!' Ben and Robert stood in front of the giant plasma screen as if they were worshipping a false god.

The first image on the screen was of a plutocrat who'd once accused our sitting president of secretly planning for another 9/11 just so his numbers would go up when he got his best chance to 'look presidential.'

But the plutocrat's words tonight surprised me. 'Susan, Susan, all we know is that at worst all Senator Logan did was maybe have a brief fling. And even that hasn't been established for sure. I say that as someone who despises everything Logan and his socialist cohorts stand for. But I think it's time that we let the law do its work before we make any judgments about his guilt or innocence.'

It was Christmas morning, New Year's Eve and the Fourth of July afternoon simultaneously, and this was Empire News channel, for God's sake. The way Ben and Robert dove for the bar foretold just how hammered they planned to get tonight.

Jane pulled herself up into a sitting position and sleepily rubbed a small hand across her right eye. I went over and she said, 'This is really embarrassing. God, did I snore?'

'You shattered glass.'

'Everybody will think I was drunk.'

'I think they probably know better than that.'

Now those sleepy eyes were narrowing and focusing on me. 'Is everything all right?'

'It will be, I hope.' Then, 'I need to get going.'

'You won't forget I'm waiting here for you, will you?'

I smiled. 'Probably not.'

TWENTY-FOUR

Moonlight on the ground frost contrasted with the shadows of the windbreak, the line of pine that overpowered the small house and made it seem even more isolated and lonesome. Smoke coiled from the chimney and a large gray cat squatted on the small porch feigning feline indifference when he got a look at me. From inside the bungalow a voice spoke much too loudly.

After knocking, I looked around the yard. A car was in the drive. The voice inside continued to pound away.

I knocked again, this time with more force. I had to compete with the diatribe. I was surprised that the door was opened with no precautions of any kind. Even though this was the country, meth had changed everything from the good old days when people left their doors unlocked and offered to help strangers. Drug dealers carried guns now and traveled the gravel roads of rural America. It no longer made much news when a body or two was found in a ditch, fortunes of a drug deal gone wrong. In Missouri a few years back two nineteen-year-old males were found in a ditch with their hands tied behind their backs and their heads missing. Apparently Mexican drug cartels had made instructional videos of how to deal with drug enemies.

'This better be good. I'm missing my show. So what the hell do you want?'

'I'd like to speak with Mark if I could, Mrs Coleman.'

'He isn't here.'

'His car is in the driveway.'

She pulled her dark terrycloth bathrobe tighter around her. A long, light-blue nightie showed beneath the bottom of the robe. 'You ever hear of somebody going for a walk?'

The man on the radio was bellering now. 'Why hasn't the American Congress – and I emphasize the word "American" – why hasn't the American Congress started impeachment proceedings against the only president we've ever had who wrote a secret letter to the head of the United Nations saying that his ultimate goal was to have the UN take over the governance of our nation? And have you noticed that our so-called president – who wasn't born here, not that that seems to bother anybody in the so-called American press – in his arrogance wouldn't even speak about this when a reporter from this show asked him about it?'

A cruel, mad smile crossed her crone lips. 'Are you hearing that?'

'Oh, I'm hearing it all right, Mrs Coleman.'

'Probably scares you, doesn't it? To know we're on to you. Your Senator Logan's a Communist and that makes you one, too, since you work for him. I told that to my Mark. He said he's pretty sure neither you or Logan are Commies. But people have seen that letter, the one to the UN. He wrote it longhand, which was a mistake because Stan on the radio had a handwriting expert on the show and the expert said that once he got a chance to see the letter he'd know if it was the president or not. Stan told him he'd heard of two people who'd seen it and they both said it looked just like the president's handwriting.'

'Kind of made it official, huh?'

'Go ahead and make fun – you'll be in prison soon enough. You and your kind.' And with that she started to shut the door.

But I put my hand on it and stopped her. She wasn't strong enough to do anything about it. 'You take your hand away right now or I'll call the sheriff.'

'I just want to ask you a question.'

'I don't answer your questions. I know what you are.'

'When I was here before you said you could smell perfume on Mark the other night. You said it belonged to his wife.'

'She's a whore. All she wants is to get her hands on this house and then get rid of me so she can live here the rest of her life and not have to pay any rent.'

Of course. Now it was clear to me. The ex-wife was driven by her overpowering desire to steal this ramshackle bungalow and spend decades living in rural luxury. Providing the septic tank held fast.

'Did you really smell perfume on him?'

'On who?'

'On Mark.'

'I said I did, didn't I? It was enough to make me sick.'

'What did Mark say?'

'He didn't say anything. He just went in and washed up. Like he was in a hurry. I was hopin' he was ashamed of himself for givin' into her. That's how she'll get him back – sex. Whores always know how to handle men. Now take your hand off the door.'

I stepped back. She slammed it so fast and so hard I was surprised by the fury of it. Such a tiny woman.

I stayed on the small slab of porch for a couple of minutes. The problem I had was her state of mind. She was clearly suffering from some form of dementia so it was difficult to know what was fantasy and what was real. But to the scent of perfume on her son, she'd added that he seemed to be in a hurry to wash up. Maybe because I wanted to believe those two details I decided that they confirmed my suspicions.

Maddy had told me – following our initial conversation on the subject – that Tracy Cabot said that some 'creep' had been hanging around the cabin and that he made her nervous. Maddy knew she meant Mark Coleman and said he wasn't a creep; just a confused vet whose wife had left him. Maddy said she considered that one more reason to despise the Cabot woman. Maddy then told me she'd had a number of conversations with Mark over the past year and liked him very much and that he was just a lost and lonely man searching for the solace of a woman. It wasn't difficult to imagine the scene if he ever came into any kind of contact with somebody like Tracy Cabot.

I started to walk back to my car. I'd known she wouldn't let me in the house where I suspected Mark was hiding. Now I'd pretend to leave, park down the road and then sneak back here. There was a chance that he would do me the favor of packing a bag, tossing it in his trunk and trying to flee. And I'd be waiting for him.

As I began to open my door, I heard, 'Put your hands up in the air. I've got a rifle pointed right at you.'

Movies and TV have taught us that when you say things like that you're supposed to snarl the words if you want to keep working in La La Land. But Mark had probably never taken any acting classes so when he said it, it was pierced with the same weariness I'd heard on my previous visit. And I knew the eyes would be the same, too. The ineluctable sorrow and frenzy of men and women who'd died psychically and spiritually on the battlefield who came home to trudge through their nightmare days.

'You won't shoot me, Mark.'

'I don't have much to lose.'

'You'd just make things a lot worse for yourself. And this would be first-degree. I imagine the Cabot woman was on impulse. She say something ugly to you?'

My back was still to him but I hadn't put my hands up.

'I know I'm a freak. I could see it in her face. I was stupid enough to go in the cabin in the first place. I couldn't help it. She was so beautiful. I thought that was all finished for me after my wife left, that I wouldn't ever want another woman again. I wasn't going to rape her or anything. I just wanted to look at her, was all. Not even touch her.'

'I believe you, Mark.' And I did.

'She wasn't scared or anything when she saw me. She thought I was some kind of handyman or something. At first, anyway. But she figured it out pretty fast I guess because she started making her remarks. I didn't blame her. I shouldn't have been there. I apologized and went to go out the back way – same way I'd come in – and I don't know why she did it. She kept saying things about me and I guess because I was walking away she came over and grabbed my sleeve and that was when she said it, that one thing.'

He paused a long time.

'What did she say?'

'That's the funny thing. I can't remember what it was now. Maybe it was somethin' about the way I walk now. My ex-wife said somethin' like that when we argued one time. I could see she was sorry right away – my ex, I mean. She even started crying and asked me to forgive her. But when the Cabot woman said it ... She doesn't know a thing about the war, what we went through, and there she was, laughing about it – laughing at me ... That was when I picked up that statue and ... I remember thinking that I really wasn't going to hit her with it, that I was just going to scare her. And I did scare her and she started to turn away and – and then she was on the floor and I was terrified—'

I faced him now. He stood near the edge of the house with his rifle. The stars were vast and alien and couldn't give a shit about this little drama of ours, the way we couldn't give a shit about the ferocity and sadness of animal life. He'd go to prison or maybe a mental hospital and I'd go on with my life, or maybe not. Maybe an eighteen-wheeler would flatten my Jeep on my drive back to Chicago. Or the headaches I got more frequently would turn out to be brain cancer. Or maybe in prison he'd figure out how to slash his wrists or his throat. Maybe, maybe, maybe.

'I want to do everything I can for you, Mark.

I'm going to hire Ben Zuckerman to be your lawyer.'

'It's not me I'm worried about. It's my mom.'

'I'll see that she goes to a very good nursing home.'

'They're really shit. They're always in the news.'

'I know a few good ones.'

'She doesn't have that kind of money.'

'I'm sure she has Medicare and Medicaid.'

A risky line but by God it worked. I can't say it was a fulsome laugh. It kind of spluttered out of him but it was an honest laugh and he said, 'She's going to say this is all a Communist conspiracy to take her son from her; she might even say that the president himself killed the Cabot woman.'

'I wouldn't put it past him. He's a sneaky bastard.'

'Well, I suppose wherever she goes they'll let her plug in her radio.'

I had the sense he was already in prison and locked away and thinking about his mother.

'Yeah,' I said, 'it's quite a country, isn't it?'

Then we allowed each other silence for a time. There was just the swarming night and those stars and that blaring, insane, hateful radio.

'I really didn't mean to kill her. I just lost it for a couple of seconds there.'

'I know.'

'I never got violent with a woman in my life

before then.'

'I'm sorry, Mark. I really am.'

God damn it. God damn it anyway.

Then I walked over to him and gently removed the rifle from his trembling hands.

TWENTY-FIVE

Someday somebody will write a book about all the politicians who got involved with their babysitters. Politicians of all stripes will make an appearance. For instance, there was the pol who paid for the entire college education of the babysitter he seduced just to keep her quiet; the pol who dumped his wife and children for his babysitter; and the pol who set his babysitter up as a staffer in his Washington office as soon as she turned twenty-one. A fetching lass, she went on to become a highly paid and quite creative lobbyist.

The press did a great deal of backtracking, of course, after Tracy Cabot's real murderer was named. The exception being *Empire*, which clung to the adultery angle. Since that was all they had against Robert they pressed on.

Our own polling showed that we'd dropped eighteen points following the story first breaking. Two days after being cleared and after appearing on *Today, NBC Nightly News* and *60 Minutes* we came within two points of tying our old pal and worthy opponent Charlie Shay. Still not enough.

I mentioned babysitters. The last time I'd spoken with Lee Sullivan, private investigator, he'd told me that his son Jason, opposition research wizard, just might have a surprise for us.

Surprise indeed. And babysitter indeed.

Seems there was a twenty-six-year-old young woman that our strapping Irisher Charlie had impregnated when she was seventeen. Jason had told Lee about her and Lee had flown to Madison to interview her. She said that she'd never planned to talk about the incident – she admitted to enjoying her affair with Charlie – but that seeing him on TV ranting about how abortion should be outlawed and abortion docs sent to prison for life ... well, she'd talked it over with her husband and her parents and was willing to cut a thirty-second spot revealing what a hypocrite Charlie was. We shot the spot immediately and found enough national money to run it relentlessly.

The press did the heavy lifting for us. Charlie had been married at the time – still was, though to a different woman – so his adultery canceled out our adultery. And his hypocrisy sank him with a good part of his base; they stayed home.

We won by seven hundred and nine votes. There were challenges, of course. There was an official recount. Robert was declared the winner and planned his return to Washington where all the good, dear true friends who'd sold him out when he was under suspicion would throw him a party and say they knew he was innocent all along. Robert would have to accept their largesse because he would have done the same damned thing in their position. There are no heroes in the US Congress on either side of the aisle – some decent people, but no heroes. The test for heroics is simple – would you give up your seat for an issue you believe in? I don't have to answer that for you, do I?

Jane spent two weekends with me and though we had a good time she decided she'd best stop seeing me, because if we got serious she'd have to consider moving to Chicago and she could never do it – unless, she smiled sadly, I would consider moving to her nice little hometown.

As for Hawkins ... he enjoyed a month or so of national media coverage. He was good at playing the reluctant hero, I'll give him that. His *Aw, shucks, me a hero?* routine made everybody in the United States of Media Hokum stand up and salute. Hell, he even came up with an explanation as to who had fired the shots at Howie in the park the night before his death. Playing on Ruskin's gambling problems, Hawkins claimed that Howie had been into a big-time gambler for a couple hundred thou and that said gambler was furious that Howie insisted the games had been rigged and refused to play. So the gambler sent him a message. He ordered that Howie be wounded but not killed. Hence the shots in the college park. He couldn't say more until his intrepid investigation was finished. The press not only understood, they swooned like a maiden taken for the very first time.

Me? I tested my conspiracy theory on a few of my colleagues and was offered looks of bemusement and pity. The only time I got any kind of direct response was the night I got hammered in a posh Loop club and was met with wild laughter by an old newspaper friend of mine who drunkenly a) brought up the subject of Bigfoot and b) suggested that ole Dev boy needed some time away from the grind.

But I still have the nightmares that started the night Howie Ruskin was gunned down ... I am in the epilogue of the original *Invasion of the Body Snatchers* ... on that rainy highway running up to cars and shouting that they have to believe me. That there will soon be an attempt to seize control of the government by ... it's really happening. Can't you see it?

So there you have it. Hawkins was a hero, a Vegas gambler hired the shooter who worked on Howie, and no conspiracy whatsoever.

But sometimes I still think about that first plot to overthrow the government led by the billionaires and that general named Smedley Butler.

If I ever meet anybody named Smedley, I'm reachin' for my gun, partner.